They had kept Julia awake, swirling around in confusion within the dark recesses of her mind. Finally she'd come to have another look at him.

There was a reasonable explanation for his resemblance to Jack. Wasn't there?

She moved closer, staring in disbelief at his beautiful features. He had everything, from Jack's hard jawline to the high cheekbones. He had her husband's determined chin and chiseled nose. He had the same lion's mane, light brown hair with pale streaks of gold.

But this man's eyes belonged to a stranger. They were the same color, a pale translucent blue, but they guarded secrets.

Julia perched on the vacant side of the bed. As if pulled by an irresistible magnet, her hands slid over the soft covers. She couldn't deny the temptation of pretending for one instant that her husband had returned to her. It had been so long since she'd slept in the warmth of a man's arms. Jack's arms...

Dear Harlequin Intrigue Reader,

Summer lovin' holds not only passion, but also danger! Splash into a whirlpool of suspense with these four new titles!

Return to the desert sands of Egypt with your favorite black cat in *Familiar Oasis*, the companion title in Caroline Burnes's FEAR FAMILIAR: DESERT MYSTERIES miniseries. This time Familiar must help high-powered executive Amelia Corbet, who stumbles on an evil plot when trying to save her sister. But who will save Amelia from the dark and brooding desert dweller who is intent on capturing her for his own?

Ann Voss Peterson brings you the second installment in our powerhouse CHICAGO CONFIDENTIAL continuity. Law Davies is not only an attorney, but an undercover agent determined to rescue his one and only love from a dangerous cult—and he is *Laying Down the Law*.

Travel with bestselling author Joanna Wayne to the American South as she continues her ongoing series HIDDEN PASSIONS. In *Mystic Isle*, Kathryn Morland must trust a sexy and seemingly dangerous stranger— who is actually an undercover ex-cop!—to help her escape from the Louisiana bayou alive!

And we are so pleased to present you with a story from newcomer Kasi Blake that is as big as Texas itself! Two years widowed, Julia Keller is confronted on her Texas ranch by a lone lawman with the face of her dead beloved husband. Is he really her long-lost mate and father of her child—or an impostor? That is the question for this *Would-Be Wife*.

Enjoy all four!

Denise O'Sullivan
Associate Senior Editor
Harlequin Intrigue

WOULD-BE WIFE

KASI BLAKE

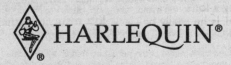

TORONTO • NEW YORK • LONDON
AMSTERDAM • PARIS • SYDNEY • HAMBURG
STOCKHOLM • ATHENS • TOKYO • MILAN • MADRID
PRAGUE • WARSAW • BUDAPEST • AUCKLAND

ISBN 0-373-22676-4

WOULD-BE WIFE

Copyright © 2002 by Brenda Canada

Printed in U.S.A.

ABOUT THE AUTHOR

At twelve years of age, Kasi Blake decided to be a writer and modestly rewrote the ending of a popular classic. She has an insatiable desire to read everything she can get her hands on. When she isn't writing or reading, she spends time with her favorite nephew, paints with oils, travels and shops until she drops. She resides in Missouri with her two cats.

Books by Kasi Blake

HARLEQUIN INTRIGUE
676—WOULD-BE WIFE

Don't miss any of our special offers. Write to us at the following address for information on our newest releases.

Harlequin Reader Service
U.S.: 3010 Walden Ave., P.O. Box 1325, Buffalo, NY 14269
Canadian: P.O. Box 609, Fort Erie, Ont. L2A 5X3

NEW
MEXICO

OKLAHOMA

ARKANSAS

• Dallas

LOUISIANA

• El Paso

• <u>Bunco</u>

TEXAS

<u>Triple K Ranch</u>

N

MEXICO

Gulf of
Mexico

All underlined places are fictitious.

CAST OF CHARACTERS

Julia Keller—Her husband was murdered two years ago. Or *was* he?

John Smith—A stranger with a familiar face. Could he be Julia's husband returned from the dead?

Jack Keller—He was killed when he made a shocking discovery.

Chalmers—This DEA agent claims he was John Smith's partner. He's hiding a dangerous secret.

Bob Keller—Jack's brother has a plan to smoke out the killer.

Roberta Keller—Bob's wife claims she had a secret affair with Jack before he died.

Sylvia Keller—Jack's mom insists that John is her missing son.

Pascal—This doctor is conveniently missing.

Cecily Carpenter—Was she John's psychiatrist... or his lover?

To my grandmother, Yvonne "Lil Gramma" Whardo,
for introducing me to lazy afternoons spent
between the pages of a good love story and for believing
I could do it even when I didn't. I miss our long talks
at the kitchen table over an ice-cold glass of Pepsi.

Chapter One

"Hey, this is where you get off."

John opened his eyes and glanced out the passenger side window. He took in the unfamiliar surroundings. Would he recognize it during the day? The note he'd found next to his hospital bed had suggested he find the ranch and it had insinuated he would find the answer to his identity. Amnesia was an odd condition. He could remember how to read and write, but he couldn't remember his own name.

John mumbled his gratitude to the trucker as he climbed out of the cab. The truck rolled forward, vanishing into the murky darkness, leaving John alone again.

He'd been lucky to find someone willing to give him a ride. The appearance of his clothing alone should have been enough to give anyone second thoughts. The only way he could escape from the hospital was to put on the clothes he'd been wearing at the time of the car accident. His blue jeans were ripped at one knee. The black T-shirt had dried bloodstains on it. Fortunately they blended well with the dark fabric.

Nothing about the land or the house appealed to him. The house was a weather-beaten gray with cracked, peeling paint. There was a wrap-around porch starting in the middle, heading to the right. A porch swing hung just outside the front door. It readjusted itself, creaking in the evening breeze. A corner of the screen door's silver mesh had come loose and was hanging at an angle.

John stood on the dirt road in front of the house. He turned to check out the rest of the place. Directly in front of the house there was a corral. As far as he could tell in the dark, it was empty. To the right of the corral was an old-fashioned red barn. At least it appeared to be red from the distance he was standing.

He hoped the trucker hadn't dropped him off at the wrong ranch, but the letters running across the entrance claimed Triple K. Right ranch. Wrong person. He didn't belong here.

The odors were odd. The sounds tormented him, making his heart beat faster.

There was a strong smell of cows and horses, manure and dirt.

John wrinkled his nose in distaste and sank into a nearby porch swing. It creaked under his weight. He stared into the darkness. He would wait until morning, ask a few questions, and then he would head back to El Paso.

The porch light snapped on. He jerked, startled. A cold, wet fear he hadn't known until that moment, seeped into his bones. A part of him he had yet to discover, the child within, cowered from the light. He had the sudden urge to hide. He jumped to his feet. The thought of meeting the owners of the ranch scared the daylights out of him.

Too late to run. The screen door flew open with a screaming whistle, banging against the exterior of the house, and a sweet old lady emerged.

The sweet old lady had a shotgun in her hands, raised and ready to fire. It whipped around and centered on his chest.

The old woman's cornflower-blue eyes widened. Her

hands began to shake. For a moment he feared she might accidentally shoot him. She lowered the rifle and took a hesitant step forward, reaching out a withered old hand. "Jack? Jack, is it really you? Or am I just dreaming again?"

John was caught completely off guard. He would have given anything at that moment to say he recognized the woman, but he didn't. He didn't know her. He said the first thing that popped into his head.

"I'm sorry I startled you."

She smiled and tears filled her eyes. "Oh, Jack. You've finally come home to us. I never doubted you would. I knew you weren't dead."

Dead? If this Jack guy was dead, why did this woman think he was him?

He shook his head, but he didn't get the chance to deny his identity. The woman touched his face, caressed it with calloused fingers. "Dear Lord. I knew you'd come home. I told them all. They didn't believe me. Guess they'll have to now. Won't they? Let me look at you."

Her eyes wrapped him in a warm blanket. She put the rifle down and her arms stole around his middle. She hugged him tightly. His hands hung uselessly at his sides, but she didn't seem to notice.

A surge of warmth shot through him. It felt incredible to have someone touch him, to have someone care about him even if the feelings weren't really meant for him. He closed his eyes, fighting the tears.

Men don't cry.

He heard the voice, a strong masculine voice repeat the words in his head. The words and voice were familiar. It was the first time since waking up in the hospital that anything had been familiar to him and he latched on to it.

Hope flooded him with relief. He was going to remember. He was going to regain his memory...someday.

The woman stepped back and grabbed his arm, tugging at him. "Come inside. You look terrible. Lost some weight. I'll fix you something warm to drink. How about coffee with a touch of brandy? You look like you could use one. Are you hungry? Silly question. You're always hungry."

She continued to ramble. "I made some fresh bread today, and we had chili for supper. I can warm some up for you. Got one of those fancy microwave things now." She blushed. "I'm sorry. I'm chattering away like an old fool. Haven't given you time to get a word in."

His stomach rumbled. He was starving. Would it be so wrong to accept the woman's hospitality? Not with his memory gone. Besides, she seemed so sure he was this Jack fellow.

He followed her into the kitchen, a brightly lit room with white cabinets and a yellow curtain hanging over the sink. The sweet smell of fresh-baked bread and cinnamon had his stomach growling. He sat at the round lace-covered table, searching his mind until his head began to ache. It was no use. He didn't remember the woman or the house.

She set a steaming bowl of spicy chili and a few pieces of bread in front of him. He dug in, content for the moment with what he had. The woman sat across from him, watching him eat with a look of pure satisfaction.

His fork froze halfway to his mouth and his eyes widened in astonishment as a pink bubble emerged from her lips. It grew bigger and bigger before popping.

She peeled it from her face and wrapped it around her finger twice before sticking it back into her mouth. She smiled, showing a full set of healthy teeth.

"Yes, I still got my own choppers. Told you I wouldn't need dentures."

John forced a polite nod. "You have a lovely smile."

"Enough small talk." She leaned in closer. "Where have you been, honey? Why didn't you call us? We've been worried sick. Where were you?"

He admitted, "I don't know. I woke up in the hospital a few weeks ago with amnesia. I was in a coma for several weeks. They called me John Doe."

"Oh, Jack. I wish we'd known. We would have been with you. How on earth did you find us?"

"Someone left me a note telling me to come here. It wasn't signed."

She said, "I should probably wake the others so they can see you, but I'm going to be selfish a little longer. Do you mind?"

"Others? What others?"

She touched a hand to one side of her weathered face. "Oh, dear."

JULIA'S EYES fluttered open. She mumbled something under her breath, a leftover thought from a dream, and reached for her alarm clock. Staring up at the luminescent numbers, she groaned. It was three o'clock in the morning. What had driven her from blissful sleep?

She got up. There was an uneasy feeling in the house. Something was wrong. She grabbed an old robe and left her bedroom while struggling into the sleeves. The robe was a few sizes too big for her. It had belonged to Jack.

Although she wasn't holding on to it because of that, she mentally insisted. She didn't stare longingly at the other side of the bed anymore. She didn't cry in her sleep for those strong arms to hold her again. The fact that she *could* sleep now boded well for her sanity. For the first few months following Jack's death she hadn't been able to sleep at all.

Julia descended the stairs with an appalling lack of grace. She could barely think, let alone walk. Voices floated up to her. Someone was in the kitchen. In her dreamy state she almost recognized them, voices from the past.

Shoving her long bangs away from her eyes, she entered the kitchen. Nothing could have prepared her for the haunting sight. Her husband—her dead husband—was at the table, calmly talking to his mother. She would have laughed hysterically if he hadn't glanced up at that moment, pinning her with his cold blue eyes.

Sylvia raced to her side, supporting her as if the woman feared she would faint. "Honey, I was just about to wake you. I wanted a moment with him first. He came home to us. You aren't dreaming. It's Jack."

Her husband stood, but didn't approach her. She went to him as if sleepwalking, hands outstretched. Any minute now she would wake up, nothing but air to grab on to.

The lingering scent of bread and chili made her nauseous. The clock behind her ticked a steady beat as her heart began a marathon. As she moved closer to her dead husband, she realized she could smell the familiar masculine scent of him.

Her hands collided with the solid muscle of his chest and she gasped. A painful bubble inflated near her heart. He was real. Jack was actually standing in the kitchen, a wary glint in his eyes as he waited for her reaction.

Several emotions, all of them overwhelming, battled for supremacy. A strong part of Julia wanted to throw her arms around him and to capture his mouth with her own. She wanted to hold him and to love him until the earth shook apart. But a stronger part of her demanded explanations.

Reacting with fury to her husband's lack of compassion for her and their child, she struck him with the open palm of her hand as hard as she could.

Sylvia gasped behind her.

She would have turned to comfort the woman, but she was reeling with shock herself. Her hand stung from the impact. How dare he leave them, let them think he was dead, and then return as if nothing had happened.

The red imprint of her hand became increasingly noticeable on his cheek. He didn't move. He didn't speak. What was wrong with him?

She cried, "Where were you? Where in the hell have you been? You let us think you were dead! I never knew you could be so cruel! Why? No call. No letter. Nothing. What kind of man are you?"

Stunned, John ironically said, "I don't know."

Sylvia touched Julia's arm. "Honey, he doesn't remember anything. He doesn't know us. He has amnesia."

Julia laughed with bitterness, fighting the tears. "Well, isn't that convenient."

"Honey…" Sylvia stroked her arm.

"Don't." Julia put distance between them and her as if they'd become the enemy.

Julia wouldn't allow him to waltz back into their lives. She wouldn't allow him back into her heart until she was satisfied with his reason for leaving. Damn him! Damn him for making a part of her wish he *was* dead.

She shook with rage, for her son more than for herself. J.J. had had to learn to live without a father. He was nine years old now. Still very much a little boy. Over the past two years he had asked questions about his father, about the man's life and his death.

Sylvia inserted, "He's been going by the name John Doe because they didn't know his real name. Someone left him a note, telling him to come here. Thank God. Other-wise, we might never have known.''

''Yes, we might never have known that Jack was alive and lying to us. Aren't we lucky?'' Julia said. ''The only reason he's here now is because he has amnesia and forgot why he left us in the first place.''

Sylvia flinched, and Julia experienced remorse. Of course the woman was happy to have her son home. Julia hated to spoil it for her, but the only thing Julia'd had left was the knowledge that Jack had truly loved her. Now, even that small treasure was gone.

Sylvia turned to her son, motioning for him to say some-thing. For the first time Julia noticed how old and fatigued he appeared. His eyes especially. Their expression seemed centuries older than his thirty-three years. They were weary, filled with a once-absent knowledge of the wicked world. There were tired lines at their corners and around his mouth.

Everything about him contradicted the facts of who she knew him to be. Jack had always been laughing, carefree, a consummate flirt. He had been able to tease her out of her bad moods. The man standing in front of her didn't know what to say or do.

She looked deeply into his eyes, searching for her hus-band's soul, and found cold emptiness.

Julia shook her head and tears filled her eyes. Just a few seconds ago she had been close to wishing him dead. Now she knew Jack was, in fact, dead. This man was an im-postor, a beautiful replica of her dead husband. He was a ghostly imitation without substance.

Her hand rose to cover her quivering mouth, and she sobbed quietly, ''You aren't Jack.''

His Adam's apple bobbed. He offered her a half nod, accepting her decision without argument. His eyes were tinged with sadness and regret. Julia realized he had wanted to be her Jack, almost as much as she had wanted it. He was a lost soul looking for a home, somewhere he could feel he belonged.

Sylvia stepped between them. "What do you mean, he isn't Jack? I know my own son when I see him. He's Jack. Look at him. Who else could he be?" She turned anxious eyes on him. "You are Jack. Don't listen to her. She's upset. You two need to talk. I'm going to bed. I expect to see my son in the morning, Julia. Don't run him off."

They watched her go with mixed reactions.

Julia cried.

John seemed angry.

Julia said, "I'm sorry I hit you."

He rubbed his face thoughtfully. "You've got a good right hook," he mused as he sat at the kitchen table.

Julia refilled his coffee mug and added one for herself. Her hands shook, but as long as she didn't look at him she was okay. So she kept busy until she ran out of things to do.

She sat opposite him with the most uncomfortable feeling. Her heart had been ripped out, stomped on, then put back in her chest.

He said, "I'm the one who should apologize. I showed up without warning, not knowing what to expect. You're in shock. It's frustrating not to know who you are. I could have a family out there somewhere."

She couldn't look directly at him. Instead she focused on his left ear. "If you do have a family, you have to find them. I know what it's like to dream about a missing husband night after night. I wouldn't wish it on anybody. Of course, my husband can't help he's missing. He's dead."

"What happened to him?"

"My husband, Jack Keller, was murdered two years

ago. It happened right out in front of the house.'' Her eyes turned to the window. ''We had been talking that morning, laughing about something. He was going to work on a broken fence that day. I needed to wash the dishes.

''I heard gunshots. His brother Bob and I raced outside. We found him slumped over the steering wheel in his truck. There was so much blood.'' Her voice faded with every word. ''He'd been shot twice.''

Tears flowed down her cheeks. Unreal, talking to her husband's face about his own death. But this wasn't her husband, she reminded herself. She had to keep that straight in her own mind.

He placed a hand over hers. ''You don't have to tell me.''

She snatched her hand away. She didn't want him to touch her. The feeling of his skin on hers was nearly revolting.

''I want to.'' She hadn't spoken to anyone about it since that day. ''Bob drove us to the hospital. Jack couldn't sit up. His upper body rested in my lap, and I cradled him. I smoothed back his hair from his face.

''I talked to him, but I don't remember what I said. I tried to stop the bleeding. I couldn't. Once we reached the hospital...they took him away. A nurse handed me his watch and wedding band to hold while he was in surgery. I held them in a tight fist. By the time Jack was dead, I had an imprint of both etched deep into my palm. Funny, the things you remember.''

John asked, ''Did they catch the guy who shot him?''

''No. The evidence disappeared. Jack's body vanished from the hospital. We didn't even get to bury him. The police thought it was a professional hit. Jack didn't have enemies. Especially not anyone with the kind of money a pro would expect. This weird card was found on the floorboard of his truck. The police thought it was connected to some other killings. But nothing ever came of it.''

John paled with each word.

He pulled a shiny, white square from his pocket and tossed it onto the table. "Did the card look like this one?"

She gasped. Emotion choked her until she could barely speak. "Where did you get this?"

"They found it on me after the accident."

Julia held the card. Her hands shook. She'd never wanted to see it again, but it had haunted her dreams. It was a hideous thing; a scrawled scarecrow with razor-like teeth and hollow eyes.

Julia looked straight at him. A painful volt hit her. The familiar face of her husband stared back at her with a stranger's eyes. "Your accident wasn't an accident. The sheriff told me this is the calling card of a professional assassin. Maybe they saw you and thought you were Jack. Must have been a shock for them."

Her emerald-green eyes finally met his, this time without flinching. "Or maybe you are Jack. I've heard that people with amnesia can develop a different personality. You could be Jack. I don't think you are. But you could be."

She shook her head hard. "Dammit, I don't know what to believe anymore! I can't believe I'm sitting here with you. Talking to you. It's crazy."

"I don't know...."

"Well, I know one thing. You can't leave until we find out the truth." Hope bubbled within. She tried to control it. "You'll have to stay here. We have plenty of room." She reminded him, "And you have nowhere else to go."

"How do we find out who I am when I can't remember anything?"

"Let's think about it tomorrow. Okay?" She forced a polite smile. "It's been a long day and you look as though a strong wind could knock you down. You can sleep in the guest room. We'll talk tomorrow. At the very least, I promise we will find out who you are. Deal?''

He offered her his hand.

She gaped down at it with barely concealed revulsion. She didn't want to touch him, but what if he was Jack?

With that in mind, she reluctantly shook his hand, half hoping she would feel the same old electricity.

Nothing. His hand was warm and strong. Even his hand resembled Jack's, but she didn't feel a thing. No sexual tension. Nothing. She might as well have been holding her brother-in-law Bob's hand for all the reaction it invoked in her.

Chapter Two

He had the face of an angel.

Miracle or cruel trick?

Julia hovered over the sleeping stranger, tempted to touch but afraid she'd wake him. He had fallen asleep without switching off the lamp. Soft light illuminated him, casting shadows on the bottom half of his face. The haunting effect had her reaching into the past for confirmation. He was almost an exact replica of Jack.

Too numb with shock, she had barely looked at him before. Now she wanted to study him in private, desperately needing to look at him without schooling her facial expressions. No one was watching her. She was free to confirm or to deny his identity in her own heart.

Julia had gone to bed, trying in vain to sleep, but how could she when the stranger with her husband's face slept right across the hall? She had tossed and turned, fighting a losing battle against questions without answers.

Questions. Accusations. Possible scenarios. They had kept her awake, swirling in confusion within the darkest recesses of her mind. She hadn't been able to deny them. After an hour of relentless badgering from the little voice inside, she'd come to have another look at him.

There was a reasonable explanation for his resemblance to Jack. Wasn't there?

She moved closer, staring in disbelief at the stranger's beautiful features. He had everything from the hard jawline to the high cheekbones. He had Jack's determined chin and chiseled nose. He had the same lion's mane, light brown hair with pale streaks of gold.

But there were hard-to-miss differences, as well. Impossible to ignore. For one thing, Jack would never have grown his hair to such a wild length, shaggy in back, long sides that swung into his eyes when he nodded his head.

And this man's eyes belonged to a stranger. She recalled from their earlier encounter that they were the same in color, a translucent pale blue. But they guarded secrets. Jack had shared everything with her. Well, nearly everything. She had seen the stranger's eyes flash with cold contempt when she had first entered the kitchen. Jack had never displayed such an emotion, least of all focused it on her.

Julia perched on the vacant side of the bed. As if pulled by an irresistible magnet she reluctantly crowded him. Her hands slid over the soft covers. She couldn't deny the temptation to pretend for one instant that her husband had returned to her. It had been so long since she'd slept in the warmth of a man's arms. Jack's arms.

What would it hurt to pretend for one stolen moment that he'd returned? If she didn't wake him, her fantasy was safe.

She hadn't been able to sleep with him so near. The very thought of him scalded her senses. She couldn't resist the urge to touch him…just this once. No one would know. He was sound asleep, perhaps dreaming of another life. Another wife.

The tips of her fingers feathered across his forehead,

down the bridge of his nose, and then rested on his sensuous mouth. His lips unconsciously parted. A soft sigh escaped, and his warm breath caressed her face. It sent a shiver through her. Jack would be dreaming of her.

His skin held the faint scent of soap. His snores were barely audible over the thunderous beating of her heart.

She wanted to kiss him.

No, she amended, she wanted to kiss Jack. A goodbye kiss. The goodbye kiss she'd been denied two years ago.

Julia swallowed. The logical side of her brain waged a private war with the part that still believed in fairy tales. He looked like Jack. He talked like Jack. Why couldn't he be Jack?

Julia leaned closer, replacing her fingers with her mouth. Gently she kissed those lips. A tender brush like a butterfly's wings. It was all she could handle.

"Cecily," he groaned.

Julia gasped, half in fright at the thought of being caught and half in stunned disappointment.

She reclined back on the bed in despair, one arm slung over her eyes. She was angry with herself. What had she expected? He was a stranger with her husband's face. He didn't owe her anything. He hadn't professed his love for her. He hadn't known of her existence yesterday.

Exhaustion swept her into a black sea. She wanted to return to her own bed, but her strength was zapped. Strange images flooded her mind; incoherent images with nothing in common trailing one to another like cars on an endless train. Jumbled pictures carried her over into a dream.

In sleep, her unconscious body gravitated toward familiar territory. She turned to the stranger, and he wrapped her in his arms. A soft caress whispered across her skin. She smiled.

Content, neither of them stirred again.

"UNCLE BOB! Mom's in bed with some guy!"

John traveled through layers of gauze, desperately reaching for the light. He had to wake up. Something was wrong. He forced his brain to take inventory. The first thing he realized was that he wasn't alone. He held something tangible yet soft in his arms. He held it close to his body, protecting it as if it was precious to him.

The second thing he'd figured out was that the first thing was a woman.

Her startled emerald-green eyes flew open and a soft gasp pierced the silence. John found his face mere inches from hers. Half of his brain was dreaming. He didn't bother to question who she was or why she was in bed with him. It seemed to him that her beautiful lips were parted, silently begging for a kiss. All he had to do was to move a breath in her direction.

Beneath the sheet one of her bare legs bumped his. The brief touch nearly stopped his cold heart, and he remembered his location. He remembered finding the ranch after discovering the note at the hospital.

John and Julia froze into statues. Neither moved. Neither dared to breathe. Their eyes locked as they struggled to reach an unspoken understanding. He had no idea what she was doing in his bed, but he wasn't complaining. Waking up next to her, entwined with her, felt like the most natural thing in the world.

"Mom, who's he?"

Mom? John struggled to sit up. He found two curious blue eyes staring at him as if he were the ugliest spider to crawl out from under a rock in a long time. The kid turned accusing eyes on his mother.

John heard footsteps stampeding their way.

Julia bolted upright, her elbow jamming into her bed partner's stomach as she made her escape.

John stifled a surprising grunt, rubbing the newly bruised area. He wasn't sure what was happening, but he knew one thing: Julia had some explaining to do.

The door burst open and a tall man with unkempt blond hair pushed past the kid. His face was red, eyes close to bulging. For a second John wondered if he was the woman's husband. Then he remembered he was supposed to be her husband.

The man's angry gaze swung to him. His expression shifted like the wind. It went from fury to confusion to fright in a sparse few seconds. The man took a hesitant step forward, arms wrapped tight around his middle.

He muttered, "Jack? It can't be."

John understood. He waved a tired hand. "I am not—"

"He has amnesia, Bobby," Julia interrupted. "He doesn't know who he is. He doesn't know his name. He looks like Jack, but…is it possible?"

Bob said, "Does he know where he's been for the past two years?"

John rolled his eyes. "I'm right here. You can ask me. I have amnesia. I'm not deaf."

Bob turned back to John, seemingly reluctant to speak to him. He scratched his head. "Okay. Do you know where you've been?"

"No," he snapped with barely restrained hostility.

Julia sent John a chilling glare. "Bob is…would be your brother if you were Jack. He's the one I told you helped us take you—I mean, Jack—to the hospital."

J.J. asked, "Who is he? Is he my dad? He looks like pictures of my dad."

Julia went to her son and knelt in front of him.

John held his breath, anxious to hear what she would say. How would she explain his resemblance to the boy's father?

She said, "Sweetheart, this is John. He'll be staying with us for a while. He looks like your dad, but he's not."

The kid's eyes narrowed. "Why does he look like Dad?"

"I don't know, honey. But we're going to find out."

"Hey, maybe he's got a kid that looks like me. That would be cool."

J.J. left the room after a little prodding from his mother, and John's eyes followed the kid out the door. The boy had brought up an important point. John could have children somewhere out there waiting for him. Or could J.J. be his son?

A son. He couldn't begin to fathom the emotions that accepting he had a son would take. For the moment he decided to put it on the back burner. He was far too numb to deal with it. Chances were he wasn't Jack Keller anyway. No need to get caught up in feelings that weren't meant for him.

The one they called Bob towered over him. "Can't you remember anything? A noise? A smell? Anything that might help us figure out if you're Jack."

"He can't be Jack," Julia said. "He isn't Jack. Jack died. We saw him, Bob…the blood…the doctor told us he died."

Ignoring her denials, John said, "I keep having this one dream over and over."

Grabbing a chair, Bob pulled it to the bedside, straddled it. "Tell me. Don't leave anything out."

John lit a cigarette as he studied the man. Bob was watching him with barely concealed suspicion. Why did he have the feeling that "Bobby" would rather he be anyone other than his brother?

"I'm in the woods," John said. "It's raining. I have a gun in my hand. I hear a voice—a woman's voice—calling me back. I want to go to her, but I can't. I have to keep moving forward. There's pain. I have blood on my hands, but I don't know where it came from. Then I wake up."

Bob whistled through his teeth. "That's some dream. If you heard a woman calling you, did you hear what she was calling you?"

"No matter how hard I try to remember, I forget the moment I wake up."

Julia said, "We have to help him, Bobby. What can we do? Where do we begin?"

"The police. They can check if he's missing. Someone might have reported it."

"I think it would be better if no one knows I'm here," John interjected. "Not even the police."

Bob rubbed his chin.

Julia said, "I think he's right. If the killer is still out there, he could come here. I won't put my son in danger."

Bob sighed. "We'll save the police for later then."

She said, "I'm going to help Sylvia with breakfast. Is there anything in particular you would like, John?"

"I don't know. They fed me oatmeal in the hospital and I hated it."

"No oatmeal then."

Bob stood and moved to close the door behind Julia. Turning back to their unexpected guest, he stared at John in amazement. "I cannot get over how much you look like him. It's unreal. If I didn't know better I would think you were Jack. But my brother died. I was there."

John climbed out of bed and pulled on his discarded jeans. If he'd ever possessed the virtue of modesty, it had been forgotten along with everything else. He went to the window and peered out. He watched the horses in the corral shy away from a cowboy as he tried to separate a couple from the herd. The man was being far too aggressive.

John turned away, his lips tight. He didn't know anything about horses. Did he?

"Tell me about your family," John insisted. "Julia lives here with you and your mother. Did Jack live here, as well? Or did she move in after his death?"

Bob's eyes narrowed suspiciously. "My brother and I grew up in this house. It's been our family home for three generations. When they married, she got more than a husband. She got an entire family. He died a month before their tenth anniversary. Julia is family to us. We love her."

"How much do you love her, Bobby?"

Was it his voice he heard asking the question? A voice as coldly manipulative as freezing rain?

John wasn't certain which of them was more shocked. He wasn't sure where it had come from. His mouth had opened and out it popped. It hadn't even completely formed in his mind.

Bob's eyes darkened. "Excuse me?"

John wasn't sure why he taunted the man. It was none of his business if Jack's wife and brother were together now. It had nothing to do with him, yet he felt compelled to weed out the truth. A burning curiosity flared to life within his empty soul.

Perhaps he had been a hard-core reporter.

He closed in on Bob until they were inches apart. His voice lowered menacingly. "You heard me. How much do you love Julia? Did you love her before your brother died?"

"How dare you come into my home and insult Julia! She loved Jack with all her heart. It's been two years and she hasn't looked at another man. She refuses to go on with life, refuses to let him go. You don't know anything about us!''

John relented. ''I'm sorry. I had no right to insinuate anything. Julia seems like a fine woman. It isn't any of my business if something is developing between you.''

Bob swore. ''Nothing is going on between us! Damn, you sound just like Jack! Maybe you are him, after all. I love her like a sister. Got it? She loves my dead brother's memory. Besides, I have a wife.'' At John's raised eyebrow, he explained, ''Roberta is on an overnight jaunt to the city. She loves to shop. You'll probably meet her later.''

John withdrew to another corner of the room. He leaned against the wall, arms crossed in front of him. He was learning more about these people than he wanted to know. If he was smart, he would leave while he could. No good could come out of his involvement with them.

''Tell me about your brother. What was Jack like?''

''I could give you a list of his good qualities, but it wouldn't mean anything to you. Jack was Jack. He wasn't always perfect, but he had a way of making people forget their problems. Dad used to say he could charm a rattlesnake.''

''Losing him was hard on you.''

''Of course it was hard on me! He was my baby brother. I never expected it to happen. So damned young. It was a waste. They never caught the guy, either. We never knew why. Sheriff thought it was a professional hit. There were no clues. Except for that stupid card they found.''

''Business card?'' John played dumb. How much would Bob confide in him?

''I guess. I don't think Julia knows about it. The sheriff

wanted to keep it under wraps in case the guy shows him-self down the line.''

''What did it look like?''

''It was white, with an ugly picture sketched in black. I remember the thing had teeth,'' Bob said. ''Hey, why are you so interested in all this?''

John shrugged. ''Curious. I don't know anything about my own past. I guess I'm trying to keep my mind occupied with other people's lives.''

A gleam appeared in Bob's eyes. ''You could help us, you know. I mean, as long as you're here you may as well help us out.''

A warning bell sounded in the back of Jack's brain. ''What do you mean? What could I do?''

''You are the spitting image of my brother. If you stay, if you pretend to be Jack, the killer might show himself. We could finally catch him.''

''You mean, he might try to finish the job?''

''I suppose. The only way to guarantee it doesn't happen is for you to leave now. Of course, you could always run into the killer somewhere else. You don't want to run for the rest of your life, do you?''

A dull ache began in the back of John's skull. The idea of running from something, anything, brought a bitter taste to his mouth. He couldn't do it. He couldn't spend the rest of his life running. His hands clenched into fists.

...can't run.

Pain. His hands covered his face and he denied the memory access. Remembering would bring more pain. At the moment he couldn't handle it. He fought it. Forced his mind to go blank. Then he pictured a serene place, a grassy meadow with a huge shade tree.

The pain receded slowly. His breathing returned to normal. When he glanced up he saw Bob staring at him, but it wasn't concern in those fathomless eyes.

"Are you okay? I thought you were going to faint for a second. You turned white. Was it something I said?"

"I'm fine, thank you. I have a bit of a headache."

"Want some aspirin?"

"No. I want answers. I have the feeling you know more than you're letting on. You think you know who the killer is, don't you?"

Bob shrugged. "I may have a clue. Nothing I can prove. I won't disclose the name to you in case I'm wrong. Will you help us?" He added wryly, "Actually, the real question is, are you going or are you staying?"

He could leave, but he would never see Julia again. In a matter of hours she had become the most important person in his life. Of course, in his present condition that wasn't saying much. She was practically the only person in his life.

John sighed. "I'm staying."

"I thought you might." A slight menacing smile tilted one corner of Bob's mouth.

Lately, John found it easy to read people. He couldn't be sure if this was a newly developed talent or a carryover from his old life. But for some reason, with Bob it was different. John could only draw a blank. Agreeing to stay might not be the smartest thing. He had the feeling "Bobby" was setting him up for something. But what?

No matter. Bob could be telling the absolute truth about finding his brother's killer. Either way, John realized, his own life was about to be put on the line. He got the strange impression that Bob hated him. Whether it was because of physical appearance or something deeper, he wasn't certain. He only knew one thing for sure.

Born in mind and spirit only a few minutes ago, he already had himself an enemy.

JULIA'S DAYS WERE HECTIC with her job at the ranch and taking care of a mischievous nine-year-old boy. She had no room in her schedule for anything else. An organized person, she was used to juggling everything with no problems. But that was before John had entered the picture.

When he was nearby, she found herself watching him. Not just watching him, but obsessing over his every movement.

When John wasn't around, she found herself thinking about him. She tried to focus on her work. She gave herself a stern mental talking to, but nothing changed. Her thoughts revolved around the stranger, the stranger with her husband's face.

And body.

She halted on the front steps, seeing him in the yard. He was chopping wood. Why?

It did not escape Julia's notice that John's body fit, in detail, every aspect she remembered Jack possessing. He was broad-shouldered with muscular arms. The tight jeans he wore accentuated every movement of his thighs. His T-shirt stretched to accommodate flexing muscles as they bunched up before relaxing.

John lifted the ax high over his head. He swung it down in an arc. It buried itself in the wood on the stump in front of him. Bringing it up, he slammed it back down. The wood splintered. It fell in two halves on opposite sides of the stump.

He repeated the procedure.

Her mouth went dry. Julia turned away, facing the door. It hurt to look at him. He was so beautiful. So Jack. Was he? Could he be?

She spun again, confused. She felt like a teenager with racing hormones and no direction to focus them. Once the numbness of first shock had faded, the stranger made her ache in places she'd forgotten. She wanted him, but was it fair to him?

Julia crossed the yard to stand directly in front of him. Her hands went to her hips. Something had to be done. They couldn't simply go on avoiding each other. They had to reach an agreement of some kind. But what?

Well, for one thing, he could stop parading around in tight jeans.

He glanced up with eyes as cold as the frozen tundra. Why did she get the feeling she wasn't his favorite person? Odd. She hadn't done anything to him.

His eyebrow arched. "Yes? Can I help you?"

"I was wondering if you would walk with me?"

"Why?"

"We need to talk." She sighed. "How am I supposed to figure out if you're my husband if you never speak to me? Maybe if we talk, something familiar will pop out of your mouth. Something undeniably Jack."

John buried the ax deep in the stump. "Let's go. Ladies first."

She headed in the direction of the barn, then passed it. He followed behind. Her back burned with the imprint of his gaze. Determined to follow through to the bitter end, Julia walked faster. She hated herself for wanting him. It felt wrong.

She was so busy denying the attraction between them that she inadvertently tripped over an exposed root.

John's hands shot out to catch her. He pulled her back sharply against his hard body. His fingers dug into her upper arms, holding her in place. He lowered his face until he could breathe in the scent of her hair.

Was it her imagination or had his lips brushed the nape of her neck through the silky strands? She shivered. It had to be her imagination.

Julia's breath quickened.

Suddenly he pushed her away as if she'd burned him, while the opposite was true.

She turned to look at him. His eyes accused her. Was he playing games? Hot one second and cold the next.

"How are we supposed to talk when you're racing over the pasture like the devil is on your heels?"

An apt description if she'd ever heard one. She shielded her eyes from the sun's glare. The huge fiery ball was just over his shoulder. Had he positioned himself there on purpose to throw her off balance?

She said, "Now that we're alone I don't know what there is to talk about. I'm new at this. I don't know what questions to ask. I don't know what to say. Maybe you could start us off."

"Right. Tell me about yourself. What kind of music do you like? Are you a morning person or a night owl? Who do you run to when your heart is breaking?"

Julia picked a blade of grass and sucked it between her teeth. The familiar sticky feel on her tongue brought things into perspective. This was her home. Confident once again, she admitted, "Jack. I went to Jack when I needed someone to talk to."

"Damn, I'm sorry. I always say the wrong thing."

"Not always." An airplane passed overhead, momentarily distracting them. She stared up at it, feigning interest. Talking to the stranger had been a dumb idea. It wasn't getting them anywhere.

John smiled and his eyes crinkled endearingly. "I bet you liked to tease the boys when you were little."

She gave him a smile. "I loved to tease Jack. He was easy. He rose to the bait every time."

"Did he enjoy teasing you back?"

She nodded. "Jack loved to laugh. He was carefree, easy to talk to. We were friends a long time before we became lovers. I can't even remember what life was like before him."

As lost as she was in the past, Julia noticed the frown marring his handsome face. She rubbed her tired neck. John's eyes fixated on her hand. She feared he might suggest taking over the task himself. She couldn't bear for him to touch her again.

He finally spoke, his voice raw with emotion. "You still wear his ring. He was lucky to inspire such loyalty. Your brother-in-law tells me you haven't wanted anyone else since his death." He met her eyes. "Are you going to carry the torch forever? Do you think that's what Jack would have wanted? Or are you simply using him as an excuse not to live? You're afraid, so you bury yourself beneath widow's rags. You can't hide forever."

She flinched as if the words had carried a punch. "I can't believe you were discussing me behind my back. What business is it of yours if I date or not? Why do you care?"

Julia twisted the ring on her finger. It felt suddenly cold and tight like a noose. There wasn't anything wrong with her being faithful to her husband. What right did this impostor have to question her motives?

He shrugged in reply to her question. "I don't know. Maybe I'm just bored."

"Well, find another way to entertain yourself."

"If my being here hurts you, I'll leave. All you have to do is say the word and I'm gone. I didn't agree to stick around to cause problems."

''Then why did you?'' She stared up at him with enormous green eyes. ''I know why I asked you to stay. Now I want to know why you agreed. Why do you stay?''

He swallowed hard before turning his back on her. His body was ramrod stiff.

Tension coiled around the two of them. She sensed there was something else, something he wanted to say to her but couldn't. Or wouldn't.

Disappointed, Julia said, ''This was a big mistake. This conversation is over. I think we should forget it ever took place.''

''What conversation?''

His eyes were on her, intense blue eyes that made her shiver. He shouldn't have her husband's face. It wasn't fair. The face she had loved since she was a child. Why did he have to look like Jack?

Chapter Three

Fifty thousand dollars was missing.

Julia kept the books in order for the ranch. She kept the debit and credit columns in check each month, making sure they always balanced. No matter the sacrifice: time, loss of sleep, routine headaches. It wasn't easy with three other people using the business account. Sylvia, Bobby and their trusted foreman, Stu, all had access to the account. Sometimes they forgot to tell her about purchases made.

However, if a large purchase had been made for the ranch, she would have noticed. She concluded the missing money had been spent on something personal. But what? What could have cost that much money?

She left the dimly lit study for the spacious kitchen. Sylvia was busy baking bread. The smell drifted through the open doorway, making Julia's stomach growl. "Mmm. What's the occasion?"

Sylvia smiled with a sort of smugness Julia hadn't seen before. "Jack always loved my bread. I'm fixing all of his favorites tonight. Would an apple pie be pushing it? Jack never liked to be fussed over."

Julia nodded absently. Her mind circled around the missing money. She didn't want to sound accusing.

She said, "Someone forgot to tell me they wrote a check

for a fair amount of money. Books won't balance. Do you know if Bob or Stu bought anything recently?"

Sylvia frowned. "I don't remember anyone buying anything. You should ask them."

It was the answer Julia had expected. She had the horrible sinking feeling that someone had purposely forgotten to tell her about the missing money.

"I wonder where Jack has gotten off to. Have you seen him, dear?"

Julia winced. "You can't keep calling him Jack. I don't want J.J. confused."

Sylvia's smile faded. Julia had watched the woman dissolve after her son's death. If only he *were* Jack.

Julia wondered if she had the right to shake Sylvia's delusions.

"I'm sorry," Julia said. "Forgive me."

Sylvia struggled to smile, but it wasn't as bright as it had been. "It's all right, dear. I understand. I wish you could be as certain as I am that Jack has returned."

Julia sank into a kitchen chair. Sylvia joined her at the table, placing a hand on hers. She had always admired the woman's strength. It was legendary. Maybe some of it would rub off on her.

She asked, "How are you so sure he's Jack? When I look into his eyes, I see a stranger. His eyes are cold, unforgiving. Jack's were tender, filled with love."

Sylvia blew a pink bubble. "Perhaps when he was with you, but I saw him when he was angry. He loved his father, but John Senior was hard on Jack. That boy's eyes could be as cold as the Nebraska wind. Make no mistake about it. Jack could hold a grudge. If you wronged him, he wasn't quick to forget it."

Julia couldn't reconcile the Jack she knew with the man Sylvia painted for her. Jack had been blessed with an even temper. He had been gentle, easygoing. She couldn't remember seeing him angry. Hurt, worried, upset—yes. But never truly angry.

Was it possible she hadn't really known him?

"Sylvia, you weren't there when Jack was shot. I saw the blood. He lost so much blood. No one could have survived it. I know you want to believe. It's easy to believe. John is practically Jack's twin, and it doesn't help matters that he doesn't remember his own name. It wouldn't be difficult to convince that man he's your son. He's alone in the world, searching for a connection. Don't make the mistake of turning him into a surrogate son. Someday he'll remember, and then he'll be gone."

Sylvia nodded slowly. The hope in her eyes withered. She aged ten years within Julia's sight. The woman pushed herself out of her chair, looking suddenly fragile. She crossed the room to check the bread.

Julia wanted to crawl under a rock. Sylvia was the last person she wanted to hurt.

Julia heard the front door open and close. It would have to be their foreman, Stu. He had given up on propriety long ago, being as close a member of the family as he could get without sharing their blood. She looked up, waiting for him to round the corner.

Stu stopped at the kitchen doorway, tall and lanky with stubble on his chin and a dusting of dirt over his work clothes. Julia rose and stepped closer to him. He spoke low so Sylvia wouldn't overhear. "I heard what you said about the stranger. You're right. He ain't Jack. I'm glad someone around here has some sense."

Julia had known Stu most of her life. He'd been close to Jack, teaching the boy to rope and ride. She trusted his opinion. "Sylvia wants to believe. Jack was her son. She misses him."

"We all do."

"Is that all you wanted?"

His eyes narrowed. "Reckon so. Why? When you called the barn I got the feeling you had something to ask me."

She took a deep breath and plunged in. "The accounts don't add up. Someone made out a check and forgot to tell me. Have you bought any equipment recently or—"

He cut her off. "I haven't written a check since we picked up that new trailer. Maybe Bob's wife bought herself a diamond tiara for her pointy head." He looked for a place to spit out a sunflower encasing and finally settled on his gloved hand. "Anyways, I gotta git back to work. You watch that new fella. Let me know if he causes trouble. I'll git rid of him."

She sighed in exasperation as she watched him go. With two huge problems biting at her heels, she didn't know which way to turn. Sylvia and Stu both denied knowledge of the missing money. That left Bob.

Julia went in search of Bob. She left the kitchen in a blur and barreled into a solid chest. Strong, familiar arms wrapped around her upper body to steady her. A sizzling current traveled through her as she gazed up into a pair of incredible blue eyes.

They were the same eyes she had gazed into on her wedding day. The same eyes she had watched drift shut in passion. The same eyes she had watched close for the last time two years ago. She noticed from his clothing that Sylvia must have given him some of Jack's clothes to wear. To her it seemed like an invasion of privacy.

Julia shoved against him, but he wouldn't release her.

"Where's the fire?"

"Leave me alone. Haven't you done enough?"

"What are you talking about? What did I do now?"

"You disrupted all our lives. That's what you did. Sylvia thinks you're her son. J.J. is confused. You have my husband's face, but you do not have his heart. Jack never would have come back if it meant hurting his family. He wouldn't have stayed away for two years in the first place. He never would have left us."

Julia turned for the stairs. She no longer cared about the money. She would worry about it in the morning. At the moment she only wanted solitude, a chance to lick her wounds in private.

He whispered behind her, "You can't run forever."

She froze, hand on the banister. Revolving slowly, she demanded, "What did you say?"

"Just thinking out loud. I guess I should watch that."

"Damn you. Why did you come here? Why now?"

He seemed about to answer her when Sylvia poked her head out. "Good. It's you. Could you carry some boxes down from the attic for me? Bob would do it, but he's vanished into thin air."

Julia hurried up the stairs before the conversation could turn to her. She needed to be alone. Her mind whirled. She counted all the reasons to believe Jack was dead. Then she listed every reason they had to think John was Jack, minus the memories.

Her meandering ended in a tie. She didn't know what to believe anymore. The biggest evidence pointing to Jack's death was the word of the doctor. Pascal, Julia had been told, had an excellent record. There would be no reason for him to lie.

There had to be something she could do to verify John's identity.

JOHN STUMBLED across a family photo album in the attic. No one would know if he gave in to his curiosity. He knew he shouldn't be snooping, but he had to look. He had to see for himself how much he and Jack Keller looked alike.

Sitting on a sturdy box in the corner, he flipped through the pages. There were several pictures of two little boys. He deduced that one was Bob and the other was Jack. One boy wore a bright smile, beaming with confidence. The other seemed to melt into the background in every photo.

He finally turned to more recent photos. His breath caught in his throat. To say he could be Jack's twin was an understatement. Gazing into a mirror couldn't be more revealing. No two people should look so much alike. No wonder he had shaken everyone up with his sudden appearance.

He tore his gaze away from Jack and fixed it on the blushing bride. He saw Julia's high school pictures. She had been a schoolboy's dream. There was no doubt in his mind why Jack had married her. A guy would have been a total idiot to let this girl get away.

Her dark hair had been a waterfall of silky waves spilling over her shoulders. High cheekbones, a generous mouth and a narrow nose made her model perfect. Her face, matured over the years, had barely changed at all. She was even more beautiful now.

John's gaze moved to the man pictured at Jack's side. Bob must have been best man at his brother's wedding. His eyes were solely focused on Julia. John wasn't certain he could label Bob's expression. Was it warmth, admiration…or was it love? Had Bob been in love with his brother's wife?

Was Bob in love with her now?

John had no right to question Bob's motives for tracking down his brother's killer or for looking after his brother's widow. It was none of his business.

A floorboard creaked. "What are you doing?"

John slapped the album closed and tucked it behind him. "I'm helping Sylvia move some boxes."

Julia flew across the room. She grabbed the album and waved it in front of his face. "How dare you invade my privacy!"

"I could be Jack Keller. It's not an invasion then."

Pain filled her green eyes, and he wished he could recall the words. There was no reason, beyond the obvious, to believe he was married to this incredible woman. Looking at her put his senses on overload. When he had grabbed her downstairs after she'd run into him, his hands had itched to move over that incredible body. He longed to touch her silky skin, to mold her soft curves.

He suddenly realized he was jealous of Jack's ghost. After two years Julia didn't seem prepared to go on with her life. She remained in love with a memory.

He should pack it in and head back for El Paso. He couldn't get involved with this woman. He didn't belong in this house.

"You are not Jack. How many times do I have to tell you? Sylvia is the only one who believes it, and that's only because she's mixed up. Losing Jack nearly killed her. I watched that woman die a little each day. I won't allow you to make it worse."

"I'm sorry. I never meant..."

"What did you mean then? Why are you still here?"

"You asked me to stay." He threw up his hands. "I need answers as much as you do. I need to know who I am. Sylvia seems to think I'm her son. Until I get proof one way or another, I'm staying right here. I don't believe in running away."

I won't run.

A screaming siren went off in his head. He bent forward, fingers against temples. He remembered the roar of thunder and the feel of rain pelting his face. He had been running from…

The memory faded in a flash. He swore beneath his breath, sure he had been close to the truth. It was damned frustrating. The memories were there, but he couldn't get a firm enough grasp on them.

Julia asked, "What's wrong with you? You look sick."

"I almost remembered something."

"Cecily?" She said the word quietly, a mere whisper. He might have missed it completely if he hadn't seen her lips move.

"What did you say?"

"Cecily," she repeated. "You called her name in your sleep. Do you think Cecily could be your wife?"

He enjoyed the jealous tilt to her mouth. "Would it matter to you if I had a wife?"

"Of course not. I hardly know you. Why would I give a fig if you're married?"

John stood beside her. There was a dusty cobweb clinging to her hair. He pulled it loose and flicked it to the floor. "She could be my sister or a friend. Just because I said her name in my sleep doesn't mean we were married. Could even be my dog." He rubbed his chin thoughtfully, a sly grin on his face. "Come to think of it, you never explained what you were doing in my bed in the first place."

"I—I h-have no idea what you're talking about."

She turned to go, but he swung her back around to face him. Her dark hair spilled over one shoulder. The bangs landed over one eye. She gasped for breath as if she was suddenly having trouble breathing.

He leaned closer, a mere inch from her face. His gaze settled on her lips. "I remember waking up next to you. Your son and brother-in-law were standing over us. It's my long-term memory that was damaged, not the short-term.''

"I was confused. You look like my husband.''

"Your dead husband,'' he supplied with no tact.

"My dead husband.'' Julia tilted her chin, meeting his eyes dead-on. "I wanted to talk to you, but you were asleep.''

His mouth twitched as he tried in vain not to smile. She was a beautiful little liar, but she wasn't very good at it. "Then you crawled in beside me to wait until I woke up. Right?''

"Don't mock me.''

Throwing his hands up in surrender, he said, "I wouldn't dare. I'm just trying to understand what happened. Did you sleep beside me the whole night? Did I touch you? Did I make love to you in your dreams?''

She glared. "Don't be obtuse. I don't dream about you. Now let me go.''

She backed away from him and lost her footing at the same time. Her back hit the wall. Her arm swung out, striking objects on the shelf. They tumbled to the floor with a great crash.

She cried, "Now look what you made me do!''

Julia went to her knees. She made a move to grab the broken bottle, but John caught her hand. "Don't touch it. You might cut yourself. Anything important?''

"It's one of Roberta's handmade ships in a bottle. She'll have a fit if she sees this.''

"Roberta?'' he asked, lowering himself to the floor.

"Bob's wife.''

"Maybe I can fix it,'' he said.

"Don't bother. It takes a great deal of patience. I've seen her work on one for days on end. She has hundreds of them. I don't know what she does with them all. Maybe she sells them. There are only a few up here. The rest are gone.''

John picked up a piece of glass and studied it. He rubbed his thumb along the smooth side, picking up a strange white residue. ''Defective glue?'' He wiped it off with a shrug and tossed the piece of glass onto the pile. ''I'll pick up this mess. It was my fault.''

Julia appeared ready to bolt for the trapdoor. She leaned toward him in an effort to stand.

John reached out to stop her. Cupping both sides of her face, his eyes zeroed in on her mouth. One kiss was all he wanted. He promised himself to kiss her once, a lightly teasing kiss. Then he would release her.

He just wanted to feel something, to blast through the icy coldness around his heart.

SHE SHIVERED at the look of desire in his eyes. He was going to kiss her. She had stopped him once before, but this time it was different. Though she might be angry with him for snooping, she was going to allow it for experimentation purposes. She had come to the logical conclusion that a kiss might be the thing that finally proved he was not her husband. No one could kiss like Jack.

Her eyes drifted shut. She would allow him one kiss. If there wasn't anything familiar about it, she would ask him to leave the ranch. On the other hand, if his kisses were echoes of the past, she would take him to her bed and remind him of the love they'd once shared.

The kiss began slow and sweet. It wasn't anything like she expected it to be. She wasn't in the mood for tenderness. She wanted passion.

His sexy mouth brushed over hers lightly at first. He took his time, igniting the fire slowly. His tongue flickered out. It traced a line from one corner of her mouth to the other. Then it slid between her lips, begging for entry.

Julia sighed and pulled him closer. Her hands dug into his shirt, the same blue plaid shirt Jack used to wear. She tugged at him. The burning desire she had thought long dead rekindled itself in the pit of her stomach. She couldn't get close enough.

John took advantage of her sigh. His tongue dove deep, sending tiny shock waves throughout her entire system. She feared he would pull back, but the kiss went on and on. She also feared the kiss would last forever. The pleasure was too intense. Too shocking.

Old insecurities knocked on her mind, demanding entry. Jack had wanted her, loved her. But this was not Jack.

Jack had died.

Her brain tried hard to latch on to the logic of it. The kiss was incredible. However it wasn't the type of kiss Jack had bestowed on her in the past. Jack's kisses had been confident, sometimes rough, not nearly as tender as John's kiss. Her Jack was gone.

And she was betraying him in another man's arms.

Julia shoved John away from her. The back of her hand made a deliberate wipe at her mouth. She had wanted the truth. What was she going to do with it now that she had it?

John was staring at her, his chest heaving as he tried to regain his breath. His fingers raked through his thick mane of hair, messing it up. Her hands itched to smooth it back down.

She didn't have the right to touch him. She should be ashamed of herself. He was a total stranger. Had she been without a man for so long that any man would do?

He seemed to read recrimination in her eyes. "Sorry," he said. "It was my fault. I shouldn't have done that."

She disagreed. "It had to be done."

"What?"

"You're not my husband."

John sighed. "You've already said that."

"But now I know for certain. You don't kiss like Jack."

He rubbed his chin and changed the subject. "I've decided to go to the police. When I came out of my coma, an Officer Nader was there to take my statement. He said I was in a car accident. He claimed no one was looking for me. There were no missing reports filed that matched my appearance. He offered to take my prints, but unless I was a criminal or in the military I wouldn't have fingerprints on record. I told him not to bother."

Julia shook her head in confusion. "Why change your mind now?"

"I've been wondering if maybe I was in the military. Those dreams I mentioned before, me with a gun…it's possible."

She threw up her hands. "Fine, do what you want. Just don't kiss me again."

"I won't kiss you again." He winked. "Unless you ask me to."

She stormed off, fighting the urge to slap his smug face. She would rather die than to ask him to kiss her again. She hadn't enjoyed it at all. Well, not much.

JOHN SMILED as he carried a heavy box down the ladder from the attic. Julia had disappeared. She was probably off thinking about the possibilities. He couldn't imagine having a woman such as her by his side all the time. His heart quickened in excitement just thinking about it.

He set the box down and started back up the ladder. He was on the fourth rung when something barreled into the ladder, shaking it. He grabbed for the rung in front of his face, but his hand closed on air. He fell.

John landed in a painful heap on the floor. His old injuries screamed in protest. The breath left his body on impact. There wasn't anything he could do but wait until it was over and pray he hadn't broken any bones. The hospital was the last place he wanted to go.

"Oh my gosh! Are you hurt?"

The high-pitched whining voice sent shivers through him. It was like listening to fingernails scrape a chalkboard. He glanced up to see the owner of the voice hovering over him.

The woman had a mess of platinum-blond hair somehow secured to the top of her head in a way that defied gravity. The powerful odor of hair spray and too much perfume collided with his nostrils, causing his nose to wrinkle in distaste.

She was incredibly tall, or at least appeared so from his awkward viewpoint. She wore a startlingly short black mini and a colorful neon blouse that nearly blinded him. And her makeup! How could she possibly hold her face up with such a heavy mask of cosmetics?

John struggled to his feet, via his knees. He was still somewhat weak from his ordeal. He looked forward to the day when he could run a mile without limping. If he enjoyed running. It was awful not knowing what he liked or disliked. Each day was an adventure. He never knew what to expect. And speaking of which...

The woman's bright pink lips formed an "Oh," and she backed away from him. "D-don't you c-come near me."

He frowned. "What's wrong with you? Do I know you?"

She laughed without humor, gazing up at the ceiling. "Does he know me? Isn't he funny?"

John looked around, confused. Who was she talking to?

The woman dropped her shopping bag. Reaching into her purse as if she were going for a tube of lipstick, she pulled out a small handgun and pointed it at his head.

Chapter Four

John's hands floated up into the air, automatically reaching for the sky.

He couldn't believe the woman with the loud clothes and painted face was pointing a gun at him. The absurdity of the situation would have made him laugh if he wasn't so afraid to twitch.

The gun itself was tiny, but he knew it could do a lot of damage.

He was unarmed. He had to use his brain to get himself out of the situation. He forced a harmless smile. "Could you point that thing somewhere else?"

She sneered, "You! I thought you were dead. I don't believe in ghosts. So you're either Jack Keller's long lost twin or you're the man himself. Which is it? Are you Jack Keller or an impostor?"

"Lady, I have no idea what you're talking about. You're actually the first person I've met who isn't happy to see old Jack alive. Did you hate him? Did you kill him?"

He realized too late the mistake of accusing a woman with a gun. Her hold tightened on the butt of the weapon, aiming it more carefully. He thought he saw her finger curve inward slightly.

"She didn't shoot Jack." Bob stepped forward. He re-

Would-Be Wife

moved the gun from his wife's suddenly trembling fingers. "She was upstairs asleep when it happened. I had to wake her up after I returned from the hospital."

"She didn't hear the gunshots?"

"Roberta needs help sleeping sometimes. She told me she'd taken a couple of sleeping pills. Not even a tornado could have woken her that morning."

Roberta turned watery eyes on John. "I wouldn't have killed Jack. I loved him." Her eyes flew to her husband's face. "I mean, he was family. We all loved him."

John felt the underlying tension between Roberta and her husband. There was something they weren't saying. John could practically hear the words humming gently beneath the surface static. He got the feeling that Roberta had loved Jack, all right, but not like family.

What was going on in this house? Was he abnormally paranoid? Julia didn't seem like the kind of woman who would cheat on her husband, especially not with his own brother. On the other hand, Roberta *was* the type to have a sleazy affair. At least she appeared to be and he was reminded of the look in her eyes when she'd mentioned poor old Jack. She'd been in love with him.

"I wasn't going to shoot you," Roberta said. "You scared the life out of me. I never thought I'd see Jack's face again." She focused a sober expression on her husband. "Who is he? Why does he look like Jack?"

"John has amnesia. He's staying for a while. We're hoping the killer might mistake him for Jack and try to finish him off. We all need to get on with our lives. Especially Julia."

Especially Julia. The words hung in the air, heavy with meaning. Bob seemed to bend over backward to single out Julia. Was it concern for his brother's widow or something more? Sylvia had told John earlier that Bob had taken a lot of pressure off of Julia in the beginning. He had arranged his brother's burial and taken her under his wing.

All the more reason for John to discover his identity quickly. He had to claim his family before someone else did. If they were his family.

John said, "I'm going to the police tomorrow. Hopefully they can tell me who I am."

Bob responded, "I thought you decided against that?"

"I need to do it. It may be the only way to find out who I am. I don't have to let the police know where I'm staying. Don't worry. Your family won't come to harm because of me."

Bob shrugged. "Don't worry about my family. I can take care of them. Do what you want."

"I can kill two birds with one stone this way. I'll make sure people in town see me. Maybe we can draw the killer out faster. If that's what you really want."

Bob gestured to the gun. "Sorry again about my wife. I wasn't expecting her back until tomorrow." He lifted the shopping bag and turned to his wife. "Is this all you bought? You were gone a whole week."

"I'm having the rest shipped later."

Bob groaned and followed his wife down the hall.

JULIA OPENED HER DOOR, her eyes raking over John's stationary form. Her hair hung over her shoulders in wet waves, straight from the shower, and she wore a plush green robe two sizes too big for her slender figure. He didn't need to ask. It had been Jack's.

"Is there something I can do for you?" she asked.

She obviously thought he was waiting at her door for a reason. He said, "I want to know if you want to go with me to see the police tomorrow. I'm going to let them print me. We'll know soon enough who I am."

She looked down, but not before he saw the apprehension in her gaze. She stroked her bottom lip, drawing his eyes to it. She glanced up, eyes large, as if she'd suddenly become aware of him and their gazes clashed. In an instant they both remembered the kiss they'd shared a short time ago.

The feelings the kiss had provoked, at least as far as he was concerned, had been a warning of things to come. The woman was fire to him. If he didn't handle her cautiously, he'd get burned.

Without a word, Julia disappeared into her bedroom, leaving the door open. Was it a silent invitation?

John entered her private chambers, the room she had shared with her husband, and immediately wished he hadn't. It was painfully obvious she hadn't changed anything since her husband's tragic death. Masculine colors, so unlike her, dominated the room. There was a brown-and-gold cover on the bed with matching curtains over the windows to block all sunlight out. Several framed photographs of the happy couple littered the dresser and night tables.

He went to them without asking for permission. His darkened gaze scanned each picture in turn. A large fist settled in his stomach. It was hard for him to look at images of himself holding Julia when he knew it probably wasn't him. He looked into the man's warm eyes and knew it couldn't be him. He'd seen his eyes enough in the mirror to know they'd never held warmth in them.

He lifted one photograph for closer inspection. Julia and Jack were holding each other as if they wouldn't ever let go. There was a look of pure joy on her face. Not a drop of sadness tinged those beautiful eyes. It was the look of a woman in love.

His gaze shifted to Jack out of necessity. It hurt to see

her happy smile, knowing he hadn't been the reason for it. Jack's expression wasn't much better. He was obviously besotted with the woman in his arms. Envious, John set the picture back down.

Julia stood in the far corner, biting her lower lip. She didn't know what to say any more than he did. He wondered why she had invited him into her bedroom. Was she trying to tell him something? Perhaps to show him she had no room for him.

He said, "It won't work."

She blinked with uncertainty. "What won't work?"

"You can push me away, but I won't leave. I have the strangest feeling being here will bring back my memory. Nothing is familiar to me yet, but I feel safe here. I feel…at home."

She shook her head. "Don't. You're not Jack, and your attraction to this place is easily explained. You're lost. You don't know who you are. We're the only people you know at this moment. Naturally you feel safe here."

"I feel like I've always known you." A shadow crossed her face, and he said, "I know you don't want to hear this right now."

She went to her vanity, taking a seat in front of the oval-shaped mirror. She brushed through the tangles of her hair with long, even strokes. His eyes fixed on hers in the reflection. She stared at him, unblinking, as he watched her every movement, totally mesmerized.

Without asking for permission, he took the brush. It slid from her hand, and he took over. He didn't know how to brush a woman's hair. If he had ever done it, he didn't remember. Taking it one step at a time, he gently stroked it through her damp hair. His other hand followed it down, smoothing as he went.

For him it became an erotic exercise. Her hair was like

silk. He dragged his fingers through it, becoming more fascinated by the second. Highlights danced in her hair, picking up a variety of shades from red to deep amber. He wanted to see it fanned on the pillow next to his in the morning.

And it smelled incredible, like an elusive perfume. He wasn't quite sure what it reminded him of. He only knew he loved it.

Julia's hand suddenly came up to grasp his, staying it in midstroke. Her eyes pleaded with him. "I think you should go. It's late."

"I'm going tomorrow with or without you. I need to know who I am. This might be the only way."

"What if they can't give you the answers you're looking for? There's a chance your fingerprints aren't on file."

He smiled, trying to appear optimistic. "I carried a gun. If I was ever arrested, they'll have my prints on file. If I was in the military, they'll have my prints. And what about Jack? If his prints are on file, they can compare them."

Julia said, "I never thought of that. You're right. Jack was in the air force. His prints are on file."

John stopped at the door. He turned for one final look at Julia. It wasn't the brightest thing he'd ever done. She looked like Venus standing in the moonlight, wrapped in the wind. Her face glowed. Her hair shimmered and a ghostly gray light encased her figure.

He had to leave the room before he did something they would both regret in the morning. As he stood there in silence, admiring her beauty, there were so many things he wanted to say but couldn't.

He settled for, "Good night."

John shut the door and leaned back against it. Had he ever wanted a woman the way he wanted her? He knew he couldn't have her, not when he didn't even know his own name.

"WHAT WERE YOU DOING in my mom's room?"

Another dilemma. The nine-year-old boy watched John with suspicious blue eyes. His arms folded over his chest, he scowled up at John. There was mud caked on the knees of his jeans and he smelled like a horse.

His son? Perhaps. There was a certain resemblance, but then, he looked like Jack Keller. Julia had asked him not to approach the boy, but he couldn't be rude. She wouldn't want him to hurt J.J.'s feelings.

Was this tiny replica of himself, all elbows and knees, his son?

John said, "We were talking about my problem. I'm going to get fingerprinted tomorrow. Maybe the police can tell me who I am."

"You're not my dad. My mom doesn't like you. Uncle Bob doesn't like you, either."

John smiled. "Don't worry, kid. I'm not going to stay for very long."

J.J.'s eyes narrowed. "Uncle Bob says you can't remember your name."

"I only remember waking up in the hospital. I was in a car accident."

"I heard Uncle Bob tell Stu a bad guy tried to get you," J.J. said. "A bad guy shot my dad, too."

"You shouldn't be listening to private conversations."

"It's easy. No one pays attention to me 'cause I'm small for my age. Mom says I'll get big like my dad someday. Gramma says he shot up like a weed. That's what I'm gonna do."

"I'm sure you will." John absently rubbed his left leg through the coarse denim. It throbbed.

The boy stared openly at John, his eyes a curious blue. "You look just like pictures of my dad. Maybe you're his brother or something."

John shook his head in denial. "More likely someone at the hospital made my face look like your dad. The doctor told me they had to reconstruct my face."

The kid made a face. "What is that?"

"Bones in my face were damaged. They had to fix my face, but they didn't know what I looked like before."

J.J. said, "That's stupid. How come they made you look like my dad?"

"I don't know, but I aim to find out."

"You're not my dad. You wish you were my dad, huh?"

The kid saw too much. John forced a smile. "Of course I'm hoping I'm your father. What guy wouldn't want a smart boy like you for a son?"

J.J. beamed in delight at the response. "Yeah. I guess so. When you goin' to the police?"

"Probably early tomorrow. Hey, shouldn't you be in bed?"

The boy's expression caved. "I was out lookin' for worms. Don't tell my mom."

"I won't. Just go to bed. Okay?" John ruffled the boy's hair and a familiar pang jabbed at his heart. Did he have a child? Was he a father?

J.J. gave him a thumbs-up and vanished into his bedroom down the hall. John waited until he heard the door click shut before he entered his own room. He hated the idea of Julia being across the hall from him. Too close, yet too far away.

Sleep was a long time in coming.

When it finally happened, he found himself tortured by familiar images of a boy holding out his hand. The child's eyes pleaded with John to take the offered hand. John reached for the boy, but the child drifted farther away.

The child faded until only his soft sobbing could be heard over the thunderous beat of John's throbbing heart.

JULIA DIDN'T GET MORE than a few hours' sleep. She couldn't erase the missing money out of her head. If her thoughts weren't whirling around the possibilities, it was racing after Jack—or John. She was confused as to which was which. She pictured him—one of them—smiling down at her, caressing her. But which one was it?

Did she love Jack enough to stay alone forever? In the beginning there hadn't been any question. The idea of allowing another man to hold her had been repugnant to her. It had made her physically ill just thinking about it. She blamed John for her sudden confusion.

John had come along, and her good sense had vanished. She was insane to even consider a relationship with him. There were too many obstacles in their way. He was the image of her dead husband. How could she be sure she wanted him for himself?

Julia went outside after searching the house. Bobby and Roberta were still in bed. J.J. was helping his grandmother cook breakfast. The only one missing was John. She hoped he hadn't gone to town without her. She needed to be with him when he spoke to the police.

Her eyes scanned the horizon. She didn't see him anywhere. Her heart leaped into her throat, nearly stopping her breath. What if he didn't come back? He could disappear and she would never know what had happened to him.

The sound of a throat being cleared made her jump. She spun around to find John watching her from the porch swing. His clothes were a rumpled mess. He had obviously slept in them. He forced himself to sit up, wincing as if in pain.

Julia tried in vain not to notice how sexy he appeared first thing in the morning. His light brown mane was a tangled mess, and his eyes were still half closed.

She asked, "Did you sleep out here?"

"Yes."

"How many times have I told you not to sleep on the swing? You know what it does to your back." The words slipped out before she could swallow them. She felt like kicking herself when John frowned.

She had confused him with Jack again. What was wrong with her? Jack had been dead for two years. Why couldn't she move on with her life?

Because she had loved him more than life itself.

"I'm sorry. I don't know why..."

"It's okay." He held up a hand. "You're right about my back, though. Sleeping out here wasn't one of the best ideas I've had. I felt trapped inside. Every muscle I have aches like the devil. You don't look like you've slept, either."

"I didn't." She sat next to him, trying hard not to think of the last time she'd sat next to Jack on this swing. "I couldn't stop thinking. What about you?"

"I have insomnia. I hardly ever sleep a whole night through."

Her lips twisted. "Jack slept like a baby. He never had a single night of insomnia. He could sleep anywhere."

John took her hand between his, capturing her complete attention. "You have to stop doing this to yourself, Julie. Even if I was Jack at one time, I'm not him now. He's gone."

"Is he?" Her voice rose slightly. "I'm not so sure anymore. Especially when you call me Julie. Jack used to do that. Sometimes you act completely opposite of him. Then you do something that's dead-on-target Jack. Sylvia believes you're Jack. Maybe I won't see it because I'm afraid of losing him all over again.''

She should have known right off if he was Jack. She shouldn't need fingerprints to tell her.

John put his arms around her. She broke down completely. For the first time in ages she allowed herself to cry. It felt good, cleansing. For too long she had put on a brave face for other people. Now someone else was being the strong one.

She dried her eyes and said, "When I woke up and you were gone, I was afraid you'd left without me. I was afraid I'd never see you again.''

"Me or Jack?'' At her hurt look, he amended, "Forget I said that. How could I go anywhere without you? I don't have a car. Besides, I don't know where the police are located. I'd just get lost.''

Julia forced a watery smile. "Well, do you want to go to the local sheriff or the El Paso police department? The El Paso police may know a few things about your accident that you don't know yet, but I don't know if they'd be willing to help us. The sheriff, on the other hand, is a long-standing friend of the family. Jack was a good friend of his son's. He would run your prints if we asked him to.''

John said, "That's where we'll go then. I don't need to talk to the El Paso police. I've already tried that. Officer Nader behaved as though I was the bad guy instead of the victim.''

"Okay, then. The local law it is. I'll just let Sylvia know.''

John grabbed her arm. "Do you have to tell her? I don't think she would approve. Do you have to tell anyone?''

Julia shook her head, pulling keys from her pocket. She jingled them. "Nope. We won't be gone long. Let's go."

John took the time to stretch. He bent and twisted his back in an oddly familiar way. She heard the expected popping sound that punctuated the movement. Jack had done the same thing every morning of his life.

Julia averted her eyes. She got into the truck and started the engine as she vowed not to let the stranger get to her. She couldn't allow herself to feel anything for him. The price would be too high.

John climbed into the truck, beside her. She half expected him to insist on driving. Her husband hadn't enjoyed being taxied around by anyone, especially not a woman. But the man next to her settled back in his seat, content to let her drive.

The town wasn't far from the ranch. She was both relieved and disappointed that they wouldn't be going all the way to El Paso. Relieved because an hour alone with him would have been pure torture. The disappointment was like a mustard seed growing by the minute: she liked having him to herself. She felt as if she could ask him anything.

"What do you want to do when you grow up?"

"Excuse me?" He turned puzzled blue eyes in her direction. They twinkled in amusement.

She blushed, not realizing she'd voiced the question out loud until he had replied. She clarified, "I mean, if you don't get your memory back, is there anything special you might want to do? With your life."

There was a lengthy pause. Either he was pondering the question or he wasn't going to answer. She glanced at his profile. It was getting harder to remember that his features had once belonged to another man, her husband. They seemed to belong solely to him. She wondered what he'd looked like before the accident. He'd told her his face had been reconstructed by the same doctor who had told her that Jack was dead. Coincidence?

John broke the silence, startling her. "I haven't given it much thought. I guess I figured I must have a steady job somewhere out there. I'll probably return to it. Whatever it is."

"What if it's something you hate doing? I've heard that people with amnesia can have total personality changes."

John said, "You've already mentioned that."

"Well, it's worth mentioning again. You could have loved peanut butter before and hate it now."

"Did Jack?"

"Did Jack what?"

"Love peanut butter?"

Her smile was tight and uncomfortable. "As a matter of fact, yes."

"I'll deal with my occupation when I find out what it is. If my memory doesn't return, I'll have to find something new, I guess."

Part of her selfishly hoped the sheriff wouldn't be able to give him any information. If he found out his identity, he would be tempted to go home.

She parked the truck in front of the sheriff's office, next to the town's only police car. John suddenly fell silent. He lit up a cigarette and followed her into the station. Julia resisted the urge to stroke his upper arm. She knew he was frightened at the prospect of learning something he wasn't prepared for. The need to comfort him was almost unbearable.

Sheriff Billings reluctantly turned off the tiny black-and-white TV that sat on his desk. Julia hadn't realized the time. Billings hated to be interrupted during "General Hospital." He never missed an episode.

He got up from his desk and maneuvered his ample

frame around to their side. He was about to give Julia the usual greeting, a smile and a quick hug, when his eyes landed on the man beside her.

Billings faltered. His eyes went from one to the other. They returned to John and he spoke through gritted teeth. "What the hell are you doing here?"

John was stunned into silence, not having expected such a reaction from the local law.

"This isn't Jack," Julia said. "I mean, he could be Jack. I guess. Sylvia seems to think so. But we don't know for sure. That's why we're here." She smiled a ridiculous smile, feeling like an underage girl telling her father she had just crossed the state line to marry a man he despised. "We want you to fingerprint him and compare his prints with Jack's. He has amnesia. The family needs to know if he's Jack. Can you do it? Will you do it?"

Again Billings's eyes ping-ponged between the young pair. Taking John by the shoulder, he steered him into a corner, saying, "I need to ask the fella something first. Be with you in a sec, Julia."

She hated being left out. Whatever it was Billings said to John put a scowl on the handsome face she knew so well. She started forward, but stopped as John shook his head. The private conversation was over, apparently ending on a sour note.

Billings ushered John over to another table. He took the prints himself. "Thanks to modern technology we can access the FBI's files. I'll be able to make a match in a few short minutes. If your prints are on record."

The sheriff's eyes were narrowed on John. Of course, Julia realized, the sheriff was probably having a hard time dealing with seeing Jack's face again. Nothing unusual there.

While John and Julia waited, a deputy poured them each

a cup of coffee. They stood in a corner together, watching the law at work. Billings continued to glance up at them. At John. His eyes were dark, clouded with negative emotions. Had there been a problem between Jack and Billings that she hadn't been aware of?

The sheriff finally waved them over, a generous smile on his face. Although she'd never had reason to doubt him before, Julia found herself wondering if the smile was genuine.

"I've got your name, son. John Smith. You work for the Drug Enforcement Administration. As a matter of fact, I took the liberty of having my deputy give them a call. He spoke to your partner, Agent Mike Chalmers. You are what is known as 'missing in action.' They had you figured for dead. You weren't supposed to leave the hospital. They were sending a plane and an escort to help you, but you disappeared.

"You had the El Paso police department looking high and low for you. But I guess the DEA taught you how to hide out, huh? Here's Chalmers's number. You may want to call him. I'm sure he can tell you more than I can."

John took the slip of paper and tucked it into his jeans without looking at it.

Julia's heart sank. He wasn't her husband. She had fought to keep from hoping, but hadn't been able to completely squash her wishful thoughts. Now she only wanted to put distance between herself and the man with her husband's face. A clean break would be best.

Julia walked out without a word, and John followed silently. Once they were inside the truck, he laughed without humor. "I can't believe it. John Smith. Your sheriff doesn't have much of an imagination."

She blinked. "What? What are you saying?"

He stared at her, the beautiful smile back in place. "You

didn't buy that garbage, did you? My name is not John Smith. I don't know what it is, but I know it's not Smith. Same as I know it isn't John Doe. The sheriff was lying through his teeth.''

"Why would he do that?''

John shrugged. "I don't know yet. I guess I'll give this Chalmers guy a call and see if he's any more convincing than your sheriff.''

"I'm not sure if you're correct about him lying, but something wasn't quite right in there. Billings was staring holes through your back. He never looked at Jack like that.''

John Smith was a ridiculous name, but it could be his real name. She had known Billings for years. Why would he lie?

Chapter Five

Julia waited outside the El Paso motel. They had decided to go to El Paso to check out Billings's story. The driver's side door flew open and John climbed into the cold cab. He motioned her over to the passenger side, wanting to drive now. Morose and tense, he had hardly said a word.

John passed her a baseball bat. She cradled it in her lap, staring at it in dumb fascination. Where in the world had he gotten a bat?

He shrugged at her silent question. "Clerk says this place has been broken into a few times in the past several months. He thought we might need the bat for protection. I told him we were honeymooners low on money. He thinks we're low on brains, too."

She nodded, accepting the explanation with a calm exterior while her insides were screaming. What had she gotten herself into?

They found the room with no problem. John unlocked the door before saying, "I hope you don't mind sharing. I thought it might be considered odd if honeymooners wanted double beds."

With that bold announcement, he left her standing in the doorway, mouth ajar. She hadn't expected to share a bedroom with him.

John ripped the T-shirt over his head, and the room seemed to shrink immensely. Julia realized the precarious situation she had placed herself in too late. John was a stranger, a very attractive stranger, but a stranger nonetheless. How well did she really know him?

Her grip tightened on the bat. She remained in the doorway, reluctant to close her only means of escape.

John lifted an eyebrow. "Are you coming in? I'm going to take a shower. Lock the door, and don't open it to strangers. If someone knocks, yell for me."

Ironically, she thought, she'd already let the stranger inside. She could get the keys while he was showering, leave him in El Paso. She could return safely to her family, but she would never know the truth. What if by some miracle he was Jack? She couldn't leave him to fend for himself. She might never see him again.

Something caught her eye. She moved closer to him, momentarily forgetting her reservations about being *too* close to him. He had scars on his stomach and back. What appeared to be two bullet wounds were in the same location Jack had been shot. Her hands began to shake.

John frowned at her. "What's wrong now? You look like you've just seen a two-headed monster."

There were a few other scars, as well. There was a long sharp cut stretching diagonally across his spine. There were a few burn marks on one of his arms, as if someone had deliberately put a cigarette out on his flesh. Jack hadn't had any of those on his body. What in the world did this man do to acquire such a wide range of scars?

He glanced down at himself. "I see you've noticed my collection. Pretty gruesome, huh? Took me a while to get used to them, too."

"Jack was shot twice in the stomach."

John nodded. "I know what you're thinking. You need

to stop doing this to yourself, Julie. I may not be John Smith, but that doesn't mean I'm Jack Keller."

He vanished into the bathroom. Julia dropped the bat down beside the bed. Her eyes widened. She couldn't believe they only had one bed. What were they going to do? She was not going to sleep side by side with him again. It had been a bad idea the first time. It would be an even bigger mistake now that she was beginning to notice things about him.

Such as the way he moved. He didn't walk like most men. He didn't swagger or strut. He was a jungle cat, moving gracefully without making a sound. For a man of his size, it was quite a feat.

She had also noticed his beautiful smile. He had nearly perfect teeth, like Jack, and when he smiled a dimple formed an indention in one cheek.

The phone rang. Julia nearly fell over the bed in her rush to answer it. No one knew they were at the motel. She assumed it would have to be the desk clerk.

A husky female voice enunciated, "The man you are with is a dangerous man. He has killed many people. Get away from him quickly. Or you may be next on his list."

Julia cried, "Who is this?"

"Hurry. While you are still able."

The line went dead, and the bathroom door opened. She froze. John emerged, drying his hair. He was back in his jeans. Whether out of modesty or courtesy for her, she wasn't sure. He stopped next to the end of the bed. Her eyes shifted to the baseball bat. She had set it down, and now it was too far out of reach.

John's cold blue eyes flicked over her. "Who were you talking to?"

She slowly hung up the phone, trying to keep her voice from quivering. "Nobody. Wrong number."

John shook his head and smiled, but it didn't quite reach his eyes. He discarded the towel he'd been drying his hair with. Before she could guess what he was going to do, the bat was in his hands. He held both ends. "Why don't I believe you?"

He approached slowly. Julia stood, then realized she was trapped between him and the wall. She leaned against it. How could she diffuse the situation? She had to say something fast. She couldn't tell him the truth. What if the caller was right about him?

He was a dangerous man. Dangerous to her, at least. She was alone in a motel room with a dangerously attractive stranger. How could she have been this dumb? Because he resembled her husband she had thrown caution to the wind and left town without telling a soul.

"I'm reminded of an old black-and-white movie," he said. "This woman was trapped in a blizzard with a charming stranger. With only a fire poker for protection, she spent the night with him. They were both fighting an intense attraction between them. She left the poker beside the door while she made tea, letting down her guard. He entered the room. Her eyes went to the poker. He picked it up, and her eyes grew as big as the Mississippi."

John continued to close the gap between them until she could feel his warm breath on her cheek. She could smell him, fresh from the shower. Now she knew for certain. Her heart was in danger.

He said, "The man went to her. It took him forever to cross the room. The woman's hands went to her mouth, choking back a scream."

Julia asked, "What happened?"

"He handed her the poker. He said 'I think you forgot something.' Turns out he wasn't a killer, after all. The woman had a wild imagination."

John held the bat out to her. When she didn't immediately take it, he used the rounded end to lift her chin. He moved closer. Julia's hands went to the top of his shoulders. It was an automatic response. She told herself she did it to hold him at bay.

Her heart skipped a beat. He was going to kiss her, and she was going to let him.

Then John took a couple steps backward, putting some distance between them. She should have been grateful for his calculating mind, able to think under any circumstance, but she wanted to pull him back and demand that he kiss her.

He said, "Keep the bat next to you tonight if you want."

He circled the bed and stared down at it as if trying to decipher the pattern of the comforter. She looked down, as well, trying to see what he saw. One bed. One tiny mattress. It wasn't big enough for the two of them to sleep comfortably.

John said, "We should get some sleep."

She twisted her lower lip between finger and thumb. How safe were they going to be in the same bed? How safe did she want to be? Neither of them had much control when in close proximity to the other.

He offered, "I'll sleep on the floor."

"You can't do that. Remember your back? We can share. I don't mind. Just stay on your side."

"On my side?" He smiled. "Have you checked the dimensions of this bed? We'll feel every breath, every sigh the other person makes."

She shrugged. "I can handle it if you can. As gorgeous as you are, I think I can control myself."

"Oh, really? Okay, then. We'll share."

"I have to make one phone call first."

His expression sobered. He nodded ruefully and returned to the bathroom while she dialed. She was in luck. Sylvia answered the phone. If Bob had answered, she wasn't sure what she would have said.

Julia gave Sylvia the number of the motel in case of an emergency. She cut the call short, not wanting to give Sylvia time to ask questions. Sylvia made it sound like a second honeymoon.

Julia sighed as she hung up the phone. Once they discovered John's true identity, it would be hard for Sylvia to accept.

"Everything okay at home?"

She glanced up to find John watching her from the bathroom doorway and her mouth went dry. His hair was a damp mess. She wanted to tangle her fingers in it. And his body? Too incredible for words.

Her eyes followed his solid chest to his muscular abdomen and down to the top of his unbuttoned jeans. He could have just stepped out of a magazine ad. Her husband had had a body like that. What if he was Jack? Touching him wouldn't be wrong then.

She pulled herself up short and said, "Yeah. Everything's fine."

He approached slowly. "You look tired."

"Thanks."

He smiled. "Get some rest."

He switched off the light, which made things worse. She could hear him removing his jeans. The zing of a zipper sliding down. The whisper of denim hitting the floor. Her face heated. She'd had no idea he was going to sleep in the buff when she'd offered to share the bed.

Well, she was going to keep her clothes on. Every stitch. She slid under the sheet, realizing he was going to sleep on top of it. That made her feel a little better. As long as there was some barrier between them, they wouldn't be tempted.

In the darkness he spoke. "I'm sorry about teasing you earlier. You looked like a deer caught in the headlights, mesmerized by an oncoming car."

She said, "Aha! You have a mean streak. I did not know that."

She felt the mattress sag as he raised up on one elbow. He was too close. Now she understood what he'd meant about the bed. It was way too small. His warm breath tickled her ear. A red neon light flashed No Vacancy outside their window. She tensed.

He said, "I want you to know that no matter what happens tomorrow, I will never forget you. You are an amazing woman."

"I'm not amazing. I haven't done anything."

"What are you saying?" She heard the disbelief in his voice. "You've been beside me through this whole mess. You had every reason to toss me out, but you helped me instead. Not many people would bend over backward for a stranger."

"It's not like I'm doing this for charity." Another wave of sadness rocked her heart. "You forget, you look like my husband. I was hoping you would wake up one day and remember me. I'm no saint. I helped you for purely selfish reasons."

His husky voice drifted over her. "I don't believe you. I think you would have helped me even if I looked like the Hunchback of Notre Dame."

Julia bolted up in bed. "Oh, my!"

"What? What's wrong?"

"Nothing's wrong. I just realized you remembered something earlier. You told me about a movie you'd seen.

You told me about it in detail. Maybe your memory is returning.''

"Big deal. I can tell you the plot of an old movie. I can't tell you where I saw it or who I was with. I can't even tell you if I liked it.''

"It's a start.'' She paused to lay back down. "I wish I could see your face right now. I have no idea if I'm getting through to you. I want you to be happy about this.''

He sighed in the darkness. "I prefer it this way. You can't see my face. You can't confuse me with him. I could be anybody. Anywhere. We could be a couple on a romantic getaway. I could kiss you right now and it would be me kissing you, not another man's ghost.''

He reached for her, and her hand went up to stop him. "I don't think this is a good idea.''

"Don't think. Just feel.''

His hand grasped the nape of her neck and he pulled her to him. Their lips met briefly at first. He nibbled lightly at the corners, teasing and tormenting her.

Suddenly she found herself on her back with him leaning over her. Their mouths meshed together in unspoken agreement. His tongue penetrated her lips. His hands smoothed down the length of her body. He was moving way too fast.

As if reading her mind he inched back, stroking her cheek. "I think that's enough for now. Talk to me. I want to listen to your voice.''

"Talk about what?''

"Anything. Tell me about when you were a kid.''

Talking to him in the darkness gave her an odd sense of calm. The words flowed naturally. She didn't consider what she was saying. She spoke freely to him. Telling her life story seemed strange to her. Growing up in a small town, falling in love with the neighbor boy, she hadn't had to do it before. Everyone knew her story.

She added, "I love horses. I remember wanting to be a veterinarian. I got married instead."

He asked, "How did you get into accounting?"

"I was good with numbers. My father taught me book-keeping."

"What happened to your father? Does he still live next door?"

An old sadness crept into her throat. "My father died a year after I married Jack. Old Gray Macready bought his land. I was pregnant at the time. Dad didn't live to see his first grandchild." She laughed. "Listen to me, talking like there'll be others. It doesn't look like I'll have any more babies."

A loaded silence followed her statement.

John quietly returned, "You don't know that. You could fall in love one day."

"Don't take this the wrong way. I want to be honest with you. I loved Jack. I loved him when I was ten, and I never doubted he was the one. We were soul mates. I was lucky to find a love like that. I don't expect it to happen again."

"You're giving up?"

"I didn't say that. I would like to love again. I have dated a few times this past year."

His tone sharpened in surprise. "You did? But Bob said…"

"Bob doesn't know everything. Anyway, nothing ever came of it. They would try to make me laugh at their jokes or try to dazzle me with their intellect. The whole time I would be mentally comparing them to Jack."

"And finding them lacking, I presume." His voice was dry with cynicism.

"As a matter of fact, yes. Look, I don't want you to misunderstand me. Jack was not perfect. He had faults like everyone else. I was a woman in love. If a man treats a woman right, she can forgive almost anything."

John's hopeful smile transcended the darkness. "At the risk of you thinking I'm a jerk, I'd like to hear the negative aspects of Jack's personality. All I've heard so far is how great he was. It would be nice to be able to view him as human."

Julia sighed wistfully. "Jack kept his feelings inside. He hid behind an incredible smile. I never knew what was going on inside his head. It used to drive me crazy." She smiled. "And he was macho. He thought he had to put on a show. It took me years to convince him I loved him for his true self. Warts and all. He also loved to tease. Sometimes without mercy."

"That doesn't sound so bad," John interrupted. "I thought you were going to give me something that would make him into a mere mortal again. Did you ever fight with him?" He doubled his pillow over and leaned against it. "Tell me about that. Remember a time when you wanted to see the backside of him."

It was hard to focus on the bad times. There weren't many. She squeezed her eyes shut tightly and concentrated on the biggest fight they'd ever had. "He came home drunk one night. His father's body had been found, buried in a shallow grave. Jack's father was murdered, but the perpetrator was never caught. He was inconsolable. He wouldn't talk to me. He acted as if I couldn't understand his pain. But my father had died, too. I understood. I pushed him to open up to me, and he walked out. He didn't come back until the following afternoon. I remember being so afraid he wouldn't come back at all."

John said, "He should have let you help him. Sometimes it takes more guts to reach out than it does to go it alone.''

''Basically, Jack was wonderful. When I was pregnant, it put us both to the test. He took care of me when I was suffering from morning sickness. He went to town every time I had a strange craving. I was overly emotional. Jack smiled when I chewed him out for nothing, and he made me feel feminine when I looked like a whale.''

The mattress shook as the man beside her laughed. ''I wish I could have seen you. I bet you were a sight.'' She punched him in the shoulder. ''Do you have pictures?''

Lying next to him in the dark, whispering to each other like naughty children after bedtime, the intimacy of the situation didn't escape her notice. It felt wrong. Yet, nothing had felt this good in two years.

HE COULDN'T SLEEP.

John stared into the murky black as he tried to recall every word the woman in his arms had uttered since their first meeting. He wanted to memorize every fact she had divulged for future use. A person never knew when something they had heard would come in handy. Information could be a powerful tool.

Her marriage had been a good one, but not a perfect one. It eased his heart to know she understood the difference. It meant he might have a chance with her if he wanted it. The odds were against him. If he was smart, he would move on.

He sighed as the woman snuggled closer to his body. He wasn't going to get any sleep tonight. His insomnia had more to do with the whirling mess in his mind than her close proximity. Although she did smell good. His nostrils detected a hint of wildflowers. And she was soft, softer than anything he'd felt since waking up in the hospital.

His lower regions stirred in complaint, so he changed the direction of his thoughts.

The dash of cold water came in the form of Mike Chalmers. He would meet the DEA agent in the morning, preferably alone. Julia had been through enough.

John lit a cigarette and considered the problem of Chalmers. If the man swore John had been his partner, how would he convince Julia that it was a lie? He needed proof.

He needed to speak to Dr. Pascal. The medicine man had a lot to answer for. Either the man had lied about Jack Keller dying or he'd given John another man's face, creating havoc on an entire family. Why would Pascal put his career on the line?

There was also the problem of Sheriff Billings. There had been something strange in the way the lawman had reacted to seeing John. He hadn't seemed surprised to see a dead man walking. On the contrary, he had been irritated by John's appearance.

Billings had taken him aside to ask him if he was faking the amnesia. That brought on another load of questions, too many to contemplate in the early morning hours.

John stubbed out his cigarette and closed his eyes. He had to get some sleep if he was going to be on his toes with Chalmers. He had to get the upper hand.

Within seconds John found himself walking through a humid jungle. The blue bandanna around his forehead was damp with perspiration, and his leg ached where he had been recently shot. He dredged on, rifle ready. His ears picked up a brief noise. Someone was trying to sneak up on him.

He spun around and fired at the enemy….

The scene changed. He was now inside a grass hut, digging a bullet out of a man's side. The man grunted, trying to suppress the pain. John smiled in amusement. ''Yell if you want. No one's around.''

The other man's eyes widened in horror.

John whipped around, grabbing his rifle. He wasn't fast enough. Knocked to the floor, he fought the intruder. A blade glinted in the afternoon light. John struggled harder, thinking it would be stupid to get killed by a man he hadn't seen. He didn't even know what the guy looked like.

John's hands went around the guy's throat. He shoved hard against the massive weight. Caught off guard, the man rolled. John went with him. His hands tightened. The man's attempts to free himself were weak.

''Stop it!'' Julia gasped. ''Let me go!''

Chapter Six

He was choking her.

Julia, jolted awake by the closing off of her air supply, could feel the strong hands enclose her throat, squeezing tighter. Her eyes flew open. John hovered. The blinking red neon light revealed his features. His blue eyes stared through her, not seeing her. He was living out his nightmare.

Asleep or not, he was trying to kill her. Her head swam dizzily as she struggled for oxygen. His bruising grip tightened. She fought him to no avail. Darkness closed in on her. In another minute she would be dead.

Julia's mind centered on her son. He had already lost one parent. She couldn't let him grow up without her. He needed her to guide him. With all of her remaining strength she slapped John as hard as she could.

John's head snapped back. His eyes blinked down at her, trying to focus. His hands fell away. He shifted away from her. His erratic breaths matched her own. The look on his face, the confusion and fear, made her reach out for him.

He shrugged her hand off. "I must be losing my mind. I tried to hurt you."

"You were dreaming," she said. "Do you remember what you were dreaming? Think hard. It could help us."

John's head tilted back and he stared up at the ceiling. He took a deep breath. "I don't know. I rarely remember my dreams."

She rubbed her bruised throat. Her voice came out a raw whisper. "Don't worry. It will all come back in time."

He growled, "How can you be so damned calm about this? I could have killed you. What sort of a man am I?"

John bounced from the bed. He hadn't gone to bed nude, after all. He wore a pair of blue briefs. She stared at them as he roughly pulled on his discarded jeans and grabbed the nearby shirt.

"Don't be so melodramatic. You were asleep. You wouldn't have hurt me."

Julia scrambled off the bed. If she didn't stop him, he would leave her. She couldn't let him go. Not yet. He had to stay, at least until they discovered the truth.

She said, "Talk to Chalmers. He might be able to shed some light on these nightmares."

John laughed harshly. "I'm not sure I want to hear it. I don't remember details about my dreams, but I know they're filled with violence."

She whispered, "You're a good man."

"I don't think you'd be saying that if you knew the real me. Unfortunately, I don't know the real me, so I can't clue you in."

"Maybe you were a cop. Billings could have been telling the truth about the DEA."

"Or maybe I was a hired killer," he said. "The point is, neither of us knows. I won't take the chance of hurting you again. I'm going on alone from here. You need to go back to your family."

John would have left, but she blocked his way, barring the door. Her eyes locked on to his.

She said, "You won't hurt me. It was a mistake. It won't happen again."

"How can you be so sure?"

Julia smiled wryly. "Well, I guess we won't sleep together again. Of course, we could always handcuff you to the bed. That might be interesting."

He knew she was only trying to distract him with sexy innuendoes. A reluctant smile grew on his strained mouth. "Why are you doing this for me? You don't know me. I'm not your problem. Is it because I look like Jack?"

Was it? She didn't know, but she had the feeling he wouldn't take that for an answer. So she kept it simple. "No. It isn't because you look like Jack. It's because you need help, and I'm the only one here."

He asked, "Am I getting under your skin, Julie?"

She walked away, certain he wasn't going anywhere. She quipped over her shoulder, "I'm going to take a shower. Get some sleep. I'll wake you in an hour or two."

Suddenly serious, he asked, "Are you okay? I didn't hurt you, did I?"

"I'll live."

She wished she could wash away the pain and regret in his eyes. She couldn't imagine John using a gun on anybody. Perhaps the dreams stemmed from a movie he had seen. He had been talking about an old movie earlier.

She sighed as she stepped into the shower's biting stream. She was grasping for explanations when the obvious one was right under her nose. John had been a bad man in his past life. There was no telling what horrible things he had done.

But did he have to return to that life? Would his old personality return with his memories?

JOHN GLANCED DOWN at his watch for what Julia thought was the millionth time since entering the nearly vacant restaurant. It was too early in the morning for the usual breakfast crowd. Julia reached across the table, placing her hand over his. She gave him a reassuring smile. She wished he would relax. He was making her anxious.

He said, "You should have stayed behind. This could be a trap. I want you safe."

A tiny thrill rippled over her skin because he cared about her. "Don't be silly."

"We don't know this guy. We don't know what to expect. You'd be safer at the motel. It's not too late for you to go back."

She laughed nervously, absently playing with her napkin. "Safer at the motel? Remember the harried night clerk giving you a bat? No, I'm safer with you."

Her eyes dropped. She had revealed more than she had intended. Until she sorted out her feelings she was better off not letting him get too close. A soft pink blush stained her cheeks. The man sitting across the booth from her could throw her thoughts into turmoil with a single blink of his beautiful blue eyes.

John opened his mouth to say something else, but he didn't get a chance to follow through. A shadow fell across their table, and he glanced up. Julia's gaze followed his.

A menacing young man with smooth dark skin and charcoal-black eyes hovered over their table. His hair fell in thick dreadlocks down his back. He tapped John's shoulder with the back of his hand. "Slide over."

"What?"

The other man laughed loudly. A waitress turned in their direction, glaring at them. The man stopped laughing, staring deep into John's vacant eyes. He shook his head in what appeared to be dumbfounded awe. "I can't believe it. Man, you really are messed up this time. You don't know who I am, do you?''

Julia looked at John, waiting for him to respond. His cold expression hadn't changed. He slid across the seat to the window, his eyes never leaving the tall intruder.

John said, ''You're Chalmers.''

The young man grimaced and mockingly repeated, ''Chalmers.'' He took a seat, taking his time, adjusting his position in an effort to get comfortable. Julia had the feeling he was stalling for time.

He finally said, ''In all the eighteen months I've known you, you never once called me by my last name. You really are messed up. What happened, man? You look okay to me.'' His eyes shifted to Julia, mentally assessing her in seconds. ''I never saw John with a woman before. Only professionally, I mean. He's usually all business. Who are you?''

John bristled. ''Never mind who she is. Who am I?''

Chalmers glanced around the restaurant as if he was looking for something in particular. His eyes finally returned to John. ''Okay. Is this amnesia thing on the level? You can trust me, you know.''

''You are the second person to ask me if I'm faking it. And I don't know if I can trust you. That's the whole point. I don't remember you. I don't know my name. Either fill me in or stop wasting my time.''

Chalmers whistled between clenched teeth. ''You've got it bad. Okay. Your name is John Smith.''

John laughed without humor. Julia recognized the danger in it. He was about to lose his temper.

''That's a lie, and I know it.'' John leaned forward, whispering even though everything in him clearly wanted to scream. ''Why are you lying to me? Who am I really?''

''I'm not lying to you, man,'' Chalmers said. ''Maybe

your name wasn't always John Smith, but it was the name I knew you by. I can't tell you what I don't know. You were all business. I asked a few questions once, and you bit my head off. You were running, hiding from something. I don't know. I wish I could help you, man. But I don't know anything."

Julia interrupted, "Can you tell us anything that could help us find his true identity?"

Chalmers returned her level stare. "All I know is it was real important for John here to keep his identity a secret. He trusted me with his life, but he wouldn't tell me anything about his past. He put his cards on the table one day. Told me if I wanted to be his friend, I would keep my nose out of his business. So I did."

She changed the subject. "What about Cecily? Do you know a woman named Cecily?"

Chalmers's booming laughter once again filled the room, echoing loudly. "Cecily Carpenter was his shrink."

John blinked. "What?"

Julia said, "He was seeing a psychiatrist? What for?"

"I wondered that, too. He wouldn't say." Chalmers shrugged. "Like I said, I don't know anything. I tracked him down one time and found him with this uptight blond woman. When I asked him if she was his old lady, he told me she was his shrink."

She couldn't stop herself from asking, "Did you believe him?"

"I didn't disbelieve him. She could have been his shrink. Struck me as funny, though, how they were meeting at her house. Her office was in town, but they met at her house every time."

John said, "You know where she lives then?"

Chalmers removed a piece of paper from his wallet. He jotted an address on the back. While he scribbled, Julia glanced at the open wallet. There was a picture of two men standing in front of a small shack. Warning bells pealed in her head, but she ignored them. She had to know the truth.

Julia grabbed the wallet.

"Hey!" Chalmers made a move to take it from her.

She turned it slowly, showing John. It was a photo of himself and Chalmers. John's face was the same; it was Jack's face. His features hadn't been tampered with, after all. Pascal had lied.

John took the wallet. "How long ago was this picture taken?"

Chalmers said, "Last year. We were in Brazil."

John's voice shook. "I don't understand. I was told my face had been destroyed in the accident. I was told they reconstructed it. But I look the same."

"Whoever told you that lied to your face, man. Your old face. You've always been this ugly." When John didn't respond to the joke, Chalmers said, "What do you need? Name it. Even though you don't remember me, I remember you. What can I do?"

John transfixed Chalmers with a probing stare as if he was trying to figure out if he could trust the man or not. Julia wondered if Chalmers was telling them the truth. She was no expert, but the photograph could be faked. Perhaps John didn't know this man at all.

John took the address and glanced at it. "It's here in El Paso."

Chalmers nodded. "You came here a lot, sometimes for several days at a time. When you returned to work, you were more sullen than usual. I got used to the bad moods. I came to expect them. I always thought you had something going with the lady shrink." He glanced at Julia. "What do I know? I'm more confused than you are."

John said, "I seriously doubt that. Is there anything else you'd like to tell me before we leave?"

"You aren't going to let me help you, are you?"

John shook his head. "Can't do it. I don't know who you are, and I don't trust anyone right now outside of this lady right here."

Chalmers grinned. "Same old John. You are the most paranoid individual I've ever met. I guess I have to respect your wishes. Let me know how it turns out."

John's eyes narrowed. "You're giving up a little too easily."

Chalmers smiled widened. Stark white teeth flashed against the darkness of his face. "You see, you do know me. I'll be around. If you need anything, just yell."

The two men stood and shook hands. Julia grabbed her purse. She was half afraid John might try to leave her behind. She hadn't come all the way to El Paso to sit in some sleazy motel room.

"There is one more thing I'd like to know," John added. "If my accident wasn't an accident, whose direction should I look?"

Chalmers's face took on a deadly serious expression. "You got proof it wasn't an accident?"

John shrugged. "Maybe. Do you know anyone who wants me dead?"

"Ask me for a list of those who don't. It would be shorter. In our line of work we don't make many friends."

John gave a brief nod before turning to the door. He didn't bother to ask what kind of work Chalmers was referring to, and Julia wondered why. Billings had mentioned the DEA, but Chalmers hadn't said a word about it.

Julia followed John to the truck and climbed in on the passenger side. She wasn't in the mood to argue over who was going to drive. He didn't seem to notice. His mind was otherwise occupied.

Julia concentrated on the road.

THE HOSPITAL looked different during the day to John. The outside gleamed like an oasis in the desert. His gaze automatically went up to the window that had been his. He had its location memorized.

They went to the information desk, and Julia took over before he could say anything. "We're here to see Dr. Pascal."

The woman glanced up with an uninterested smile frozen to her face. "Do you have an appointment?"

"No, but I'm an old friend. I need to see him. We'll wait if necessary."

The woman punched up a number of letters on her computer screen. "I'm sorry. Dr. Pascal is on vacation. He won't be back for an entire week."

John said, "Convenient."

Julia sent him a warning glance before asking the woman, "Could you tell me when he left?"

"His vacation started this morning. He was actually supposed to work, but he called in."

"Do you know where he's gone?"

The woman shrugged. "Maybe he's playing golf."

John interrupted. "Can you give us his address?"

The woman's eyes narrowed suspiciously. "I thought you were friends of his."

Julia said, "We are. But he recently moved. I don't remember where his new house is located. Could you give me a hint?"

"Sorry. I'm not allowed to give out that sort of information."

John motioned for Julia to follow him. He was leaving.

Life was too short for a wild-goose chase. He would skip
Pascal and talk to Cecily. If one lead failed, you picked
up another.

Now where had he learned that?

A woman in dusky-pink scrubs entered the building and
smiled at him. "John Doe. I was one of your nurses. Remember me? Do you know your name yet?"

John fixed her with a bright smile. "Actually, no. I have
a few leads. Dr. Pascal is out, so I can't talk to him about
my case. Do you know anything about it?"

"Well, I can't give you your file or anything. I do know
what your injuries were. Why did you cut out in the middle
of the night? Dr. Pascal nearly had a cow. Two men in
suits came looking for you. Things were intense. Pascal
seemed almost…frightened."

"I was sick of hospital food." The nurse giggled and
he continued, "What were my injuries?"

"Well, head trauma for one. That caused your coma.
You had a broken leg and lacerations on your face."

Julia asked, "Did Dr. Pascal have to reconstruct this
man's face?"

The woman barely glanced at Julia. Her adoring gaze
returned to John. "Of course not. There was nothing
wrong with your face that a few stitches couldn't cure,
sweetheart. No, you've always looked this good. I can
barely see a trace of a scar now. And only because I'm a
trained professional."

John said, "You've been a big help. Thanks."

The woman reluctantly walked away, a disappointed
turn to her lips as if she expected more from him. She was
cute, but he wasn't interested in dating her. If he was going
to date anyone, he wanted it to be the stubborn woman
beside him.

"This is your original face," Julia said. "We've heard it from two sources now, but why would Pascal lie?"

John scratched his chin. "Because he didn't want me to find out my true identity, I guess."

"Why?"

John said, "You tell me. You met Pascal before. Didn't you?"

"I only met him once, when he cared for Jack. Pascal pronounced Jack dead. What in the world is going on? Why would he lie? Why would he risk his reputation?"

"I don't think Pascal had a choice. Someone else is behind this, someone bigger."

"But who?"

"Perhaps the same person who tried to have me killed."

She took his arm and pulled him toward the automatic doors. "We need to see the police. This is getting out of hand. They can protect you."

He laughed. "Protect me? Honey, I may have been a DEA agent. If I couldn't protect myself, the locals can't do any better. No, I have to find the guilty party on my own."

Still holding his arm, she gave it a light squeeze. "You aren't going through this alone. I'm going to help you, like it or not."

"I don't want you in the center of this. It's dangerous. I'd never forgive myself if anything happened to you."

"Nothing will happen to me." She said, "Besides, if you're Jack and there are people out there who want to kill you, they already know I'm your wife. They'll assume I love you. They could use me to get to you. It's better if I stay by your side."

A smug smile transformed his handsome face. "Admit it. You care about me. More than you want to."

She rolled her eyes as if annoyed. "Fine. Have it your

way. I care about you. But that doesn't mean we'll be together when this thing finishes playing out. I need to know if you're my husband. You need to know."

His expression sobered and he asked, "If we find out I'm Jack Keller, your husband, and I left you, would you ever be able to forgive me?"

"I don't know. Depends on why you left." She forced a smile. "So, are we partners now?"

"Partners."

"Shake on it."

Julia stuck out a hand. He grasped it lightly with his, then pulled her to him. "I got a better idea. Let's kiss on it."

Before she could object, his mouth captured hers. It was a searing kiss meant to seal more than a deal. The background noise faded. He couldn't hear anything beyond the beating of his own heart.

He was in danger of a different kind.

Chapter Seven

Julia rang Cecily Carpenter's doorbell.

John stood off to the side, partially hidden behind a bush. Julia could feel the tension holding him ramrod straight as they waited for a response. The lacy white curtain in the window rippled. Someone was home. John and Julia waited, but the door remained firmly shut.

Julia knocked again.

There was a soft click. The door moved open an inch, far enough for Julia to see the gold chain holding it in place. A frightened brown eyeball peeked through the slit.

"What do you want?"

Julia said, "We need to talk to you, Dr. Carpenter."

"I'm not Dr. Carpenter. She's...unavailable at the moment."

The door began to shut. John moved fast, sliding a foot inside before it closed. He held it immobile, staring at the woman. At least what was visible of her. He said, "We aren't leaving until we speak to her. Do you know me? Have we met?"

The woman's eye widened, and he quickly explained, "I have amnesia. I need the doctor's help. I have a feeling she could shed some light on my situation."

"I know who you are. Cecily is my sister. She moved away. I don't know where." Her voice broke. "If I talk to you, I might never see her again. They could be watching.''

'''They'?'' Julia raised an eyebrow at John.

The woman's eyes darted up and down the street. "The people she works for. My sister works for a government agency. I don't know which one. Very hush-hush, you know.

"They showed up a few days ago, packed her stuff, said they were relocating her, but I wasn't allowed to know where. I don't even know if she's still in the country. Cecily didn't seem scared. She went willingly.''

John said, ''I'd be grateful for anything you can tell me. Did you know me? Did we ever talk?''

The woman swung the door shut. Believing she wasn't going to speak to them anymore, Julia turned to leave. Then she heard the chain fall. The woman reluctantly stepped outside. She was like a tall glass of lemonade, cold with only a hint of sweetness.

The lady wasn't bad-looking. There were still traces of beauty beneath the fine wrinkles and the circles under the woman's brown eyes. There was no sign of life in her features, neither happiness nor depression.

A few strands of graying blond hair fell loose from the tight bun secured with dark bobby pins to the back of her head. She wore a long, beige dress with a woolen green sweater pulled over it. No artificial color adorned her face.

Julia was startled to see herself in the woman's lifeless eyes. Had it not been for her son, Julia understood, this woman would be her, this woman who had obviously given up on life.

After Jack died, Julia had wanted to crawl under the covers and never emerge again. If it hadn't been for her son, her dear sweet beautiful son, perhaps she would have done so.

''I'm Clarise.'' The woman smoothed back her graying

blond hair with a nervous hand. "I'm sorry I gave you such a hard time. I didn't want to turn you away. I'm just not sure what's going on. Cecily and I have lived together over ten years now. She takes care of me. Or she did until 'they' took her away. Come in before someone sees you."

John said, "We don't want to bring you any more trouble, but we need answers. Who was asking about me?"

She threw up her hands. "Better to ask who wasn't. I had visits from the local police, the FBI, and a young man with the DEA. He called himself Chalmers, but I can't vouch for him. You'd mentioned him a few times, of course, but I didn't know him personally. There were also a couple of women calling about you. Of course, I didn't tell them anything. None of them. I insisted I didn't know you."

She stepped back, allowing them into her home. It was small, crowded with decorations. The woman had quite a collection of oddities: toy trains, dolls, miniature tea sets, a colorful set of throw pillows on the sofa, lacy doilies, and several thimbles locked behind glass cabinet doors.

There was an interesting odor of lilac, herbal tea and Ben-Gay ointment. It was a bit strong. Julia could not picture a psychiatrist living in the cluttered mess with a neurotic sister.

Julia asked, "How long was John in your sister's care?"

Clarise made a face. "I don't think John was actually a patient."

Julia blinked. "Oh? I got the impression he was a patient."

"Well, he just wanted someone to talk to. He confided in Cecily. Nothing odd about that. We all need someone to talk to on occasion. She doesn't actually practice full-time anymore. She took John on as a favor to a friend."

"Who was the friend?"

Clarise shrugged.

"Well, what kind of things did John talk about?"

"Cecily was strict about doctor-patient confidentiality. Even though he was talking to her more as a friend, she kept his confidence. She'll never tell anyone what was discussed here. Not even you, John." She turned huge eyes on him. "Hey, is this a test? Did they send you to see if I would talk?"

John leaned forward in his floral-print chair. "I need you to talk to us. I have amnesia," he stressed. "It was brought on by a car accident. I don't remember who I am or what I was working on at the time. I need you to tell me anything you can, no matter how small. It's important."

Clarise wriggled as if uncomfortable in her seat. "If this is a trick, it's a good one. But I don't know anything. We only ever talked about the weather and such. Nothing crucial."

John sighed his frustration. Julia could see it was tearing him apart.

She asked, "Does your sister keep files on her patients here?"

"Who are you? I didn't catch your name." Clarise turned suspicious eyes on Julia. "John never mentioned a girlfriend."

"I'm Julia Keller."

The woman ignored Julia's outstretched hand. She appeared to flinch at the name and withdraw further. What reason could this woman have for disliking her?

Julia asked, "Do I know you? Have you heard my name before?"

"The name Keller sounds familiar, but I'm not sure."

John asked, "Are the files here or not?"

"There were files in the office, but those men I told you about packed them up."

John swore. "Dammit, what are we going to do? Whoever 'they' are, they're always one step ahead of us."

Julia asked, "Would you mind if we looked around the office?"

Clarise shrugged. "I suppose Cecily wouldn't mind if John snooped a bit."

"Wait a second. You knew me as John?"

"Yes." She smiled. "John Smith. I always thought it was a fake name. If Cecily knew your real name, she didn't say."

She led them to a small room that had been, until recently, an office. File cabinet drawers were ajar. The desk drawers were open and empty. A few stray papers littered the floor, torn and discarded, rubbish to the people who had packed Cecily's belongings.

Clarise left them alone in the room. They searched it quietly. The minute Julia became certain they wouldn't find anything, she spotted a folder stuffed behind a metal cabinet. The name, printed in bold black, jumped out at her: John Smith.

"Find something?" John asked.

"Yes and no." She explained, "There's a file with an alias on it, but it's practically blank. There's no useful information here. Just sleeping habits, fantasies, and the word 'psychotic' is mentioned."

John grinned. "What sort of fantasies?"

"It says you have fantasies about killing people and becoming ruler of the universe. Also, you want to own everything in sight."

"Oh, is that all?" John laughed, but it sounded hollow. "What does it say about my sleeping habits?"

She read it out loud. "'The patient sleeps ten hours a night. No need for sleeping pills. Borderline psychotic personality. Sociopathic tendencies.'"

"Can't be me." John shook his head. "Doesn't sound like me."

"No, it doesn't." Julia agreed.

"Here, let me see that." He took the file from her, reading it over himself. With a frown, he closed it. His frown deepened. "Wait a second. What is this?"

"What?" Julia hovered beside him, watching in fascination as he peeled back the loose label with his name on it. Underneath was another name. B. Keller.

Julia gasped. "It can't be Bob. Why would he see a psychiatrist?"

John raked a hand through his thick mane, and once again Julia was caught up in the past. It was another of Jack's gestures. One more familiar quality that John possessed. Julia was beginning to think she might never know the truth.

But another fear ran deeper, chilling her bone to the marrow. The more time she spent with John, the less she cared if he was her husband. The more tempted she became to throw caution to the wind and to get to know him on a deeper level.

John said, "Don't say a word about this file to anyone." He tucked it beneath his dark shirt. "Let's go."

Julia watched as John shook hands with Clarise on their way out. "Thank you for your help."

Julia watched as the other woman grasped John's hand and said, "You be careful. They may be after you."

John laughed. "You've been watching too many old movies."

"You used to watch them with me while you waited on my sister. I'm sorry you don't remember."

"One more thing. Have you ever seen this before?" John removed the shiny white card from his pocket.

She replied, "It's the Scarecrow. He's a professional hitman."

"How do you know?"

"My sister mentioned him. She wanted to do a book about him. You know, what drives a person to become such a monster."

Clarise trembled as she twisted her broach until Julia feared the woman would tear the thin cotton material of her dress. Clarise's eyes fell to the floor. She refused to reconnect her gaze with John's.

John said, "It was good seeing you. Take care."

Clarise closed the door behind them. He shrugged at Julia. She wished she could read his mind. What was he thinking? Was he feeling defeated? She wanted to know the secrets behind that mysterious blue stare.

He said, "Do you think she was lying?"

"About what?" Julia blinked, trying to focus on the conversation. "She hardly said anything."

"My name is not John Smith."

Julia pointed out, "Chalmers would disagree. So would Billings. Why would three people who don't know each other repeat the same lie?"

"What makes you think they don't know each other?"

Julia shook her head as if to clear it. "Chalmers told us he didn't know Cecily, and Clarise just confirmed it."

"And of course she wouldn't lie. You are an innocent if you believe that, Julia." He handed her the keys. "You drive. I need to think."

She was grateful for the diversion. "Maybe I am naive, but it's better than being paranoid."

"Even paranoid people have enemies," he reminded her.

"How long have you known my husband's killer was a man named Scarecrow? Don't deny you knew. I saw your face back there. She said exactly what you were expecting to hear when you flashed that card in her face."

John said, "I don't know why it sounds familiar."

Julia started the truck. "Where to?"

"Police station. I'm going to get something out of them."

Julia saw a shadow move behind the curtains. Clarise was watching them. Had the woman lied to them? Was it a big conspiracy, as John suspected?

THE YOUNG FEMALE OFFICER watched John with wary brown eyes. Her fingertips clicked across the keyboard as she entered the data he'd supplied. Every few seconds her puzzled gaze raised up. From his current position, John couldn't see the green glow of the computer screen. From the strained expression on the officer's youthful face he could tell it wasn't good news.

Frustrated, John spoke slowly. "Yes. I don't know the exact date, but I do remember the policeman who took my statement after I woke up in the hospital. It was Nader. Officer Nader."

The female officer stared at John as if she didn't understand a word of English.

An older uniform approached them. "We don't have an Officer Nader working here. You must have the wrong precinct."

"I don't have the wrong place," John insisted. "This is where he told me he worked. He showed me his badge."

The female officer turned to the older one. "This gentleman claims he was in a car accident, but I have no record of it."

"I'll take over."

John said, "I didn't imagine waking up in the hospital. I was in a car accident. An Officer Nader took my statement after I came out of the coma."

The older officer picked up the phone. John listened as the man called the hospital and asked about his case. When he hung up the phone, the man said, "No one's heard of you over there. Go home and sleep it off before I lock you up.''

A flash of memory slapped John in the face. The police officer behind the desk, along with another officer, had dragged him down the corridor and locked him up in a cell.

''You mean, like you did before?''

The man behind the desk shook his head. ''You are nuts. Go home and sleep it off. I won't tell you again.''

John said, ''One more thing, please. Have you ever seen this before?'' He flashed the Scarecrow card in spite of the little voice in his head screaming a warning at him.

The male officer's expression did not change, but the female officer standing to the side went pale. She gasped, dropping a load of files. There was a look of pure terror in her brown eyes.

John returned the card to his pocket. ''Thank you.''

Taking Julia by the arm, he pulled her from the building. An instinct buried but not forgotten told him to hurry. They had to get as far away from El Paso as possible. The ranch was their next destination. He told himself it wasn't exactly running away. He was making a slight retreat to work on strategy for his next move.

Julia asked, ''Why didn't you give him time to answer?''

''I wouldn't believe a word he had to say.'' He paused on the stairs in front of the building. ''I forgot something. Wait here.''

She said, ''I thought you were in a hurry?''

John had noticed a wall of pictures near the front desk. He went back inside and inspected them carefully, searching each one for a familiar face. In their uniforms it was hard to tell them apart. A multitude of partially shadowed faces stared back at him.

The one he was looking for—Officer Nader—stood

proudly in the second-to-last row. So Nader did exist. He hadn't lied to John. He was probably the only one who hadn't.

The older officer glanced up from the telephone to see John staring at the incriminating photograph. He nearly dropped the receiver. His jaw slackened.

John said, "I forgot my pen."

He glanced around, patted his pocket and smiled. "It was in my pocket the whole time. My mistake."

He left quickly, joining Julia on the steps, and something familiar crowded his other emotions. The most familiar sensation he had experienced since waking up in the hospital. It was the sensation of being hunted.

She asked, "What was that all about?"

"I'll tell you later. We should go."

They walked away with two different perspectives. Julia didn't think they'd accomplished anything; John knew better. He had learned more than he'd intended, more than he'd wanted to know. His life was in real danger, and he couldn't trust the police.

BACK AT THE MOTEL John paced like a caged tiger while Julia gathered the items she'd insisted on purchasing from the local drugstore. There wasn't any way to make her hurry without scaring her. He wanted to protect her. He should have left her at the ranch.

If Julia hadn't been a target before, she was now. Thanks to him. His eyes followed her around the room.

She turned a bright smile on him. "What now?"

The phone rang. "I guess I answer the phone."

It was Chalmers. He spoke rapidly. "Leave town now! Go! You're being erased! Go now!"

John asked, "What do you mean 'erased'?"

Chalmers said, "Call the hospital, man. They're saying they've never heard of you."

"I know. Police are the same way. What gives?"

Chalmers explained, "All the doctors and nurses who cared for you have been relocated. Whoever is doing this is serious. They have heavy connections. It looks like an entire organization could be after you."

"DEA?"

Chalmers said, "DEA. FBI. CIA. ABC. Who cares? I've never seen people relocated so fast."

"What do you mean, they've been relocated? Dead?"

"No, man. At least I don't think so. Some are on vacation. Some have new jobs. Your file is gone. The DEA is pretending they've never heard of you. Get it? Now I don't know what the hell you did, but it must have been bad. Keep your head low and good luck."

John opened his mouth to ask more questions, but the connection died.

Julia asked, "What is it?"

He sighed. "I'm being erased."

"Excuse me?"

He stared at her, point blank. "I'm being erased."

The room exploded. Shards of glass flew in every direction. Bullets ripped by their faces. John grabbed her by the wrist, pulling her to the floor. His body landed on top of hers in an effort to protect her. A grunt of painful surprise burst past her lips and was muffled by the carpet.

Chapter Eight

Bullets continued to rip through the door.

Julia found herself on the floor, nose pressed against the dusty gold carpet. It hurt to breathe, in part due to her allergy. Although most of the difficulty stemmed from the one hundred and ninety pounds of warm male flesh lying on top of her. John had moved like lightning, knocking the breath out of her.

She tried to move, using the floor as leverage.

He grunted in her ear. "Stay still. They may not be finished."

They? She felt the steady beat of his heart pulsating through the back of her green blouse. Odd, his heart didn't thunder. He was calm while she wanted to run in any direction. If John wasn't pinning her down, she would bolt for the door.

Terror clawed at her throat. Another time. Another gunshot. She was blasted back to the past. The scent of blood assaulted her nostrils. The feel of Jack's life seeping from his dying body. She had fought for him, desperate to save his life, desperate to keep him with her. The failure to do so presented its own consequences. Now she was sentenced to a life without him.

"Get off me!"

"Not yet." His body shifted, but not enough to give her the freedom she craved. "I don't think they've gone."

"What do we do?"

"Don't worry. I'll think of something."

"And if you don't?" Her voice quivered.

John stroked her cheek. "I won't let anything happen to you."

Did he think she was worried for herself?

She asked, "What about you? I don't need you to play hero and get yourself killed. That isn't a real turn-on for me. I'd rather have a live coward than a dead hero."

He froze in midstroke. Had she finally reached him with her concerns? A new tension seized his entire body, and her senses went on red alert. It was more than a sudden chill in the air, more than the Arctic blue of his cold eyes. The feeling that something had changed came from knowing Jack's expressions.

John moved. On his knees he went for the baseball bat. He grabbed the end with both hands and rose up, holding it high above his head. He shook his head at her, signaling for her to remain on the floor. There was no time to question his judgment.

To Julia it happened in slow motion. The door burst open. An enormous man carrying a gun appeared in the doorway. He spotted her immediately. Gun raised, he smiled through a row of crooked teeth.

John swung the bat down. It connected with the back of the would-be killer's head. The giant fell to his knees and John didn't hesitate to swing the bat again. This time it struck the assassin between the shoulder blades. He collapsed in a heap on the floor.

When John lifted the bat a third time, she rushed forward. "No! You can't kill him!"

"Why not?" He glared at the unconscious man. "He was going to kill us."

"We're better than him."

"No, honey," he corrected her gently. "You are better than him. I'm not."

"Yes, you are. You are better than him."

John's eyes glowed. He turned away from her probing gaze. Instead, he chose to look at the empty doorway. "We should leave. He might have a partner."

"Oh," she gasped. "Yes, but I think we should call the police. They can arrest him before he tries to shoot someone else."

"He isn't going to try to shoot anyone else. He was paid to take care of us. Or rather, me."

"Do you think this is the Scarecrow?"

"Could be. Or he could just be another hired gun. The police could be in on it. We can't trust them."

Julia couldn't believe her ears. The police were the only hope they had, and he was talking as if there was a conspiracy. Jack hadn't been a suspicious person.

She stated, "You are so paranoid."

"So you've said. Call them if you want." She made a move in the direction of the phone, but he caught her arm at the elbow. "Not now. We'll stop at a pay phone on the way home."

She caught his slip of the tongue, but didn't point it out to him. He had called the ranch "home."

She darted out to the truck with John close behind. She took the driver's seat. There was a need deep inside of her to take control.

John's eyes scanned the parking lot. "Step on it."

She threw the truck into Reverse and gunned the engine. The tires squealed in protest. She slammed it into First gear and hit the gas. Her eyes went to the rearview mirror, checking for a second shooter. The parking lot appeared to be empty.

John said, "Relax. We aren't being followed."

"How do you know?"

"Instinct."

All the same, she kept her foot on the accelerator. Once on the road leading home, she found she couldn't slow down. Fear had her speeding past all the other vehicles. They had to make it back to the ranch. They would be safe at the ranch.

Surprisingly, John wasn't complaining about her driving or offering to take over. In fact, he was abnormally quiet. The silence in the cab disturbed her. She turned to him, unprepared for what she would see.

John stared down at his stomach. He had pulled back the plaid shirt to expose a dark stain on his turquoise T-shirt. He examined it, gently peeling the material away from the wound.

She gasped.

Julia lost control of the truck. It swerved into the oncoming traffic. Several horn blasts accompanied her folly. John grabbed the wheel and steered them back onto the right side of the road.

"Watch it! Are you trying to kill us?"

Julia's eyes snapped back to the road, but she couldn't erase the horrible image of John bleeding from her mind. A sense of déjà vu clung to her with razor-sharp tentacles and wouldn't let go.

"Were you shot? You're bleeding!"

"I was probably hit by flying glass. I don't feel a thing."

A wave of dizziness slapped her in the face, and anger surged to life within her breast. He had mumbled the words casually, as if reading off a grocery list. He might have been shot! He could die!

He could die.

The words swirled like rain in a cold March wind. Her

heart was breaking again. "I'm turning around. We need to get you to the hospital."

"No! Keep going. It isn't safe in El Paso. I'm not going to the hospital there. I'd rather bleed to death."

"Don't say that! You can't die on me now!"

"It's okay." He placed a hand on hers. "Just a scratch. Doesn't your town have a doctor?"

"Yes. Dr. Lloyd."

"He can stitch me up then."

Julia bit her lower lip to keep from arguing with him. It wouldn't do any good. He was a stubborn man, a grown man. He could take care of himself. Who was she to insist he seek medical attention? She wasn't his mother.

The truck sputtered and died. Muttering an unladylike curse, she steered to the shoulder of the road. Once the truck had come to a complete stop she tried in vain to reengage the engine. It coughed but didn't quite catch. She didn't know anything about trucks.

John rubbed his forehead in exasperation. "What did you do to it?"

She uttered a string of expletives. Then she said, "It's an old truck."

His blue eyes turned in her direction. "I don't think I've ever heard you curse before."

"I've never been this mad! I can't believe this! We need to get you to a doctor before…" Tears flooded her eyes.

He smiled at her in a way that set her heart to pounding even harder. "I'm not going to bleed to death. It's not that bad. Don't worry about me. I won't die."

I won't die. Jack had uttered the same words on the way to the hospital. He had reached out to her, tried to reassure her. He had forced words past his lips, past the pain.

Pulling herself together, she said, "The nearest phone is several miles back. I'll flag down a car. We aren't that far from the ranch. Maybe we can get a lift."

John was leaning the way Jack had before collapsing against her in the truck on the way to the hospital.

He asked, "Do you need help?"

She put on a smile to reassure him, the same smile she'd pasted on for the family while her own world shattered. "I think I can manage to hold my thumb out. You stay here and rest. You'll need your strength later."

His eyes twinkled. "Oh, yeah? What are we going to do later?"

Sometimes he was so much like Jack it tore her heart in two. She wanted to slap him and kiss him all at the same time, but she refrained from doing either one. It wasn't easy. Her emotions were on overload and his cavalier attitude wasn't helping one bit.

Did he have any idea how beautiful he was?

His long, dark lashes fluttered. "Are you sure you don't need my help?"

"You'd be a hindrance, not a help. Men won't stop for other men like they'll stop for a woman."

He bit off half a laugh, then groaned in pain. "Show some leg if all else fails. You have great legs."

"How would you know?"

He didn't respond; he was unconscious. She had to flag down a ride quickly and get him to a doctor before he died. She wasn't going to lose him. She had lost Jack. Whoever this man was, she was not going to lose him, too.

IT WAS FUNNY how you could be hurt and not feel a thing until you saw the wound. The sight of blood set off a chain reaction. His heart doubled in tempo. Perspiration sprang to life on his face. His wound began to throb and burn like a razor cut.

His vision blurred for a moment, hazy like a dream. Then he saw Julia hovering over him, his own private guardian angel. There were tears in her eyes and she was shaking. He wanted to tell her it was okay, but he couldn't speak.

Of course, she wasn't actually there. Julia was on the side of the road, desperately trying to flag down some help. Apparently she had told him the story of her husband's death so well he could picture it as if it had happened to him. He could practically taste the saltiness of her tears as they rained down on his face. He could feel the blood draining out of his chilled body.

It felt real, but it couldn't be. Julia was certain he wasn't her husband. Almost a hundred percent certain.

But wasn't Sylvia just as certain that he was her son?

They both couldn't be right. He knew which way he was gambling on. If he was Julia's missing husband, he wouldn't have to win her trust or love. They would already be his.

Julia poked her head in. "No one will stop. How are you holding up?"

"You sang to Jack on the way to the hospital. Didn't you?"

"How do you know that?"

"Bob must have mentioned it."

His eyes drifted shut, and the song pulled him back through the years. A sweet melody, it taunted him with familiarity. Then left him without something to grab on to.

HER WORRIED GLANCE traveled back to the truck. As far as she could tell, John hadn't moved since she'd left him. Time dragged by, and she wished she had thought to bring her watch. How long had she been standing on the side of the road? Hours? Minutes?

Julia stuck her thumb out as three cars zoomed by. Not one of them even slowed down. Perhaps John had been right about showing some leg. Too bad she was wearing jeans.

Another car rounded the bend, and Julia automatically went into position. The car passed her. The brakes squealed. The car backed up, returning to her side.

She bent to look inside, smiling with relief. To her the driver had been heaven sent.

Or dispatched from hell.

Chalmers nodded. "What's up? Julia, isn't it?"

She stumbled over the words. "John's been shot. I mean, he might have been shot. He's bleeding. He says he was hit by flying glass."

"Where is he?"

"In the truck." Her eyes drifted to the vehicle. "He's lost a great deal of blood. The truck broke down. I didn't know what to do. I thought I could catch a ride, get him to the ranch or to a doctor."

He gave her a brief nod. "You did the right thing."

Chalmers shut off his car. He followed her and climbed into the truck. First, his fingers went to John's throat, checking for a pulse. Then he laid his hand on the other man's chest. She assumed he was checking his heartbeat, breathing, or both.

John's blue eyes parted. He stared at Chalmers through narrowed slits.

Chalmers asked, "How do you feel, man?"

"Been better."

"You were lucky I came along."

Something strange and disturbing entered John's expression as he mumbled, "Yeah. Lucky."

Julia asked, "Can you walk?"

John shared a smile with her. He stroked one side of her face, staring at her as if seeing her for the first time. Tears filled her eyes at the tender way he touched her.

Julia sniffled and glanced away. It hurt to look at him, but she wasn't sure why anymore. Was it because he looked like her dead husband or because she was beginning to feel something for the man himself?

"I can walk," he insisted. "Just point me in the right direction."

Chalmers helped John from the truck. The two of them walked to Chalmers's car with Julia lagging behind, studying them. There was something strange in the way they interacted. John had slung an arm over Chalmers's shoulders, and Chalmers had gripped John around the waist, half carrying him to the vehicle. It was as if they had done it before, as if it had been rehearsed.

John ducked his head to get inside the car.

Julia said, "Careful."

Chalmers smiled. "Easy there, man."

Julia slid in beside John because there was no back seat in the vintage sports car. It didn't matter. She preferred sitting next to John. Chalmers started the car, and they were on their way at last.

She fought with the memories. The situation wasn't exactly the same as before with Jack. They were in a car, not a truck. John was awake and lucid. But other things were familiar.

She could tell John was watching Chalmers through his eyelashes and wondered if the other man could feel the intense blue gaze.

Julia said, "You can drop us off in the next town. After we see a doctor, my brother-in-law will come get us."

Chalmers shook his head. "I'll take you where you need to go."

Her mouth compressed. "Fine. I'll give you directions when we get closer to the turnoff."

Silence reigned for several minutes. The tension was almost tangible. Julia wanted to say something, but she didn't know what. Chalmers took charge. "What happened to him?"

John's eyes opened all the way. "Why don't you ask *me?*"

Chalmers said, "Sorry, man. I thought you were out of it. So who got to you?"

"Someone's hired gun."

Chalmers laughed, seemingly unaware of the building tension in John's body. "And how do you know that? Did the man give you his business card?"

John stiffened.

Julia interrupted, "No. He showed us his gun."

John struggled to pull a card from his back pocket and flashed it at Chalmers. "Do you know what this is?"

Chalmers nearly ran the car off the road. He twisted the steering wheel sharply, bringing it back under control. His face registered surprise for a brief second. Then nothing. "So, you've had it all this time."

"You've seen it before?"

Julia glared at the card in John's trembling hand. It was horrible, a macabre figure in black. She remembered the day Billings had first showed it to her, insinuating that Jack had been murdered by a professional. What did it mean? She waited along with John for the answer.

Chalmers said, "It's the Scarecrow's calling card."

Julia blinked. "How do you know about the Scarecrow?"

"John and I have been working the case for almost two years. The Scarecrow is a pro. He does a lot of work for organized crime figures. His modus operandi changes quite frequently, but he always leaves his card. We can't get close to him. I think you finally figured out who it was, man. Then you vanished. We thought he got you. The police found the card at the scene of your accident. How did you get it?"

John admitted, "It was tucked inside my jeans when I put them on at the hospital."

"That's weird, man. The police claimed they lost it. Why would someone leave you a clue?"

"I don't know." John sat up straighter. "Do you have a gun on you?"

Julia's hand settled on John's arm. Fear shone in her eyes. He smiled at her reassuringly and waited for the other man's reply. Chalmers withdrew a pistol from under his jacket. He handed it to John as if it was a delicate flower.

John turned the gun on Chalmers without hesitation.

Neither Julia nor Chalmers saw it coming. They were both caught off guard. She watched the two men interact, terrified of what she didn't know. They could be friends. They could be enemies. She wasn't sure anymore. In fact she wasn't sure of anything.

Chalmers shook his head. "Man, you are messed up."

"I'm sorry, if you are who you say you are." John aimed the gun at Chalmers's head. "Pull off to the side. We need to borrow your car. I'll see to it that you get it back."

Chalmers's voice sharpened. "I love this car. You scratch it, and I'll kill you."

The car swerved to a stop at the side of the road, and John motioned for Chalmers to get out. "If you are who you claim to be, then you know I can't trust anyone right now. I apologize for my insolent behavior. Now get out."

Chalmers laughed. "That's the John I remember. Okay. I'll get out, but we'll be seeing each other again. Leave my gun in the glove compartment. I love that gun. I sleep with it. It's seen me through more than one jungle."

John's breath caught. His hand shook harder.

Chalmers's hand moved. Julia wasn't sure if he was going to grab the gun and turn it on them or grasp John's shoulder, helping him through whatever stress was weighing down on him at the moment. Julia couldn't give Chalmers the chance to do what she feared most.

Her hand closed over John's, holding it steady. Her finger slid over his on the trigger. She said, "I'm sorry. He doesn't know whether to trust you, and I only trust him. Please understand. We need the car. I'm sorry for the inconvenience."

"It's more than inconvenient, sugar. It's stupid. He needs me. He just doesn't know it yet."

"He has me now. Goodbye, Chalmers."

"It's not goodbye, sugar. We'll see each other again, real soon."

The threat lingered as he got out of the car. Julia would have climbed over John to drive, but he slid into position and gunned the engine himself. He didn't appear to be in any shape to drive. She didn't say anything. She wanted to put as much distance between them and Chalmers as possible. The man frightened her as few men could.

The gun rested in John's lap. She stared at it, wondering how easily he might turn it on her. His eyes had been like ice while he had pointed the gun in Chalmers's direction. She had no doubt he would have shot the man if provoked. Chalmers must have sensed it, too.

As if reading her mind, John handed the gun to her, butt first.

She held it gently, staring down at it. "You told Chalmers you didn't trust anyone."

"I trust you." He smiled at her again, and the warmth she knew so well was back in his eyes.

She placed the gun in the glove compartment, her heart soaring. John's trust meant a lot to her, especially considering everything he'd gone through. In his situation he shouldn't trust anyone, but he trusted her.

"Maybe I should drive. You look terrible. We need to get you to a doctor."

He said, "I'm okay. Don't worry. I'm tougher than I look."

"I know you are." She smiled, placing her hand over his as he shifted gears.

THE DOCTOR WHISTLED while he worked. He sat on a tall stool, head bent as he stitched together John's wound. Julia waited in the background. John would have rather had her closer to him. She hadn't said much since they'd left Chalmers behind.

Dr. Lloyd said, "You could have knocked me over with a feather when I saw you walk through the front door. Jack Keller was a patient of mine. I delivered him. He came squalling into this world like—"

Julia interrupted, "Dr. Lloyd, are you almost done? I'm anxious to get home to my son."

His head bobbed up and down with rapid movement. "Of course you are. Just give me a second. Now, how did you say he got shot?"

"She didn't." John chose his words carefully. "It was silly really. I'm usually careful with guns, but I was cleaning it and didn't bother to check the chamber. Sure enough, there was a bullet in it."

Lloyd grunted. "Hope you learned a lesson, son. Handguns kill more owners than thieves."

"It won't happen again."

Lloyd turned to Julia. "How did you two meet? Must be strange having a look-alike in the house. Is Sylvia okay with this?"

Julia pasted on a pretty smile. "I guess you could say it was fate. We ran into each other, and the family is fine with it. They understand he's not Jack. Is he okay?"

Dr. Lloyd grunted as he continued to work with a cultivated patience few people could muster. "Uh-huh. It wasn't so bad. It might have seemed like a great deal of blood to you, but it wasn't. Bullet just grazed him. Tore the skin. I've seen worse."

John threw an I-told-you-so smile over the doctor's shoulder.

Dr. Lloyd slapped John on the knee. "There you go. Don't do anything to strain the stitches. They could pop open." He glanced at Julia while washing his hands. "I'm going to have to report this. It's the law."

Julia's eyes widened in panic. John knew the warning signs. She was going to explode; she was going to spill the truth.

John said, "I've already spoken to the law. You can check it out. I spoke to Chalmers. He's with the DEA."

"DEA?" Lloyd's eyes grew bigger than Julia's.

"Yeah. He and I go way back. He's done all the paperwork by now. He'll notify the local law."

Julia said, "I'm sorry, Dr. Lloyd, we really need to go. Thanks for everything."

John stood up. He was beginning to ache as the local anesthetic wore off. A burning sensation buzzed closer. He joined Julia at the door, more than ready to go home.

The doctor pulled John off to the side. Julia couldn't hear him as he said, "You have an interesting array of scars there. Were the others caused by cleaning loaded guns, as well?"

John asked, "What are you getting at?"

"Where were you the past two years?"

"What difference does it make?"

Dr. Lloyd said, "I care about the family. You know that. I want to know why you're pretending to be somebody else. I knew it was you the second you came through the door, Jack."

Chapter Nine

Julia saw the unmistakable cloud of pain in John's eyes the second she entered the kitchen. Those eyes that reminded her so much of Jack. They held hers intimately as he waited for her to speak.

She supplied, "Dr. Lloyd called to warn me about you. He seems to think you're playing us."

"He's going to believe what he believes."

She said, "Well, it's good to be home."

"You look like you slept well."

She smiled smugly as she readily admitted, "Like a cat. What about you?"

"I guess I dozed off a few times. I must have, because I remember having some more odd dreams."

He looked tired, more so than usual. Dark circles underlined his eyes, and there were strain lines around his mouth. And still he was incredibly handsome. It wasn't fair.

"Was your side bothering you?"

He shook his head, lifting a steaming mug of hot coffee to his lips. He took a sip before saying, "Not really. I just can't seem to sleep for any great length of time. I'm either plagued with bad dreams or I can't get comfortable. I have trouble shutting my mind off at the end of the day."

Jack had never had any trouble sleeping. Taking the chair across from him, she mentally admonished herself for her thoughts. He wasn't Jack. They had all but proved it beyond a shadow of a doubt. It was that one lingering shadow that killed her every time she looked at him.

She remembered Cecily Carpenter's file, the file that said he slept ten hours a night. Why had the name B. Keller been replaced with John's name? What had Cecily been trying to tell them?

She asked, "How long has it been since you had a full night's sleep?"

"I can't remember." He laughed at the irony.

Her hand crossed the table to lie on top of his. She stroked his fingers lightly, wanting to comfort him, but she wasn't certain how much comfort he would accept from her. "John—"

"I'm fine," he interrupted. "A touch of insomnia. That's all."

"Have you tried warm milk, counting sheep, meditating before bed?"

"I've tried everything." His sexy somber tones washed over her. Goose bumps formed on her bare arms. "What's that saying? No rest for the wicked? I must have a guilty conscience."

"How can you joke? My brain won't function without my allotted eight hours."

He shrugged. "Maybe I'm delirious."

"That's not funny."

He stood and circled the table in the time it took her to blink once. His hand enclosed her wrist and he yanked her from her chair. She fell into his arms. They wrapped around her securely, holding her tight.

He said, "I guess I can't be held responsible for anything I do in this state. I can't think straight." His hand slipped down the length of her thigh. "I have no idea what I'm doing right now."

"Stop it, John. This isn't funny." She feebly pushed against his solid chest.

He narrowed the gap between them, closing the inches until a sheet of paper couldn't pass between them. "You're right. There's nothing funny about the way I feel when I'm holding you in my arms."

She rolled her eyes. "Oh, please."

"I'm serious."

She placed a hand on his forehead as if to check for a temperature. "You really are delirious, poor baby."

Who was she kidding? She wanted to kiss him as much as he wanted to kiss her. Maybe more.

She breathed, "Kiss me."

He didn't have to be asked twice. John's mouth captured hers. The kiss was like no other kiss she'd ever experienced. With one earth-shattering kiss he transformed her into a new woman.

She felt giddy when his tongue pushed past her lips. It stroked her senses. The velvet softness of his tongue slid against hers and wrapped around it. She whimpered and pressed her body closer to his.

Her fingers dug into his strong shoulders. She wanted the kiss to last forever. It breathed to life emotions she thought long dormant. She marveled at the effect one lone man could have on an otherwise sensible woman.

John's hands curved around her face, holding her steady as his kiss deepened. She melted against him. Mundane things such as breathing didn't seem important anymore. She wiggled closer to him, but close wasn't close enough.

The sound of voices penetrated her brain. Someone was coming. She tried to push away, but John held her firmly.

His kiss deepened even more. Worried he didn't hear the voices, she struggled harder against his muscular chest.

John released her mouth with a breathy, short kiss. He whispered against her forehead. "Relax. I hear them."

John placed one last kiss on the tip of her nose. His arms dropped to his sides, and a cold chill filled her. She would have given anything to be able to walk back into those arms.

Bob and J.J. entered the kitchen. The boy held on to his uncle's arm, tugging at him. Bob's glare immediately sought out his brother's double. "You're back."

It was more accusation than statement. Julia watched with wonder as John simply nodded. His expression remained blank. It didn't provoke or ignore. She envied him for being able to hide his emotions. Although part of her worried he could do the same with her.

J.J. asked, "Where'd you go, Mom?"

She ruffled his hair. "We went to El Paso. John needed to see a doctor."

J.J.'s concerned eyes went to John, and Julia felt her heart drop to her knees. She hadn't realized he was getting closer to the man who looked like his father. She couldn't allow her son to be hurt, not even if it meant giving up the one person in the world who could make her heart beat again.

J.J. said, "Are you sick?"

John replied, "Right as rain."

"Cool. You wanna help me with the go-cart? I'm building it myself."

Bob interjected. "I thought I was helping you?"

The boy shrugged. "You're always busy. John can help me."

The lines of dissent shifted. J.J. didn't notice his uncle's anger at being replaced, but Julia did. Her son had inadvertently given Bob another reason to dislike John.

John said, "Sure, kid. I don't know how much help I'll be, though. If I ever built one, I don't remember."

"No problem. I'll show you."

Julia wanted to get her son out of the room. "Honey, go wash your hands, please. They're filthy."

"Yeah." The boy grinned. "I'm having a blast outside. See ya."

Bob grasped Julia's arm below the elbow. "May I have a word with you?"

She would have declined, but Bob was already pulling her from the room. Telling John she'd be right back, she could feel his eyes bore into her as if searching for something. Perhaps a plea for interference?

Out in the hallway Bob demanded, "Where did you go with him?"

She sighed. "I told you. We were in El Paso."

"And you saw the doctor? Or was it the police?"

"Both, actually."

Hands on hips, he glared down at her. "Have you been helping him delve into his past?"

She crossed her arms over her chest. "So what if I have?"

"It's dangerous. We don't know anything about this guy. Leave his past alone."

"Why?"

He repeated, "Leave his past alone."

Bob turned his rigid back on her. She stared at it as he disappeared up the stairs. What was the matter with him? He didn't like John. That was obvious. But why should he care if she helped John discover his past?

JOHN STARED at the Scarecrow card in his hand. It filled him with an awful foreboding. He wished he could remember something. Anything. If Chalmers had been telling the truth, he could already know the identity of the elusive killer. He thumbed the edge of the card, bending it. Somehow he needed to reach deep into his mind and to pull the memories forward.

"Whatcha got?"

J.J. had entered the kitchen in a quiet manner for once, throwing John off guard. He hadn't expected the kid to sneak up on him. The child was followed closely by Roberta. She held a bottled ship close to her chest.

She said, "Yes, John, what is it?"

He ran a hand over the card and it vanished. He hadn't thought about it. He had simply made it happen. Like a professional magician, he had made the card disappear into thin air. He wasn't even sure where it had gone, it had happened so fast. He was reasonably sure it was safely tucked into his sleeve, but he couldn't check without giving away its location.

He said, "Nothing."

"Cool!" J.J. exclaimed. "How did you do that?"

"Do what?"

"Make that thing disappear? Aunt Roberta, did you see? He made it disappear!"

The woman's alabaster skin seemed unusually pale. She said, "Yes, I saw it. Good trick. J.J., have you seen your uncle Bob or has the magician made him vanish, as well?"

Her voice was tight, but the boy didn't seem to notice. "I think he's outside." Once she flounced off in the opposite direction, J.J. said, "My mom says to ignore her. She can be rude."

John smiled. "So I've noticed."

"You don't like Aunt Roberta, do you?" He fetched himself a bottle of Coke. "It's okay. She doesn't like you, either. I heard her tell Uncle Bob you give her the creeps. She wants you out of here.'' He opened the bottle against the edge of the sink. ''I thought what you did was a good trick even if Aunt Roberta didn't. Where did you learn it?''

''I honestly don't know.''

Julia entered and smiled at her son. ''Sweetheart, go outside and play, please. I need to talk to John.''

''Okay. Come outside when you're done, John. I'll show you my go-cart.''

John turned to Julia after the boy was gone. ''What did Bob want?''

She sat across from him. ''He wants us to drop the search into your past.''

''Why?''

''He wouldn't say.''

''Don't you think that's odd?''

''Yes.''

''Are you going to stop helping me, Julie?''

''No.''

John smiled. Did she have any idea how beautiful she was? Her green eyes made such a contrast to the dark hair framing her pale face. He told her, ''You can back out if you want to. I won't hold it against you.''

She raised her chin high and declared, ''Bob is not my father or my husband. He doesn't dictate my actions. I want to help you. I'm going to help you. Together we will find out who you are and where you belong.''

John's smile faded as a serious thought forced its way to the forefront of his mind. ''I don't want you to get hurt.''

''I won't.''

''There are no guarantees.''

She leaned closer. ''I feel…safe when I'm with you.''

His face went hot. "That's sweet, but I'm not Superman, honey. I can't protect you twenty-four hours a day."

"So who says I need to be protected? It's the new millennium, John. Get a clue. Women can take care of themselves these days. Actually, we always could. We just let men think they were taking care of us to make them feel better."

"All right." He laughed. "You don't have to convince me. You can take care of yourself."

She rose and circled the table to lean close to his ear. "That doesn't mean I don't need assistance once in a while."

Her lips brushed his cheek, and he couldn't contain his smile. She was quite a woman. He only hoped he would prove worthy of her once his true nature came to light.

JOHN SHIELDED HIS EYES as he stared into the distance. Two figures emerged from the barn. The flamboyant pink dress could belong to no other than Roberta, but who was with her? He was a tall, lanky cowboy. It could be Bob or Stu or a half dozen other men who worked at the ranch.

John returned his attention to the boy. J.J. twisted the last screw into place. He smiled up at John, pleased with the work they'd done on the go-cart.

Julia stepped out onto the porch. "How's the project coming?"

"Great, Mom! Look! John helped put the wheels on!"

She tweaked his nose. "I hope you'll watch for pedestrians."

J.J. rolled his eyes heavenward. "Oh, Mom!" He turned to John, all business. "I need to get more wire."

He scooted off to the barn and Julia said, "I'm sorry my son cornered you into helping him like this. He can be a bit pushy."

John shrugged. "I don't mind. He's a great kid."

"Yes, he is. I don't know how to say this, but I'm afraid J.J. may be getting too attached to you. I don't want to see him hurt."

"Neither do I." He stared deep into her emerald-green eyes. "What do you want me to do? Leave?"

Her heart nearly stopped. She trembled. The thought of him leaving cast a dark shadow over her life. Someday she knew he would have to go, but not yet. She hadn't prepared herself yet. Her stomach tightened.

"No. I don't want you to go."

"Then what?"

"I don't know. Don't make yourself indispensable to anyone here." Her lower lip quivered and he realized she was close to tears. "Okay? J.J. can't be allowed to use you as a substitute father."

"I'd never hurt the kid on purpose."

"I know." She touched his hand as he reached for a wrench and their eyes locked. They held. Neither of them wanted to be the first to look away. A tremor sizzled just beneath the surface of Julia's skin.

He said, "Maybe I should leave. All I seem to do around here is make people uncomfortable by reminding them of a painful loss."

Julia didn't get a chance to respond. Stu interrupted them with business. He wiped the sweat from his brow, ignoring John as he spoke directly to her.

"Randy broke his arm, and we got a mustang that needs to be broke."

She said, "You could—"

"No, ma'am. I don't do that sort of work no more. Too old. We agreed on that."

She said, "But just this one time can't you—"

"No, ma'am," he cut in.

"Isn't there anyone else?" Desperation edged her voice.

"No, ma'am. Unless..." His eyes shifted to John. "Do you ride?"

Julia said, "He doesn't work here."

"But can he ride? If someone don't break that mustang, we're in trouble. Patterson already paid for that horse. He wants him tomorrow. The horse is almost broke. He just needs another ride or two to settle him." He spit a sunflower casing out the corner of his mouth.

Julia met John's concerned gaze. She said, "He's exaggerating."

Stu said, "You think so? If Jack was here, I doubt he would agree with you."

Tears pricked the backs of her eyes. She couldn't believe Stu had thrown Jack into the mix. He had no right.

"Where's the horse?" John asked.

She felt the angry tension radiating from him, pushing him to try something for which he wasn't trained. There was going to be a fight. Under normal circumstances, she was certain that John could pulverize Stu. But he'd been injured. He had stitches. They would get ripped open.

"You can't ride that horse!" Julia cried. "You'll be hurt!"

Stu hid his grin from her, but not fast enough. He turned to John. "Follow me. I'll show you where you put your foot."

"I know where I'll put my foot." He muttered, "I also know where I'd like to put the other one."

"John, you can't do this! You'll rip your stitches open!"

He ignored her and followed Stu to the corral. She had no choice but to follow. John was going to need medical attention when he finished. How could one man be so stubborn?

"John, you can't do this!"

J.J. joined them at the fence. "Is John gonna ride a horse, Mom?"

She nodded slowly, stroking her son's hair. "Yes, honey. Maybe you'd better go in the house."

"I'm not a baby, Mom."

Her eyes drifted to the sight on the other side of the fence. John had ignored her warning. Stu held the mustang's reins while he gave John a few last-minute instructions. Her mind floated back to the days when Jack had broken the horses. He had been a born rider. He and the horse had become one being.

She snapped her mind back to the present. John was climbing onto the wild horse. He took the reins, and Stu jumped out of the way. The horse went crazy. It bucked hard, changing directions in mid jump.

Julia held her breath. She crossed her fingers and sent up a quick prayer for the foolish, stubborn man she had come to care for.

John managed to hang on for several seconds—it seemed like hours to Julia—then was thrown. He fell to the ground with a grunt of pain.

Julia gasped.

J.J. said, "Wow!"

She bit down on her lower lip, willing John to get up.

"Look, Mom! He's getting up!"

John rose, brushing the dirt from his backside. She waved him in her direction, but he ignored her. He turned to the smug, wild gaze of the mustang. Smiling, John bent his face to the captive horse. He appeared to be talking to it. She couldn't help but recall that had been one of Jack's tricks.

John climbed onto the horse for a second round. The

horse bucked, but not with the same enthusiasm as before. John twisted his body with the horse and held on tight.

Julia's heart thumped painfully in her chest. Stu swaggered over to the fence. He spit another sunflower seed shell out the side of his mouth. Then he grinned at her, shoving his hat back a little.

He said, "I can't believe it. I haven't seen anyone ride a horse like that since..."

Stu's eyes centered on hers, and she felt her blood run cold. He had been about to compare John with Jack. She had already noted the similarities. But she couldn't afford to become too hopeful. No amount of wishing could bring back the dead.

She said, "You shouldn't have goaded him into riding. He could have been seriously hurt. What were you trying to prove?"

Stu grinned and walked away.

J.J. exclaimed, "That was cool! Did you see that, Mom?"

"Yes, honey. I saw. He did a good job."

John climbed over the fence to join them. Layer upon layer of dirt had been ground into his jeans. There was a rip in one knee, exposing torn flesh. The sight of blood fueled the fire already raging within her.

She said, "You shouldn't have ridden that horse. That was stupid. Did your stitches open?"

He grinned. "Tell me. If something had happened to me, would you have missed me?"

She gaped at him, stunned by his heartless statement. Tears stung her eyes. She wanted to slap him. Suddenly she didn't care if he had ripped stitches or not. Let someone else worry about him.

He took a step forward, as if to apologize. "I'm sorry, Julie."

She fled without a word.

Chapter Ten

John flinched as the doctor restitched his wound. The anesthetic didn't seem to be working. Either that or the wily doctor had decided not to use very much just to teach him a lesson. Whatever the reason, his side burned as if on fire, and he was sure he felt each prick of the needle.

To keep his mind off the pain, John turned his thoughts to Julia. He hadn't seen her since he'd broken the mustang. After the wild ride he had been pumped up and hadn't realized what he was saying to her until it was too late. If she didn't speak to him again, he had no one to blame but himself.

Stu stood on the other side of the room. He stared in every direction but John's. The foreman looked positively green. The sight of blood didn't bother John.

Dr. Lloyd said, "Do I need to repeat my earlier instructions?"

"No, sir."

"Good. Are you taking the antibiotics I gave you?"

"Yes, sir."

"What about the painkillers?"

John said, "I took one the morning after you stitched me up. I didn't need them after that."

The doctor raised an eyebrow. "Haven't you been in pain?"

He reluctantly admitted, "Well, yes, sometimes. But..."

Stu said, "He's a tough one, Doc. John don't need no sissy pain pills."

The doctor rolled his eyes at them both. "I have never understood the macho mentality that says a man's a wimp if he feels pain. Pain is real. The next time you feel it, take a pill. Clear?"

John nodded. He wanted to get away from the doctor. The walls were closing in on him. He had been noticing his claustrophobic reaction to being inside more and more lately. It wrapped around his chest, compressing until he couldn't breathe normally.

"You okay?" Stu asked. "You look a little green. Blood turns my stomach, too."

"I need some air."

The doctor released him with one last warning, and they stepped out into the bright sunshine. John stopped to take a deep breath. When he glanced around, he saw Chalmers across the street. The man's dark head was bent as he spoke to an elderly woman.

The woman shook her head, a tentative smile on her face.

John grabbed Stu's arm and ducked into a nearby store. John observed Chalmers's every movement through the glass door. Chalmers stopped each person along the street, showing them something. A piece of paper.

John had a bad feeling.

Stu asked, "What's goin' on?"

"Do you see that man over there?" John pointed.

"The stranger? Yeah. Do you know him?"

"He's looking for me. I don't trust him. I'm not willing to take a chance with Julia's life."

Stu took another look at Chalmers, sizing him up. "You want me to get rid of him, boss?"

Not much surprised John these days, but Stu offering to

help him almost knocked John off his feet. Maybe it was the pain or the loss of blood. Perhaps it was the combination of them both. He should have been able to think his way out of this situation. He shouldn't need help.

"I don't want him hurt. I just want him to stop asking questions."

Stu nodded. "I'll take care of it, boss."

John didn't understand the "boss" label Stu had suddenly pinned on him. Did the man call everyone boss or was he confusing John with Jack?

Stu crossed the street to talk with the stranger, and John watched. A horn honked. Stu tapped the side of the passing green Chevy. The driver yelled a friendly greeting as he continued on.

Stu stopped in front of the tall black man, arms crossed over his chest. Chalmers flashed the paper and Stu shook his head. Then Stu pointed off somewhere down the street. The two gentlemen chatted for another minute or so. Chalmers appeared to be smiling. John broke into a cold sweat. He wished he could hear what they were saying. Was Stu helping him or selling him out?

Chalmers got into the car. It must have been a rental. John hadn't had the chance to return his vehicle he'd borrowed.

Waiting for Chalmers to vanish before he left the safety of the store, John grimaced.

Stu raced across the street. His smile was wide. "I got rid of him, boss. Told him I saw you but you left the other day. I kind of led him to believe you might be headed upstate."

John had an uncomfortable feeling about the whole situation. "What was he showing everyone?"

"A picture of you and him together. You looked pretty chummy to me."

"Maybe I know him, but I may not be able to trust him. No way for me to know."

Stu shrugged. "Don't trust him. Don't trust anybody. That's my motto. You live longer if you only trust yourself."

"You're a cynic."

Stu beamed. "And proud of it."

A flash of Roberta exiting the barn with a tall cowboy made him ask, "How well do you know Bob's wife?"

Stu's face reddened. "She lives at the ranch. I see her once in a while. She can be a pain."

John said, "I saw her leaving the barn right before you suggested I ride the mustang. Was she with you?"

Stu's eyes diverted south. "No, sir. Why would you think she'd been with me?"

"I saw her with a tall man in a cowboy hat. The sun was in my eyes. I was just wondering why a woman dressed like she was would be in a barn. Isn't it dirty in there?"

Stu laughed. "You got her pegged right. She wouldn't be in the barn unless she was trying to cause some trouble."

"Trouble? What kind of trouble?"

"I probably shouldn't say."

John wasn't in the mood to play Twenty Questions. His lips tightened. "Come on, Stu. Tell me what you know."

"The thing is…Roberta Keller isn't exactly faithful to her husband. She's slept with more cowhands than I can count."

John nodded. "Does Bob know about his wife's infidelity?"

"Hard to say. He's a bit tightlipped, and he seems to think the sun sets on his wife. She's been with nearly every guy on the ranch. She slept with Jack, too, and Bob may have known about it. The two of them had a huge fight a few weeks before Jack was murdered. I had to break it up. I thought they were going to kill each other.''

''How do you know she was with Jack?''

''She told me. She's not real good at keeping secrets.''

John wasn't as surprised by the news as he should have been. Bob was too cool, too calm, whenever his brother's murder was mentioned. His reaction had bothered John from the start. In the beginning John had suspected it was because Bob had been in love with Julia, but perhaps it ran deeper.

He asked, ''Did Julia know about the fight?''

''I think so.''

Stu spit a sunflower casing into his hand. ''What's with the questions? I helped you out with your friend, and now you're givin' me the third degree. I don't like it.''

John nodded, deciding to leave it alone for the moment. Stu was beginning to like him. It wouldn't be smart for him to put the man on the defensive.

John turned and headed for Stu's truck. Roberta had been fooling around, giving Bob a motive for murder. The pieces were finally starting to fall into place. He only hoped he could see the whole picture before the killer decided to strike again.

HIS SIDE BURNED as if it were on fire. John entered the house and quietly shut the door. He wanted to avoid a run-in with Julia if at all possible. If she saw how much pain he was in, her anger would resurface. She had every right to be angry. He had done a stupid thing, taken a risk in the name of pride.

He realized now he had only attempted to ride the mustang in an effort to impress his would-be wife. He should have known an act of simple kindness would have reached her frozen heart faster than a stupid stunt.

John limped past the living room on his way to the staircase, but a whining voice cut short his escape.

"Hey, you, come in here."

His head fell forward in defeat. Light-brown hair spilled into his eyes. Roberta was second on the list of people he didn't want to see at the moment. He shifted mental gears and stepped into the spacious room.

Roberta sat on the floor between the couch and the coffee table. She patiently maneuvered another piece into a bottle, attaching it to the nearly completed ship inside. Her eyes remained fixed on her work. She didn't bother to glance up in his direction.

"We've hardly had a chance to talk. One good thing about having you here, my tummy hasn't been so full in months. Sylvia wouldn't hardly boil water while Jack was missing. She spent all of her time on the phone, trying to find him, or in her bedroom staring at the wallpaper. Now we can't get her out of the kitchen."

"I'm not Jack."

"I didn't say you were. Poor Sylvia. She's a bit flaky. The rest of us know you aren't Jack. So when are you planning to leave? You can't stay here forever. It wouldn't be fair to Sylvia. She has to face the truth sooner or later."

John refused to answer. It wasn't any of her business how long he planned to stick around. He wasn't quite sure what his plans were yet himself.

She continued. "Sylvia isn't the only one acting strange, either. Bob can't sleep at night. I think you scare him. And Julia's poor kid. The little tyke is confused. He doesn't know what to believe. Don't you think it would be better for everyone if you left?"

John's face relaxed into a smile. Roberta wanted him gone. Of course, he suspected she wasn't the only one.

He hunkered down and looked Roberta right in her startled, vacant eyes. "I'll leave when I'm ready. Unless you can think of a reason why I should go now."

She returned to her ship. "Go. Stay. I don't care. I was just thinking of Sylvia."

John turned for the stairs. He wanted to take a pain pill and a nap. His forehead was damp with perspiration. He hoped he could make it up all those steps. It would be embarrassing to tumble down them in front of Bob's annoying wife.

JULIA RACED OUT the front door, check in hand. She was fuming mad. When she got her hands on Bobby, he was going to be a changed man. She couldn't believe his nerve. He had looked her straight in the eye and lied to her. Sometimes she wondered if she knew him at all.

She was in such a hurry, she barreled into John. He was standing on the edge of the porch, staring out at the scenery. His expression was calm, until he saw her.

He demanded, "What's wrong?"

"Have you seen Bob?"

"I saw someone go into the barn a minute ago. It could have been Bob. I couldn't really tell from here. I can check it out for you."

Her legs were already moving in that direction. "I'll go."

John trailed after her. "What is it? What did Bob do that has you so riled up?"

The words nearly caught in her throat. "I found this check in the trash. Every month the bank sends me the checks that have gone through so I can balance the books. Someone got them first and threw this one in the trash."

"And that's why you're mad?"

"No," she snapped. "I'm mad because this check was made out for fifty thousand dollars. The missing fifty thou-

sand dollars. It was written out to some company called
Straw Man, Inc. It was signed by Bob.''

John whistled between his teeth. ''Fifty thousand dollars. What was it for?''

''That's what I'm about to find out.''

Julia ripped the barn doors open. It was abnormally dark
inside. The horses were out in the corral. She stepped inside and listened. Not a single sound met her straining ears.
There didn't seem to be anyone around. She called, ''Bob?
Are you in here, Bobby? I need to talk to you.''

John settled in behind her as she moved through the
quiet barn, calling for her brother-in-law. His hands went
to her waist, staying her. Her stomach muscles betrayed
her, contracting with desire. She didn't have time to play
his game of seduction at the moment. She pushed his
hands away and continued ahead alone.

There was a strong odor mixed with that of fresh hay.
John's nose wrinkled as he tried to identify it.

John said, ''I smell gasoline.''

Julia sniffed. ''Me, too.''

''I don't like this. Let's get out of here.''

''Yeah. I think you're right.''

They carefully retraced their steps. John was the first
one at the closed doors. He pushed against them, but neither gave way. He pushed harder, grunting with the strain.
The doors wouldn't give an inch.

''The doors won't open. I think something is blocking
them.''

Julia glanced around for the source of the sudden flick-
ering light. There were flames licking at the outside boards
along the eastern wall. The flames crackled, eating more
boards.

She screamed, ''The barn's on fire!''

''What?''

Julia grabbed John's arm and steered him in the direction of the flames. The barn was indeed on fire. Half of the wall had already been devoured and it was spreading fast.

John said, "Let me go! I have to get the doors open!"

"There's no time!" she yelled. "There's a trapdoor under the barn and a tunnel! It might be blocked now! I don't know. Jack and Bob used it when they were kids, playing soldiers and stuff. We can use it now."

"Where is it?"

Julia led him to the center of the barn. "I think it's here somewhere under all the hay."

John thumped down on his knees and started to dig for it. She glanced at the fire even though every survival instinct she had told her not to. The entire wall was on fire and it was spreading. Flames licked hungrily at the roof. Soon the whole roof would collapse on top of them.

"I think I found it!" John's voice exploded behind her.

She helped him remove the remaining hay so they could find the edges of the trapdoor. Her fingers dug between the grooves as she tried to lift it up. It was stuck. Just like the doors.

She cried, "The barn is going to fall on our heads!"

Smoke choked her. She grabbed on to his arm. "I'm sorry for getting you involved in this! You shouldn't be here! They think you're Jack!"

"That remains to be seen!" John wasn't about to give up. He continued to tug on the trapdoor. She heard a soft splintering sound followed by a loud crack. The door suddenly flew open.

"Get in!" he yelled.

John shoved her forward headfirst. She hung on to the side to keep from tumbling down the rotted wooden ladder. Her fingers scraped and bruised, she refused to let go until her feet were safely on the ground.

John jumped down, landing beside her on his feet like a cat. "I can't see a thing."

Julia concentrated hard, trying to remember what Jack had told her about the tunnel. She knew it ended somewhere at the line of their property, if it hadn't caved in. No one had used it since Jack was a boy of eleven, and no one outside of Bob knew about it. She and Jack had long ago decided to keep it from their son. Tunnels could be dangerous places to play.

John said, "Come on. We need to get as far away from the fire as possible. I don't want to die from smoke after everything we went through to get this far."

He started down the tunnel, but Julia latched on to his arm. "Wrong way. If we go in that direction, we'll wind up under my father's old ranch. Macready's probably had it boarded up by now."

Julia took his strong hand in hers. She walked carefully through the tunnel, sliding her feet forward so she wouldn't trip. Her heart pounded hard in her chest. As a child she'd had nightmares about being trapped in such a place. Even now the fear ate at the corners of her mind. But in her dreams she had been alone.

Julia squeezed John's hand to reassure herself that he was real. His fingers entwined with hers in a steady grasp. Her heart beat faster. She was safe as long as he was with her.

What was she thinking? She had been worried J.J. would attach himself to the man and get hurt, but what about her? Each day she spent in his company made it harder to imagine life without him. Someday he would leave them—her—and it would be like losing him to death. It would be like losing Jack again.

Jack never veered far from her thoughts. Although she could tell the two apart now, sometimes her mind distorted the facts and they were almost the same person. She had to be careful not to mix them up. If John was Jack, he would belong to her. But he wasn't Jack. Fate wouldn't be that kind.

John said, "I think I see a light at the end of the tunnel."

Julia laughed at his clever observation. There was light and it grew brighter by the second. She rushed forward. In her haste to make it to safety, she tripped.

John's strong arms caught her. He fell to one knee, holding her close to keep her from impacting with the hard earth. Her body was protected by his. Her arms wrapped around his middle as they fell. Still, the breath was knocked from her.

She gasped. "I'm sorry. I didn't see that rock. Did you hurt yourself?"

He lifted a shiny object with sharp ends up into the light for her inspection. "You didn't trip over a rock. It was this thing."

A shovel. She shook her head in confusion. "I don't understand. No one has used this old tunnel in years. That thing should be rusty, but it practically glows."

"It's brand-new, honey. Someone has been down here recently."

"But who? And why?"

John said, "My guess would be Bob. Maybe he buried the fifty thousand dollars out here. He might be saving it for a rainy day."

She glared at him. "The check went to Straw Man, Inc."

"Straw Man. Scarecrow. Could be one in the same. Bob could have hired a hit on someone."

John stood and pulled Julia to her feet. The shovel, she noted, was still in his other hand. They walked to the ladder and climbed up. Julia first. She was quiet, but her mind was moving in circles. How could she prove Bob was innocent? She had to believe he was innocent. If not, then he had just tried to murder her.

She shielded her eyes from the bright sunlight and looked north. Billows of smoke caressed the sky. She hoped the cowhands had put the fire out. She didn't relish the idea of having to build another barn.

She said, "We'd better get back and let everyone know we're okay."

He grabbed her arm, his fingers digging into the tender flesh of her wrist. "Not so fast. There's a killer roaming around. I don't know which of us he was trying to kill today, but I want you to accept the possibility that the bad guy could be someone you care about."

"I can't…"

"Yes, you can," he insisted. "You can and you will, for your son's sake. You have to be extra cautious now. Don't go anywhere alone. Don't go anywhere with Bob period."

Julia wasn't ready to crucify Bob yet. She had known him for years, and she was positive he wouldn't do anything to hurt her. In fact, she knew Bob a lot better than she knew the handsome stranger with her husband's guileless blue eyes.

Another scenario occurred to her. What would be more deceptive than to use her husband's memory against her? If there was indeed a hired killer after her, he was being paid by someone with a lot of money. That sort of person could also afford to pay for a bit of plastic surgery.

Julia cut her own thoughts off with a violent shake of her head. She was being ridiculous. Poor John had been shot and almost burned in a fire in the course of three days. He was a good man. She didn't know much about him, but she did know that much. He would never hurt her. At least not intentionally.

She said, "I don't want to accuse Bob. Let me handle it."

"You can't handle everything on your own. You take on too much. Let me help you. I can share some of that burden. Two backs are stronger than one."

Julia gazed up into his Arctic-blue eyes and melted. Two of his fingers brushed the hair from her eyes. A small voice deep inside her screamed a warning. She couldn't allow it to happen. She couldn't fall in love with this man. In the end, it would be the death of her.

She said, "I can't learn to depend on you. You won't always be there."

"You don't know that."

Julia turned away from him so he wouldn't see her crestfallen expression. She did know he wouldn't be around forever. She was afraid his leaving was inevitable.

She started to move in the direction of home. "We'd better get back."

John fell into step beside her, keeping her pace. "Do me a favor. Don't tip your hand to Bob. Don't ask him about the check. Not yet. Give me a chance to find out the answers on my own."

"Why should I? What's the point of you getting involved?"

"In case you haven't noticed, Julie, I am involved. I have a feeling tonight has something to do with me, my past. I don't know. Please give me the chance to put it all together. I'm only asking for a few days. If I haven't found out anything, you can go to Bob then."

"You can have the time on one condition."

John raised one eyebrow at her. A smile began to form. "And what is that?"

An answering smile lit her face. "I'm going to be with you every step of the way. I will be there for every ques-

tion you ask and every dead end you come up against. I'm
not a wilting wallflower. I won't stay at home and bake
cookies while you play the hero. Got it?''

He held up his hand in mock surrender. ''Got it.''

Chapter Eleven

She didn't mean to eavesdrop.

Julia passed by John's room on the way to her room. Whispered words, half groans, caught her attention and drew her closer to the door. At first she thought he was talking to someone. The one-sided conversation held a desperate tone. Her curiosity piqued. Who could he be talking to?

J.J. was in bed asleep. John didn't like Bob or his wife, and Sylvia was downstairs sewing. Perhaps he was on the phone. But who could he possibly be talking to at this late hour?

She pressed her ear to the door, hating herself for invading his privacy. What sort of woman was she turning into? She never would have listened in on Jack.

John's voice was hoarse with emotion. "Don't have a family. Don't have anything. Don't hurt Julia. I'm not Jack. I can't be Jack."

Julia had heard enough. She no longer cared if listening at doors was wrong. John was talking to someone about her. He knew he wasn't Jack. He was pretending to be her husband in disguise. It sickened her to think of John as anything but good. Still, she had to believe her own ears.

She pushed open the door, ready to give him hell, but another shock awaited her.

He was asleep. Sprawled across the bed in jeans and a T-shirt, John clutched the bedsheets in tight fists. He writhed like one tormented by invisible demons. A thin sheet of perspiration covered his golden skin. He twisted in the grasp of some unknown evil and cried out, *"¡Madre de dios! ¿Donde esta mi esposa?"*

Where is my wife? Jack didn't know Spanish. If she'd had any doubts about this man's identity, they had been banished. In his sleep, in his subconscious, John knew he wasn't her husband. But he had stated he had no family. How could he have a wife and not have a wife at the same time?

Tears welled up in her eyes. Some might say she was the queen of denial, but she couldn't put a good spin on this one to save her life. Deep in her heart she had wanted—no, she had needed—him to be Jack. Part of her had even believed he was her dead husband, despite her claims that he wasn't.

What was she going to do now?

Would John remember his dreams? It was possible that John would wake up with his memory intact.

What if he didn't? Would she be able to tell him the truth?

John rasped, "Got to save her...what do I do? Car tailing me. Gaining on me. Gonna hit me. Scarecrow...I know who the Scarecrow is."

She leaned closer and asked in a soft voice, "Did the Scarecrow run your car off the road?"

He hesitated. "Don't know. Headlights blinded me. Can't see. Car hit me...behind. Forced me off road. What do I do? Can't die. Gotta save her. Blood. So much blood. Too dark. I hear him coming."

"Who's coming, John?"

"Scarecrow...going to kill me."

Her hands went to his face, smoothing back the damp hair. She wished she could crawl into his dreams and save him from the phantom killer. There wasn't anything she could do to comfort him. She could wake him, but first she had to know if he had seen the killer's face.

"John, who is the Scarecrow?"

"No...stay away from them! Leave them alone!"

"Who? Leave who alone?"

Was he dreaming of another life? Another family?

She gently shook his shoulders. She'd heard enough. "Wake up. John, you're having a bad dream. Wake up."

"Huh?" His eyes slowly opened. "What? What's going on? Is something wrong?"

"You were having a bad dream. Do you remember it?"

His eyes narrowed as he tried to remember. A frown marred his beautiful face, and fear filled her lungs until she couldn't breathe. Then he slowly shook his head. "I don't remember dreams. Was I screaming? Did I wake you up?"

She admitted, "I wasn't asleep, and you didn't scream. You were tossing and turning like a madman. Are you okay?"

He sat up straight. "There's something you aren't telling me."

"You were talking in your sleep."

"Why didn't you tell me that before? What did I say?"

"Nothing of any importance." She sprang off the bed. "I need to check on my son."

Thankfully he let her go with that explanation. Although she read the doubts in his eyes. He didn't believe her. He knew he had said something important while he was dreaming. But how was she going to tell him he wasn't her husband? He would leave the ranch and she would lose him forever.

JOHN STUDIED what was left of the barn: two partial charcoal walls and an ash floor. The roof was gone. The loft had been demolished. The fire had apparently started on one side, quickly spreading to the front of the building. The arsonist had stood on the left side of the barn in broad daylight as he poured the gasoline and struck the match.

John walked halfway across the floor. Bending, he scooped up a handful of ash and stared at it. This barn had nearly been his grave. Not to mentions Julia's. Her knowledge of the secret tunnel had saved their lives. He hadn't been able to do anything to protect her.

He should leave her, disappear like her husband. She would be safe then.

Bob stood outside the invisible third wall. "Stay away from Julia."

John blinked. Had his conscience come to life? The other man couldn't have approached him at a more reasonable time. Problem was he had no intention of leaving Julia. He couldn't. There were too many mysteries left to be solved.

Bob's hands clenched at his sides. He moved forward with a grimace as if he feared something might fall on him. "Did you hear me? I want you to leave Julia out of your plans before you get her killed."

John wiped the black dust from his hands. "I heard you. Doesn't mean I'm going to do it. Julia and I are grown adults. We don't have to answer to you."

"If you cared about her—"

"Don't even go there." John cut him off. "I care about her more than you can possibly understand. What I want to know is how much do you care about her? What is your relationship? Do you love her, Bobby? Are you in love with my—with Julia?''

Bob gaped in horror at John. ''How dare you insinuate that I would mess around with my brother's wife!''

''I didn't say you were messing around with her. I think Julia is too classy for that. However, I do believe you want her, have wanted her for a very long time.''

''Where do you get off accusing me of something like that? You don't even know me.''

A hard smile curved John's lips. ''You're wrong about that, buddy. I know you only too well. I bet you were in love with her before your brother died. Maybe you even had a little something to do with his untimely death.''

''Damn you! Damn you to hell for coming in here like you own the place and making judgments on us! Who are you?''

A devilish gleam entered John's eyes as he glanced over his shoulder at the other man. ''Who do you think I am?''

Bob wobbled as if his legs could no longer support his weight. His face paled. ''You! It's been you the whole time! You've been pretending this whole time!''

A cloud of despair settled over John's heart. It was cruel to make Bob think he was his brother when neither of them knew the truth. Deep in his heart he wished it was true, but wishing didn't make it so.

Bob cried, ''Does Julia know you're lying to her?''

''I—''

John didn't get the chance to deny his own words. Bob launched at him with furious fists. Unprepared for the attack, John was knocked to the ground by the other man's flying tackle. A fist connected with his jaw, stunning him.

They rolled across the ashen floor. John tried to push Bob away with one hand planted on his chest, but Bob was determined to fight.

John managed to free himself at last. They were both on their knees, struggling to stand. Bob took another swing at John's face.

John ducked.

Bob lost his balance, pitching forward, and John threw himself onto his back. He pinned him down. As far as John was concerned the fight was over.

Bob spit out ash. "Damn you, Jack! You aren't going to get away with playing us for fools! Julia loved you so damn much she almost died when you did!"

"I'm not Jack. I'm sorry. I shouldn't have goaded you into believing I was him. I just want you out of my business. Julia and I are none of your business."

Bob sagged, the fight draining out of him. He rested on the side of his face. "I don't believe you. I knew you were Jack the moment I saw you and Julia in bed."

"Now that wasn't what it appeared to be. She was confused. She came to talk and fell asleep next to me."

"Doesn't matter. You're still Jack. I thought your amnesia was real. Now I know. Do you remember the talk we had with Billings before you got shot?"

John said, "No."

"You're a liar, Jack. You're trying to make us pay for past imagined sins, aren't you?"

John climbed off the man's back. He stood, taking the time to brush off his jeans. "What?"

Bob jumped to his feet and spat, "You accused me of having an affair with Julia. Remember that? I confronted you first. I saw you and Roberta together. Then you turned it on me, accused me of sleeping with your wife. You never deserved Julia."

John said, "Maybe I was picking up on your interest in her. She may not have given in to you, but you wanted her. Admit it. You've wanted Julia since day one."

Bob threw his hands up. "Forget it. I tried to explain things to you. I won't waste my breath a second time. You don't deserve her, and I'm going to try my best to make sure you don't get her back again. You've lied to her. You've deceived her." He glanced pointedly at the charred barn walls. "And you almost got her killed."

John rolled his eyes. "I'm not Jack Keller."

"Right. Stay away from her, Jack…or John. Whoever the hell you are. Stay away from her."

John shook his head in wonder as he watched the other man stalk away. His head began to throb. The pointless conversation had driven an invisible nail into his skull. At the moment the only thing he desired was a warm bed in a dark room.

JOHN SAT AT JULIA'S DESK in the study and stared at the computer. The screen demanded the password. The eerie green glow illuminated the otherwise dark room. He glanced at the closed door, wondering if a person passing could see the light beneath it.

His fingers returned to the keyboard. He tried to get into a DEA file. He had to know who he was, what he was working on at the time of his accident. Without giving it much thought, his fingers punched in a code. The screen called up a menu for him. He was inside.

Sweat broke out on his upper lip. He knew the password. Billings and Chalmers had been telling the truth. He worked for the DEA. Rather, he had worked for them.

John took the cursor down until a file on current agents lit up. He pressed enter and waited.

A long list of names rolled up the screen. John's eyes searched in vain for a familiar one. There was no listing for Keller, Smith or Chalmers. So he returned to the main menu.

Next, he went to discarded agents.

The name John Smith was listed along with Chalmers. Chalmers had lost his standing with the DEA. Skipping his own name, John went to the file on Chalmers and scanned it quickly. Chalmers's services had been recently terminated. It didn't say why. It did, however, say the DEA was currently looking for Chalmers in hopes of questioning him about something.

A shaft of light hit John squarely in the face. Julia stood in the now-open doorway. He motioned for her to come inside and close the door. He trusted her. He could tell her about the files.

"What are you doing in here? I didn't know you knew anything about computers."

"Neither did I."

She stood behind his chair. "What is it?"

"A DEA file on Chalmers. He lost his job."

Julia asked, "Then why is he here?"

"I have no idea."

He returned to the list of names and Julia gasped. "They have John Smith listed. Have you looked at it?"

"Not yet."

"Well, open it."

John reluctantly hit the button and the screen blinked once before lighting up again. A picture of him with the name John Smith written under it flashed onto the screen, but there was no information. Instead, a huge white bar crossed over the screen. Written on the bar: deceased.

Julia's voice dripped with awe. "They think you're dead."

"So it would appear." His mind whirled around the possibilities. Did they actually believe he was dead or were they hoping to make it true? Someone in the organization could have sent Chalmers to terminate his services.

Chalmers's current status with the agency could be a cover up in case he got caught trying to put John to rest.

John didn't know what to think anymore. He didn't know who to trust, outside of the woman beside him. His hand lightly rested on hers. She smiled down at him. She had no idea the danger she was in being with him. But he wouldn't let anything happen to her. He would die before he let anything happen to her.

THE RHYTHMIC CREAKING of the rocking porch swing was somewhat comforting to Julia's rattled nerves. She hadn't seen John in a few hours, and her conscience was bothering her. Should she admit he had revealed his true self while in an unconscious state?

He was John Smith, not Jack Keller. Although she had thought herself prepared to hear such news, her heart had plummeted all the way down to her worn leather boots.

Of course he wasn't Jack. Hadn't she told herself from the beginning that Jack was dead and no amount of wishing would return him? The logical side of her brain hadn't doubted the facts. It was her heart that kept insisting on miracles when there were none.

How long could she avoid John? The ranch wasn't that big. Sooner or later she would run into him, come face-to-face with those startling blue eyes. She would be forced to tell him the truth. As a result she would lose him forever.

Julia felt like pulling her hair out. She feared she was mixing John up with Jack again. She couldn't lose Jack. He was already gone, and she didn't have any emotions invested in John. Did she?

Bob placed one foot on the porch and leaned forward. "Can I talk to you? It's important."

"Sure. Is something wrong?"

"You could say that." Bob frowned, scratching his head. "I don't know how to tell you this. Jack isn't dead, and he doesn't have amnesia, either. He's playing games with us, Julia. He's not right in the head, honey."

Julia took a deep breath and silently counted to ten. "Why do you think he's Jack?"

"He practically admitted it. Ever since he first showed up he's been asking questions about our relationship. You and me, not me and him. Anyway, he attacked me earlier today."

Bob pointed to the tear in his shirt. Her eyes traveled down. Bob certainly was a mess. He looked as if he'd had a fight, but it was hard to believe John had started it.

"Bobby, I know for a fact that he is not Jack. Okay?"

"It's Jack! Look, I never told you about the fight we had before Jack died—"

"What fight?" she cut in.

"Jack thought you and I were having an affair."

She gasped. "I don't believe that."

"It's true. Jack didn't like it that we were friends. He mistakenly thought I had feelings for you. I do care about you. I always did. Just not the way he thought. One day right out of the blue Jack verbally attacked me over it. He wanted me off the ranch. Jack had a hot temper when it came to you. He was afraid of losing you."

Julia couldn't reconcile what she knew about her husband with his brother's version. Jack hadn't been jealous. He had always treated her well. Trusted her completely. But why would Bob lie? What could he have to gain?

"I'm sorry. You're wrong. Maybe Jack was mad at you for some other reason."

"He told me to my face, accused me of loving you. He told me to leave. When I refused, he took a swing at me.

He was out of control then and he's out of his mind now. What sort of man pretends to have amnesia?''

Julia's mouth fell open in amazement. Bob actually believed John was Jack. It was ludicrous. She snapped her mouth shut and turned away. She could tell Bob about John's talking in his sleep, recount everything she'd learned from John, but she needed to tell John first.

Bob said, "You aren't taking this seriously."

She sighed. "Oh, I'm taking this extremely seriously. I need to be alone for a while to think. Do you mind?"

"I guess not. Just don't let Jack weasel his way out of this one. We need to get that boy some professional help."

Julia nodded absently. "Give me some time to think. I'll get back to you."

Bob grumbled as he walked away. He kicked a loose rock, obviously disgusted with her. Things were such a mess. She would have to talk to John about him talking in his sleep.

Julia stood. Her eyes scanned the ranch, the land that Jack had loved so much. John would leave them, but she would be fine. She would pull herself together and move forward. She'd done it once before. She could do it again.

She started for the front door. A soft click made her stop. She glanced around. The sound was familiar, but she couldn't quite put her finger on it. Frowning, she went inside.

Chapter Twelve

Later that day Julia caught Chalmers peering in the kitchen window as she returned home from a long ride on horseback. Her lower body ached. She longed for a soak in a warm tub. Then she spotted Chalmers. Fortunately he hadn't seen her.

Chalmers ducked. His fingers latched on to the kitchen window frame as he knelt beside it. Had he spotted his prey already?

She had to warn John. The problem was, she didn't know how she was going to get into the house without being seen.

Chalmers peeked into the kitchen again, unaware of her presence.

Julia prayed the man's peripheral vision wasn't up to par. She made a mad dash for the back of the house. Her shoulders tensed as she ran. She half expected to hear a gunshot ring out behind her.

She slammed open the back door and rushed into the kitchen. Julia froze in the doorway. Sylvia was in the room with John. Julia didn't want to alarm the woman. Taking a deep breath, she entered the kitchen. "John, could I speak to you for a moment, please?"

He hesitated. His eyes dropped to the vegetables laid out on the cutting board. A sharp knife rested beside it.

Sylvia said, "Go talk to your wife. I can handle this."

Julia's lips pursed together. She made a mental note to have a talk with Sylvia as soon as possible. She couldn't let the woman go on believing her son had returned to her.

John placed a hand on the small of Julia's back. They stepped into the hallway. "What's wrong?"

"Chalmers is here—"

Sylvia's shrill scream ripped through Julia's explanation. The woman flew from the kitchen, yelling at the top of her lungs. "Where's my gun? We got a Peeping Tom!"

Sylvia flew up the stairs, and Julia pivoted to face John. "Like I was saying… It's Chalmers. He's outside. He was watching you."

John nodded. His hands grasped her shoulders. "You stay here. I'll deal with him."

"I'm not a quaking infant. I'm coming with you. He might have a gun."

"Oh, good." Sarcasm dripped off his every word. "Then we can both get killed. I don't think so. You're staying in here."

"No, I'm not. I'm coming with you. Now we can stand here and argue the point until Sylvia fetches her shotgun, or we can deal with him together."

John's blue eyes softened. The tips of his fingers traced the line of her cheekbone. His gentle touch nearly brought tears to her eyes. He reminded her of Jack. That was all there was to it. He had her husband's face and a few of his mannerisms. He was familiar, but love didn't enter into it. She wouldn't allow it to.

John said, "You are a stubborn woman."

"And don't you forget it."

"At least let me go first."

"You're the boss."

John cautiously stepped through the front door. He reached back, placing a hand on her hip to keep her firmly behind him.

She appreciated his concern for her, but it wasn't necessary. She could take care of herself. She had been doing just that for the past two years.

Chalmers was waiting for them, his face a mask of defiance.

John stepped directly behind the other man. "Looking for something?"

Chalmers revolved in slow motion, his hands in the air. "You still move like a panther, man. Glad to see you haven't lost your edge. I have a feeling you'll need it before this is over."

John smiled wryly. "See anything interesting?"

Chalmers let his arms drift slowly down until they were at his sides. "Glad to see you're in one piece. Did you find out who set you up to get killed yet?"

"No. I've been busy. Why are you here? What do you want?"

"I wanted to see if you needed my help." The man shrugged. "Guess not. I don't suppose you've remembered anything?"

John's eyes turned in Julia's direction. She read the question there. Once again he was wondering if he had said more while asleep than she was admitting to. She had meant to tell him before now. She couldn't very well give him the truth in front of Chalmers. She wasn't yet sure if they could trust him. In fact, she was leaning toward the negative on that one.

John's eyes returned to Chalmers. "I haven't remembered anything, no."

Chalmers handed him a square piece of paper. "That's

the number where I'm staying. When your memory returns you'll want to call me.''

John grinned. "Why would I want to do that?''

It was as if they were speaking in code. Julia was having trouble following the conversation. She understood the words themselves, but buried deep beneath she felt the stirring of a troubled current. Did John remember Chalmers after all?

Chalmers said, "Believe me, if you remember you will want to contact me. I can help you. You can't trust anyone else.''

Chalmers shot a knowing glance in her direction. It sent a ripple of gooseflesh up her arms. The man couldn't possibly know she had hid the truth from John about his identity.

Unless he had the place bugged.

Julia's spine straightened as she met the man's gaze head-on. Did he know something? It was hard to tell. His gaze shifted to meet John's, and he repeated, "I am the only one you can trust. When you regain your memory, you'll understand why.''

"I don't trust anyone who spies on people through windows instead of knocking on the front door.''

"I wasn't sure you would agree to see me.''

John said, "So you decided to sneak around instead.''

Chalmers sighed. "I explained that, man. I just wanted to make sure you were okay. Is there anything you need?''

Julia stepped closer to John and slid a hand into the crook of his arm. She wasn't certain of her motives. It was a reflex action. She didn't like the way Chalmers looked at John, as if he could read everything about him in a glance. Perhaps it was jealousy on her part. Perhaps something deeper.

John smiled down at her. "I have everything I need right here."

Chalmers frowned. "Don't get used to this place, man. You won't want to stay here when you remember. Believe me. You won't want to stay here."

The last sentence had been directed at her, a sort of warning.

Then Chalmers left as quickly as he had appeared. The two people on the porch watched him make his way down the dirt drive until they could no longer see him. Julia shielded her eyes against the sun. She didn't want to look away. Fear set her teeth on edge. She had had the distinct feeling that Chalmers had threatened her.

John said, "Pay no attention to him. If he knew me, he didn't know me well enough to make judgments on what I would or would not do."

She forced a timid smile. "I wish you could remember."

"He was wrong. I won't leave you when I remember."

"Don't make me any promises, John. Neither of us knows what's going to happen in the future."

He stroked her cheek with a new tenderness that made her want to melt. "Nothing could ever make me want to leave you. Absolutely nothing."

An icy finger touched her spine, and she shivered. A sense of foreboding wrapped around her like a dark cloak. One day soon John would be gone. As soon as she told him the truth he would go. She opened her mouth to speak. She had kept the secret long enough.

Sylvia barreled out with a shotgun in her hands. "Where is he? Did you scare him off already?"

John nodded, grasping the end of her shotgun and pointing the barrel at the ground so it wasn't pointed in his direction. "He's gone. I don't think he'll be coming back."

Julia wasn't so sure. Chalmers had a plan. She had seen it in his eyes. For some reason the man wanted to take John away from her and she wouldn't give up without a fight. There was still the possibility that John would want to be with her in the end.

ROBERTA ENTERED the kitchen in skintight pink spandex pants and a lime-green halter top. She stopped abruptly. Her narrowed eyes fixed on John as he glanced up from his writing. He had decided to keep a journal. The idea seemed like a natural progression for him. He would keep a record of his thoughts. Someday he would look over them with his memories intact.

John slapped the book closed. He pushed it aside, hoping the woman wouldn't try to get a closer look.

She said, "Seeing you still weirds me out. Sorry I haven't been more gracious. You are a guest, after all."

"No harm done. Forget about it."

"Thanks." She slid a finger down his bare arm. "You're a lot nicer than Jack. I don't know how I ever mistook you for him. You got something going with Julia?"

John didn't like the direction the conversation was taking. "Not really. She's trying to help me figure out who I am."

"She doesn't think you're Jack then?"

"No. She never thought I was Jack. Why?"

The woman shrugged. "No reason. I should have been able to tell you weren't Jack. I knew Jack very well." She leaned closer. "You get my drift?"

"I'm not sure."

Roberta laughed from deep within her throat. It was

meant to be sexy, but it had John cringing. "We were lovers, you idiot. Somehow Julia managed to corner Jack into marrying her. He didn't want to. He wanted to marry me in the beginning, but I married Bob. I thought since Bob was the oldest he would inherit the ranch. Not so. Jack was going to get it all. Their father didn't trust Bob to run things."

"So you married Bob for the money?"

"No, I didn't marry Bob for the money. What a thing to say. You aren't listening. I wanted them both, Bob and Jack. I married the oldest because it's better to marry rich than poor. Anyway, you missed the point, sir."

"Which is?"

"Jack wanted me. When I was no longer available, he turned to Julia."

John found that hard to believe. Jack Keller would have had to have had a screw loose to marry Julia for anything other than love. She was a precious wonder, a heavenly entity. What man could resist?

He grabbed his journal and stood. Escape was foremost on his mind. He wanted to put as much distance between him and the viper with the screeching voice as possible.

Her fingernails dug into his arm. "I hope I didn't say anything wrong. I'm only telling you what I know to be true. I was there. You weren't."

Her eyebrows inched upward, and John retracted his arm from her steely grip. He reached for a cigarette. Lighting it, he stared down into her malicious gaze. She was poison.

He blew out a stream of smoke and said, "Why should I believe you?"

She giggled. "Ask Bob. He knew about it. He and Jack hated each other. They fought over me."

A spider raced across the table. Her fist slammed down

on it. John jumped, startled. She wiped it away with a napkin and tossed it with a vicious smile.

John said, "I find that hard to swallow. Now Bob is obviously smitten with you. He can't see past the end of his nose when you're in the room. But Jack? He was married to a beautiful woman. What would he want with you?"

Roberta's smile faded. "That was a rude thing to say. You know nothing about my relationship with Jack Kel ler."

"You're right. I don't know, and I don't want to know. You just make sure you don't spread these nasty rumors around town. Julia doesn't need you rubbing her nose in her husband's alleged adulteries. I don't want to see Julia hurt. Got it?"

"Got it."

She saluted him, a mocking gesture rooted in defiance.

JULIA HEARD the last of the conversation. John didn't want to see her hurt. She couldn't imagine what Roberta could do to hurt her. The woman was an unimaginative piece of fluff. But it warmed her heart to know John cared about her.

Julia entered the room. Her eyes fell on Roberta, taking in the brittle smile. Julia tugged on John's forearm. "I need to talk to you."

Roberta said, "I can take a hint. I'll see you both later."

Julia pulled John away from the open doorway. "There is no such company as Straw Man, Inc. It's a front for something else."

John said, "We don't know for sure that the check has anything to do with Jack's murder."

"But Straw Man could be a front for the Scarecrow. You pointed that out yourself. I'm going to ask Stu about the company. Maybe he's heard Bob mention it. As a matter of fact, I think I'll go speak with him now.''

''You aren't going alone.'' He slid an arm around her waist. ''We're dealing with a dangerous person. You can't trust anyone. Not Stu. Not Bob. No one.''

''Except for you, of course.''

His eyes hardened. ''You can't trust anyone. Not even me. How can I tell you to trust me when I don't know who I am?''

She knew who he wasn't. It was the perfect opening for her confession. She could admit he had said more during his bout of sleep-talking than she had originally admitted. Her mouth opened. The words formed in her mind.

John asked, ''Where do we find Stu at this time of day?''

''Uh, I don't know. We can check his room first. He might be out on the range somewhere. In that case, we would have to wait until tonight.''

John lifted his hand. ''After you.''

Julia crossed the room with John directly on her heels. She experienced his burning gaze on her back. They went straight to Stu's quarters, a two-room addition connected to the back of the bunkhouse.

She rapped gently on the door. Her eyes avoided John's. She had the distinct feeling John knew she was hiding something from him. She would tell him soon. She promised herself, she would tell him soon.

She said, ''I guess he's not here.''

John's hand wrapped around the doorknob. He pushed the door open and peered inside.

Julia gasped. ''What are you doing? We can't invade his privacy like this.''

John glanced over his shoulder at her. ''We're dealing with a cold-blooded killer here. I think your foreman would understand under the circumstances. Are you going to help me or are you waiting out here?''

She reluctantly entered Stu's room. John was going to search the foreman's room with or without her help. She reasoned it would make more sense to help him. With her assistance they could finish faster and get out before they got caught.

He said, ''You check the desk. I'll take the closet.''

Working in tandem, they quickly moved from one area to the next. Julia didn't find anything. She didn't expect to find anything. There was no way Stu could be involved in Jack's murder. Stu had admired Jack. Even loved him. Everyone had.

Everyone accept for one person: his killer.

Julia glanced through the man's private papers. She found bank statements, letters from a woman and receipts. Nothing important.

She found charcoal drawings shoved inside the drawer next to his bed. Stu was a frustrated artist. He loved to draw, mostly horses. Julia thumbed through the pictures. She was surprised to find several drawings of a naked woman. The face was averted in every one of them. Only the body was detailed.

Julia put the drawings back without showing them to John. Guilt rode her hard. She shouldn't be invading Stu's privacy. He'd never done anything to warrant such treatment. He was her employee. It was none of her business what he did in his spare time.

She turned to John. ''This is stupid. I told you he wasn't involved. Let's get out of here now. I don't want to have to explain what I'm doing here to a good friend.''

John shrugged. ''Okay. We'll go. I haven't found anything incriminating either.''

''And you won't.'' She moved closer to the door. Her

eyes fell on a piece of paper sticking out from under Stu's dresser. Curious, she picked it up, telling herself she only wanted to set it safely on the dresser. It could be important.

Her mouth fell open as she read the check over and over. The check was from Straw Man, Inc., in the amount of ten thousand dollars. What in the world could Stu have done for this much money?

John snatched it out of her hand. "Well, it's not a smoking gun, but it's a start."

Julia disagreed. "There could be a million explanations for this."

"Yeah? What about this?" John held up a charcoal drawing. It was the Scarecrow drawing found on the card. "Your foreman is quite the artist. The question is, did he copy this from the card or is this the original drawing?"

"WHAT DO YOU MEAN we can't call the police?"

She was beautiful when she was angry. Her emerald-green eyes flashed, reminding him of the jungle after a rainstorm. Green mist.

He sat beside her in the living room and said, "We can't call the police because we don't have any real proof. There isn't a law against drawing pictures. We need actual proof that he killed your husband. Baby, we need more proof than this."

Her blood chilled to ice. The mere thought of the gun that had killed her husband being close enough for them to find turned her insides cold. She didn't want to see the gun.

She said, "We can at least tell Billings we know who did it. He can dig up the evidence himself."

John threw up his hands. "What makes you think we can trust him? We need to finish this on our own. Otherwise, we risk scaring the killer off."

Her eyes dropped. "I can't believe it's Stu. Well, I can but I don't want to. He was a good friend to Jack."

"You saw the drawing. Don't let sentimentality blind you. You have a son to think about. Remember that, and you'll be able to handle Stu when the time comes for action."

"My son! He's outside. I have to get him. J.J. could be with Stu right now!"

She raced to the door, but John detained her, by grabbing her wrist. There was a hard glint in his eyes. "If you run out there and drag the kid inside, you'll give the entire show away. We have to remain calm."

"You remain calm! If your suspicions are correct my son might be playing games with a cold-blooded murderer right now! I have to get him!"

John's hand tightened on her arm. "I'll go get him. Okay? It'll look less suspicious if I do it."

Julia trembled. Her son was the only thing she had left in the world. John was afraid she might do something stupid and get herself killed. She stared him squarely in the eye. "Do it then. Bring him in. Now."

John groaned. "Woman, you are going to be the death of us both."

Julia watched impatiently as John stepped out onto the porch. He motioned for her to stay inside. She hid behind the door and waited. He hoped she would listen to him for a change. If she wasn't careful, she would get them all killed.

John shouted, "Stu! Have you seen the kid?"

Stu yelled, "Yeah, he's playing in the field. Why?"

"He promised to help his grandmother with a project of hers today. Can you send someone to get him?"

Julia's fingernails dug into his back. Any second now

she would fly past him. He wanted to get J.J. himself, but he knew he had to hang back and keep her quiet.

Stu yelled, "I'll tell Randy to get him. He ain't doin' nothin' worth crowin' about anyways."

John said, "Appreciate it."

John shut the door and Julia struck him in the chest with her balled fist. She swore, "Dammit, are you crazy? Stu could have gone after J.J. himself. He still could. You go get him."

John grabbed her arms. "You're nearly hysterical already. I'm not going to leave you in here by yourself. Randy will bring the kid home. Don't worry. Stu has no idea we saw the drawings or the check. I put them back in place. He won't know anyone was in his room."

She shivered. "Unless we were seen."

"We weren't seen." John caressed her small fists until they relaxed and the fingers fell open. "Relax. I won't let anything happen to J.J. or to you. Got it?"

She replied, "Got it."

John's arms wrapped around her. Holding her felt good. He never wanted to let her go, but the door swung open behind them. Her son stuck his head in, giving them both a nasty glare. "Why do I have to come in?"

Julia pulled back. "I want you to go upstairs to your room for a while."

"Why? I didn't do nothin'."

She tried to pat him on the head, but he moved beyond her reach. She said, "Honey, I just need you to go to your room. Please."

He glared at John. "I know you're my dad, and I wish you were dead!"

Chapter Thirteen

John paled.

Without considering the consequences, he reached out to the kid. His fingers barely brushed the boy's shoulder. Fury erupted in J.J.'s eyes as he backed away from the hand, avoiding what he obviously thought was his father's touch. The rejection stung, but John was more concerned for the boy than for himself.

J.J. screamed, "Leave me alone! I hate you!"

Julia gasped. "J.J., what is the matter with you? John is not your father."

"Yes, he is!" The boy's eyes flooded with tears. "I heard Uncle Bob tell you. I tape-recorded you. You liar!"

He raced up the stairs, taking them two at a time in his haste to escape. Julia ran after him. John had no choice but to follow. He hung back, waiting in the hallway, feeling like an intruder. If Julia needed him, he wanted to be nearby.

John watched Julia sit on the boy's bed as he sobbed into his pillow. His slender shoulders shook with grief. Her hand stroked his hair. "Honey, he isn't your father. Uncle Bob was wrong."

J.J. lifted his tear-stained face. "How do you know?"

"Well, for one thing, John was talking in his sleep. I

heard him. He isn't your father. Plus, we have fingerprint proof that he isn't your dad.''

John swayed against the outside wall. Like a deflated balloon, oxygen and blood left his body in a violent rush. The woman had lied to him. He had trusted her and she had lied to him. He wondered what other lies she had told him.

John heard J.J. ask, ''What did he say?''

''I can't tell you right now. I haven't even told him yet.''

''I'm sorry, Mom.''

''So am I.'' She asked, ''As for the tape-recorder, I've told you several times not to eavesdrop on people. Do it again and you'll be grounded.''

''Right.''

John drifted across the hallway to his own room. Behind the closed door he was safe from prying eyes. It was not his intention to pack his belongings—the few things he had managed to acquire during his stay with the Kellers— but that was exactly what he found himself doing.

He had an extra pair of jeans, three shirts and a journal. He stared down at the folded shirt in his hand. If he stayed, Julia would lie to him again. He couldn't trust her. Without trust how could there be anything more?

John didn't hear the faint knock on his bedroom door. It swung open to reveal the ''Delilah.'' She hesitated in the doorway. Her gaze immediately fell to the overnight bag.

John shoved the shirt into the bag. No time for second thoughts. No time for regrets. He had to go whether he wanted to or not. He avoided Julia's eyes. She had no right to reproach him with a bitter look.

''You're leaving us.'' The color drained from her already-pale cheeks. ''Just like that?''

"What did you expect?"

A flicker of pain danced in her eyes. She glanced away quickly, but not before he'd seen it. "I...kind of thought you wanted to...stick around for a while."

"Why?" He snarled at her, "Why would I want to stay here? I'm surrounded by secrets and lies. No man in his right mind would choose to live here. Now I understand why you thought your husband might have faked his own death. He probably wanted to get away from you."

She rotated on one foot and grabbed the doorknob. Her voice came out choked, barely audible. "Fine. You'll at least say goodbye to Sylvia I hope."

"It won't work."

Her pain-filled eyes met his. "What won't?"

"Trying to use that sweet old lady to change my mind. I can't stay here. I'm not Jack. You know it for a fact, but you didn't tell me. Why? What did you hope to gain by the deception?"

Her eyes, sparkling with unshed tears, gazed up at him. "I never meant to hurt you."

"Famous last words."

"I just wanted more time. Is that so wrong?"

He dropped the wrinkled T-shirt he'd been strangling onto the bed, missing his bag. "Why did you need more time, Julia?"

"I don't know. Maybe I needed to prepare Sylvia for the truth. Or maybe I wanted time to digest the truth myself. I was hoping you were Jack. Finding out you weren't...it was like losing him all over again."

A tear slipped down her cheek, and his finger automatically brushed it away. It was the wrong thing to do. Touching her burned his skin. It warmed his blood, fueled his desire for her.

He wanted to kiss her. He wanted to hold her, but their

time was at an end. He wasn't sure where he would go. Anywhere as long as Julia Keller wasn't there. She was a complicated, confusing woman and he no longer wanted any part of her. Especially when she wouldn't even admit the truth to herself.

"The truth is you didn't want me to leave because you're starting to like me. Me. Not Jack Keller. You want to be with me. You want to get to know me."

Her voice raised a notch and the stubborn thrust of her jaw returned. "You have got to be out of your mind. I don't even know who you are."

"Not knowing doesn't necessarily mean not wanting. Our attraction is more than mere physical. I'm sure of that. But I'll settle for lust right now."

She started for the door again. "Well, I won't. I think you were right the first time. Maybe you should leave."

"Oh, honey. It would almost be worth the grief it would cause me to stay here and prove you wrong." His expression hardened. "But I won't. The only way I'll stay is if you admit you want me and not Jack."

She remained stubbornly silent.

He headed for the door, overnight bag in hand. His fingers locked on the knob. He forced himself to keep moving. He told himself it would get easier. He wouldn't look back. He wouldn't dare look back.

She whispered huskily, "Don't go."

At first John thought he had imagined the words spoken so softly behind him. He froze. Warning bells screeched in his head. He had to leave. He would have to leave eventually. If he turned back now, it would hurt more later. It would be harder the second time around.

She moved closer until he could feel the heat of her body at his back. "Please don't go. I need you."

"No, you don't need me. You're strong, stronger than

I am. Tell me the truth, Julie. You want me. Physically, at least.''

She placed a hand on his arm. "Look at me."

John turned around. His back was rigid with tension. Would she finally admit the truth?

JULIA DESPISED the cold triumph of his gaze. He thought he had won, but she couldn't tell him what he wanted to hear. Not yet. Maybe never.

"I want you to stay. That's all you're going to get from me. I won't beg."

He sighed. "I didn't ask you to beg. I asked for the truth. You are a lonely widow encased in two years' worth of ice. I would thaw you out, but I'm not sure anymore if you'd be worth the effort it would take."

"How dare you," she gasped.

"No. How dare you. How dare you stand there with your pretty little nose up in the air, acting as if you couldn't care less about me when all you want to do is jump into my arms. Be honest for a change. I want to hear you say the words just once before I leave. I'll still go. Just give me the words, Julie. I need something to keep me warm at night."

Her vocal chords tightened. She couldn't do it. It would be a slap in the face of Jack's memory. She couldn't possibly get involved with her husband's impostor. She couldn't possibly fall in love with a look-alike.

John grabbed her by the shoulders. He spun her around as if reading her thoughts. "Dammit, look at me! I want you to see who you're talking to. I'm not Jack Keller. I'm John Smith, and you'd better get that straight in your pretty little head."

"I can't," she choked out. "I can't say it." Her slender

shoulders shook. "I'm sorry. I don't want you...not like that."

"Then how?" He pressed his advantage. His hot breath hit her in the face and she trembled like a leaf in the wind.

"Please don't..."

"Please don't what?" He shook her. "Please don't hold you? Please don't kiss you? Please don't go crazy with wanting you?"

Tears slid down her cheeks, and John's hands dropped. Without him to hold on to she sank down to her knees. She hadn't cried much since the day at the hospital, standing in the hallway with Jack's ring and watch cutting into her tender palm. She had made herself strong for her son and for Sylvia and for Bob, but now the floodgates opened. Her emotions shattered like glass.

Her body shook under the stress of racking sobs. A bout of hiccups joined the chorus. She was no longer in control. She couldn't stop crying. She couldn't speak. She felt as if a feather would make her splinter into a thousand pieces.

"Don't cry," he commanded. John knelt next to her and wrapped her in his strong embrace. His words softened. "Don't cry. I'm sorry. I can be a real bastard sometimes. I'll go now if you want me to."

She shook her head hard, unable to speak. Her fingers clutched at his arm. She pressed her mouth into his throat as he stroked her hair. He held her without saying a word, allowing her to ride high the tide of her emotions.

HOURS LATER—or maybe it was minutes—John carefully swung her into his arms and carried her to her own bedroom. She was afraid he would leave her there, but he didn't. He settled into the bed with her still wrapped close.

She snuggled deep and closed her eyes, certain she had won the first round. John would stay, at least for the night.

She said, "I should probably check on J.J."

"I'll look in on him. You stay here."

She latched on to his wrist. "You're coming back, aren't you?"

He said, "I couldn't leave now if I wanted to. For better or for worse, I'm not going anywhere tonight."

His use of the signature wedding vow made her inwardly cringe. She could still hear Jack's voice as he'd recited those same words to her. She watched John leave to check on her son with mixed emotions. What was she doing? The man didn't belong to her. She had to let him go.

But not yet, she pleaded with the fates. She just wanted him for one more night. She wanted to sleep in his arms. The joy of having him hold her throughout the night would probably have to last her a lifetime. There would be no more men for her. Jack had clearly been her only true love. She couldn't replace him. She didn't want to.

John came back with a wary glint in his eyes. She feared he would say he had changed his mind and had to leave, but he didn't say a word. He slipped into bed beside her, and switched the lamp off.

He finally said, "J.J. is fine. He's asleep. I have to go in the morning. We can't keep drawing this out. It isn't fair. I'll explain things to Sylvia before I leave."

"I know you're right." Her fingers tightened on his arm. "Just hold me tonight."

She slid into his arms before he could respond. Her cheek rested on his chest. She wished he would remove his shirt, but she was afraid to make any demands on him. Instead, she pressed her face against him and listened to the steady beat of his heart. It thundered along with her own.

His fingers curled in her hair as he fiercely whispered, "This is insane."

John pulled her upward until her mouth hovered above his in the dark. She closed her eyes, wishing she could see his face but content with his touch. The tip of his tongue licked the groove between her lips.

The tiny sting of pleasure made her gasp. As if it was the reaction he had been hoping for, his mouth urged upward to capture hers. Thrilling shock waves shot through her system. A little voice deep down warned her not to go too far. The logical side of her brain tried to control the situation, but her emotions overrode it and the heat of his kiss melted her defenses.

His hands tangled in her hair, holding her steady for the tender assault. His palms slid down her back. He molded her to him, covering every inch with his curious fingers. He left nothing unexplored.

Then his hands fell away, but the kiss continued. His head drifted back to the pillow and she followed, eagerly taking the lead. Her tongue thrust between his lips, reveling in each new discovery.

She sucked his lower lip between her teeth, gently biting down on it, and he rewarded her with a hungry groan.

Julia's fingers went to his shirt, wrenching it from his jeans. She wanted to be closer to him. The clothes were in the way. It seemed a simple enough solution to remove them.

John's hands closed over hers, stopping them from their intended task. He whispered, "We should stop."

"I don't want to stop." Saying the words made her realize how true they were. She didn't want to stop. This felt right. How could it be wrong? "I want to make love with you."

His breath hissed between tightly clenched teeth. "Dammit, Julie. Be fair."

In the darkness she recognized Jack's furious tone and his old demands. *Be fair, Julie.* Every time Jack had thought her unreasonable he had repeated those words.

Julia couldn't take it. It was one thing after another. She was running on fumes at the moment, and John had just crossed the line.

"Stop confusing me! You aren't Jack. Why do you keep talking like him?" She tried to get up, hands pressed hard against her own ears. She didn't want to listen to his sexy voice, didn't want to look into his bluer-than-blue eyes.

John caught her by the arm and swung her around to face him again. "I may not be Jack, but I can make you purr for me."

Another of Jack's sayings. She was losing her mind. She knew this man wasn't Jack. He couldn't be Jack. Jack was dead.

John's hot mouth lowered to her throat, teasing the tender flesh with hot, nibbling kisses, and her thoughts whirled out of control, fading into nothing. There was nothing left but sensation. Tears slipped down her cheeks unnoticed.

Her fingers curled around the back of his neck and she tilted her head back, exposing her throat further to his burning assault.

She could barely breathe beneath his huge frame. His body moved between her thighs. He rocked against her in a steady rhythm. She wanted to laugh and cry at the same time. He was doing crazy things to her senses. By the time he finished there would be nothing left of her. She would disintegrate, shatter into a million tiny fragments.

He undid the buttons on her shirt and peeled the sides back, exposing her hot flesh to the cool night air. Her nipples puckered, longing for the feel of his hands and the glory of his mouth. She desperately wanted to experience his touch there, but she didn't know how to ask. She hadn't had to ask Jack. He had instinctively known.

Oh, Jack. Why did she keep thinking of him? She finally had a chance at some happiness, but she couldn't seem to put her dead husband's ghost to rest.

John stiffened, feeling the change in her.

"What's wrong now? I thought you wanted this."

"I do. I did. I'm just…I guess I'm afraid."

"Of what? Of me?" She heard the incredulity in his tone.

"Of course not," she quickly assured him. "I'm afraid of loving another man. I'm afraid we'll wake up and find everything changed tomorrow. You name it and I'm probably afraid of it. I'm a coward."

"You are not a coward." His lips caressed her cheek. "You are the strongest woman I've ever known."

She smiled in the dark. "That's not saying much since you can't remember the other women you've known."

His fingers laced with hers as he brought them to his mouth. The shadow of whiskers on the lower half of his face scraped against her skin like sandpaper. The friction fueled her desire.

He said, "I want to make love to you, but I can wait."

She wasn't sure she could wait. What if there wasn't a tomorrow for them? She had believed she had plenty of time with Jack, time to hold him and love him, time for long talks, but their time had been cut short.

"I'm sorry. You must think I'm a nutcase. I promise, no more distractions. I want you. I do." She whispered, "Make love to me, John."

"Are you sure this time?"

"More sure than I've ever been."

"I want to know everything about you. I want you to tell me what you like and what you don't like. I don't want you to have any regrets."

She smiled, tired of thinking about the past. "Shut up and kiss me."

His mouth lowered, but before it could connect with hers they were interrupted by a loud rap on the door. John gritted his teeth. "I don't believe it."

"It might be J.J."

Sylvia called out, "Jack? Are you in there?"

John groaned. "I'll have a talk with her about timing."

Sylvia knocked harder and yelled, "Jack! Are you in there? Julia?"

John went to the door. "Yes."

The woman's eyes darted past him to Julia who was trying to cover herself with a discarded sheet. "Do you remember that man you shooed off the other day?"

"What about him?"

"He's back." Sylvia added, "I saw him sneaking around the bunkhouse a few minutes ago. Want me to get my shotgun?"

John shook his head with a tight grin. "No, thanks. I think I can handle it."

"Want me to call the sheriff?"

John raced down the stairs without answering, and Julia forgot her modesty. She straightened her disheveled clothing as she blasted past the older woman. She considered getting the shotgun herself, then dismissed the idea. So far Chalmers hadn't tried to harm either of them.

Which didn't mean he wouldn't now.

Julia flew out the front door. She raced for the pasture, desperate to catch up with John. Fear clutched at her throat. She couldn't lose him. Not now. He was her only hope at having a life again.

She caught up with him halfway to the bunkhouse and grabbed his arm. ''I hope you aren't going to just barge in there. Don't you have a plan or something?''

He sighed in exasperation and shoved a hand through his wild mane. ''What are you doing out here? Go back inside.''

''No.'' She tucked several strands of dark, windblown hair behind her ear and lifted her chin high, defying him. ''This is my ranch. Chalmers is trespassing. I have every right to be there when you question him. Besides, someone has to make sure you keep your cool.''

He lifted a finger in front of her face and opened his mouth, then shut it.

Chalmers headed straight toward them, a huge smile on his face. He held his hands out. Julia wasn't certain if the gesture was intended to show he had no weapons or if he thought John was going to welcome him back.

John and Julia walked out to meet him. They cut across the gravel to the corral fence, passing by Bob's truck.

A small blast, not unlike a firecracker, cut through the silence. It was trailed by two more.

The windshield of Bob's truck exploded. Julia covered her head and face, ducking beside the truck. Fragments of glass hit her. Her clothing proved to be no protection.

She screamed, ''Get down!''

John remained where he was as if frozen. He didn't move. He didn't try to push her down, didn't try to protect her. He stood in the open, an observer rather than a participant. Julia watched John sink into some sort of trance.

And then Julia realized why he was staring ahead with a grim expression. Chalmers had been hit by at least one bullet. The man staggered forward, refusing to fall.

Julia yelled, ''Get down!''

She clawed at the ground, crawling toward John's feet.

She wouldn't let anything happen to him. She couldn't lose him the way she'd lost Jack. If it meant her own life, she had to save his.

"John, please get down!"

He glanced down, staring at her as if he'd forgotten she was there. His hands shot out to help her. He pulled her to her feet. "It's okay. I saw the shooter. He took off through the trees. He's gone."

She collapsed against him in relief, but John pushed her away. Before she could ask him what was wrong, he took off across the field. She had forgotten Chalmers.

Julia joined them. "I'll call for help."

Chalmers made a grab for her arm and missed. "No need. I have to tell you something."

John said, "Save your breath. You can tell us later."

"No." Chalmers smiled. Blood trickled down the corner of his mouth. "Time for the truth. I lied to you, man. You told me about your past. You told me your true identity."

John's eyes sharpened. "What did I tell you?"

"You are Jack Keller, man."

Chapter Fourteen

"You're Jack Keller, man."

Julia swayed on legs suddenly no more consistent than melted butter. Her eyes flooded with tears. She desperately tried to blink them away. She had to see John—Jack. Whoever. She had to see his expression to know if Chalmers was telling the truth, but her vision was hopelessly blurred.

Chalmers continued. "You were running, man."

"Running from what?"

John's voice sounded distant. Julia reached out to touch him, but he stepped to the side, avoiding her grasping hand. The horrible truth hit her like a slap in the face. John had wanted her, but Jack didn't. Jack had left her behind on purpose. If this man was her husband, he had left her behind.

Chalmers interrupted her thoughts. "You were convinced someone here was trying to kill you. I don't think you knew who, but you suspected…"

"Who?" John's voice hardened. "Who did I suspect?"

"You said…the killer…Bobby. You got a…tip. You weren't sure…didn't believe it."

Julia's horrified eyes swung in John's direction. They had suspected Bob, but to hear the words. Bob was Jack's brother. Sure they had had their differences over the years, but they always stood together in the end.

"If it's true…if Bobby had something to do with the Scarecrow trying to kill you, it has to be a mistake." John delivered her a chilling glare to which she added, "He needs help."

John sarcastically said, "Anyone who would marry Roberta obviously has a mental deficiency. That's beside the point. He tried to kill me."

"No. He 'might' have tried to kill you. We don't know for sure. We only have Chalmers's word for it. There's no proof."

Chalmers's eyes drifted shut during her defense of Bob. John searched the man's wrist for a pulse. Then he slowly stood to his feet and announced, "Well, I guess I'll have to take your word for that. Chalmers is dead."

"Did you see the person who shot him clearly enough to describe him to Sheriff Billings?"

"No. The damned sun was in my eyes. He was tall wearing jeans and carrying a gun."

Julia pointed out, "That nails half the men on this ranch. We need more than that."

John growled, "We don't need anything! We know who the killer is!"

"No, we don't! We know who Jack suspected. We don't have any proof or motive. Why would Bob want to kill his own brother?"

"I don't know. Let's find out."

"Don't you think it's a bit odd everything points to Bob all of a sudden? For two years there wasn't a single clue. Now we're being bombarded with them. What about Stu? What about the drawings we found in his room? Not to mention the check."

John's laugh was laced with bitterness. "You want me

to suspect anyone other than your precious Bob. I wonder why that is. Tell me, darling, are you in love with Bobby?''

Julia was stunned. But he was upset, she reasoned. He had just been shot at and he'd seen a man, possibly a friend, die. Naturally he was angry. He didn't know what he was saying.

She smoothed a hand down his arm. ''You are the only man I want to be with.''

John pivoted. He headed for the house, fists tightly clenched at his sides. His back was ramrod stiff with fury. His muscles bunched beneath the thin cotton shirt he wore. He looked angry enough to kill someone.

Bob was at the house. Julia couldn't let the two men get within ten feet of each other until John cooled off.

She raced after him, taking a shortcut. Her feet pounded against the dry grass. John's long legs carried him across the yard in record time. She pumped her legs harder, running as fast as she possibly could in stiff boots. A painful stitch tore at her side, but she pushed forward. She had to beat John to the front door.

Another obstacle stood in her way. The pasture fence, three beams high, lay directly in front of her. She hadn't jumped over it since she'd been a young teenager. She had to make it. Her family needed her. John needed her.

Julia's hands landed on the top beam. Rough splinters gouged at her palms. Without hesitation she swung her legs off the ground. They flew above her head and went over the fence. She was silently congratulating herself when she lost her balance and her hands lost their grip.

She fell.

A short-lived cry burst from her throat. She hit the ground hard on her left side. Pain shot up her back. She gritted her teeth, waiting for the aftershocks to stop.

Julia closed her eyes against new tears. She had failed John. He was in the house by now, racing up the stairs to confront Bob. He would blurt out the truth. J.J. would be confused, hurt. If Bob was the killer, there was no telling what he would do when cornered.

A hand landed on her arm, startling her. Her eyes flew open and she found herself staring into John's baby blues. Now how long was she going to refer to him as John? Chalmers had called him Jack before dying. Why would a dying man lie?

John asked, "Are you okay? What in the hell possessed you to try a stunt like that? You could have broken your silly neck."

Julia laughed in relief and John's scowl deepened. She sat up. Their faces were mere inches apart. She wanted to kiss him, but she was sure he wouldn't allow it. He was burning mad.

She said, "I wanted to stop you from making a big mistake. You can't just charge in there, pointing fingers at people. Poor Sylvia would be caught in the middle. She loves you both. She couldn't possibly choose sides."

John's eyes widened. They glistened suspiciously and his hands started to shake. "I'm Jack Keller. I'm Jack Keller. It's true. I knew it was true the second Chalmers told us."

"I hope so." He glared at her and she amended, "We only have Chalmers's word for it. You didn't trust him before. What about the fingerprints? Jack didn't speak Spanish, but you did in your sleep."

"A person can learn another language, Julie. As far as the fingerprints, Billings is lying."

John stood and pulled her to her feet. His hand went to her shapely backside, wiping off the dirt. The even strokes sent a tingling sensation spiraling through her narrow frame. His touch was familiar yet disturbingly different from anything she'd ever known.

He swallowed. She watched in interest as his Adam's apple bobbed. His eyes snared hers. Then they shifted away as if he didn't want to look at her.

He rasped, "Stop looking at me like that."

"Like what?"

She stepped closer. The tip of her tongue snaked out to moisten her lower lip. He groaned deep in his throat and his eyelids lowered to half mast. The sleepy, seductive expression she knew so well relaxed his facial muscles and renewed her hopes. He was going to kiss her.

He leaned down until she could feel the warmth of his breath on her face, but his words chilled her to the bone. "Now I know who I am. Who are you?"

"What?" Her smile faded. "We were married, if you are Jack. We are married. We need to talk. If we prove that you are Jack, if your memories return, are you prepared to be my husband again?"

He shrugged coldly. "I don't have any plans at the moment. There are a few things I need to know before I can make an intelligent decision. For instance, where have I been for the last two years? Also, I'd like to know why I left you in the first place. If our marriage was so perfect, why did I leave?"

Hurt, she turned her face away. "My marriage was perfect as far as I'm concerned. Maybe you didn't agree, but I was happy, and you never gave me any reason to believe you weren't. Assuming you're Jack."

"Let's say that I am." He smirked. "In other words, we didn't communicate."

She spun around. Her green eyes glistened. "You don't remember our marriage, so don't try to minimize it. We were happy. We...were...happy."

John sighed. "Maybe. My leaving could have nothing to do with you. Chalmers said I suspected someone here was trying to kill me. Bob...or someone else."

"You don't suspect me, do you?"

"Of course not."

He did! He suspected *her* along with everyone else. A cold, undying sadness was born within her heart. Even if he couldn't remember her, he should know deep down she would never hurt him. Where was the Jack Keller she'd known and loved?

"I don't believe anyone here was involved in your death. Jack's death. No one here would murder anyone."

He glided a finger down the smooth slope of her face. "Are you willing to risk our lives on that assumption? I think it's time to ask yourself how much you loved me. I realize you don't know me now and you don't owe me anything, but for old time's sake perhaps you could ask yourself how much you loved me. Then ask yourself if you're willing to risk my life and yours on the assumption that you know your family better than I did."

"You're confusing me. I don't think..."

"Don't think!" He snapped, "Don't use your mind. Use your heart, your gut. What are they telling you? Was I a paranoid person, Julie?"

She shook her head reluctantly. Jack had seen the good in everyone. It would have taken a lot to convince him that someone on the ranch was trying to kill him. Anyone, let alone his own brother. He had hand-picked practically every one of their workers.

And his family? It was unthinkable.

He grabbed her shoulders in a firm grasp, forcing her to look up at him. "You have to help me, Julie. I can't do this without you. I need you."

She stared up into his smoky-blue eyes and searched

them carefully. He was using her nickname. He was talking as if he knew her intimately. Pulling out every trick in the book. He was playing games with her. Who was this devil in disguise?

She asked, "What do you want me to do?"

"I don't want you to do anything. Not yet. Later on, I want you to help me convince everyone that my memory has returned. In the meantime you'll have to fill me in on several key components of our family. I need them to believe I remember everything. Then the killer will try again. Only this time I'll be ready for him."

She said, "I'll do it on one condition. Keep an open mind. I don't want you to solely focus on Bob. If it isn't him, you'll be leaving yourself wide open for an attack from another direction. Now that I've found you, I don't want to lose you again."

He smiled, but it didn't quite reach his eyes. There was no warmth to be found in them as he leaned close and whispered, "Don't worry. I won't rule anybody out."

Which meant her. He wasn't going to exclude her from his list of suspects. Julia wondered if their marriage would survive this new world without trust. Once his memories returned would Jack be his old self again, or would he remain the suspicious John?

HE WAITED beside Chalmers's body. His eyes focused on Julia and the sheriff as they approached him with wary expressions. John had asked her not to call Billings, but Julia had insisted they contact the law.

John didn't trust the man. In fact, his resentment grew stronger as Billings neared, his meaty hand on the small of Julia's back. She seemed uncomfortable. Her eyes avoided her husband's gaze, choosing to stare off into the distance instead.

Billings said, "Now, I had to set 'General Hospital' to taping so I could come out here. I wouldn't have bothered if the Keller family weren't the important people they are. I woulda sent a deputy instead. Now Julia tells me this here fella told you you are Jack Keller. Is that true?"

John frowned at her. No wonder she had averted her eyes. He could wring her neck. He'd told her not to share any more information than she absolutely had to.

Billings continued. "'Course I already knew that. You told me you were gonna enter the Witness Protection Program. You asked me to look after everyone until you could come back."

Julia's eyes swung to the sheriff, huge emerald orbs in a pale face. "The Witness Protection Program? Why didn't you tell me? Jack's body vanished from the hospital and you never said a word. I was going nuts thinking Jack was dead."

"Whoa there, sugar. I had no idea he wasn't dead until I was contacted by the FBI a couple months ago. I mean, things like that don't happen in real life. I expected to see Luke and Laura and all the other faces from 'General Hospital,' but I never in a million years imagined I'd see Jack Keller alive again."

Her eyebrows pulled together. "But you said Jack told you he was going into the program. So how could you not know?"

"Getting shot wasn't part of the plan. He wasn't supposed to leave for another few days. Then he was going to disappear. He was supposed to come back for you and the kid. I guess he finally did. Maybe he was on his way back when the accident occurred."

John said, "It wasn't an accident. Somebody tried to kill me."

He studied the sheriff's reaction to the news. Billings barely blinked an eye.

Billings shrugged. "Well, you're here now. That's all that matters. You're a good sight luckier than this fella here. Can you tell me anything about him?"

John replied, "He's that DEA agent, Chalmers. He's the one you told me to contact. Says we worked together on a few projects. The only proof he had was an old picture of the two of us."

"Did you look friendly in the picture?"

"I guess so. I wasn't smiling, but I was standing close to the man. I can't say if we were on the same side. I don't remember him."

John clamped his lips firmly shut. He had already said more than he'd intended to. He didn't trust Billings. The man was too curious, even for a lawman.

Billings stared at him, waiting for him to continue.

Julia stepped in. "Why was Jack going into the program? I thought only people who testified against the mob were involved."

"From what I gathered the FBI suspected Jack's father had been killed by a professional hitman dubbed the Scarecrow. Jack was also on the list of targets. Although the FBI still don't know who put the contract out on him. There are no witnesses. There isn't a paper trail to follow. It's like it never happened."

She said, "That doesn't make any sense. Why would anyone want Jack or John Senior dead? They were ranchers."

"The FBI didn't see the need to fill me in," Billings said. "I'll have to let them know about this man's death, of course." His black gaze swung to John. "You'll need to contact them, see what they want to do about you now that you've come out of hiding."

John felt Julia stiffen beside him. She was afraid he would leave her. He would have reassured her, but under the circumstances he couldn't make any promises.

He said, "If you don't need us for anything else, Sheriff, it's been a trying day. I think I'll turn in early."

"Go right ahead. I want to get back to my show anyway. I'll send a couple of deputies for the body."

John took Julia's hand in his and led her to the house. They were greeted by an anxious Sylvia. "Are you two okay? What happened?"

John stared at the woman. This was his mother. Knowing it as a fact changed things. He saw her in a whole new light. He wanted to put his arms around her, wanted to tell her he was home. Only Julia's presence stopped him. He had to talk to her first.

Julia briefly explained what had happened to Chalmers. Then the two of them went upstairs. John wasn't much in the mood for talking at the moment. He hadn't lied to the sheriff. He really was tired.

John parted from Julia in the hallway, automatically turning for his door. Her quivering voice stopped him.

"Don't you think you should sleep in here tonight? If you want to convince everyone you're back, you should sleep in your own bed...with your wife."

He shook his head wearily. "Not tonight. I'm exhausted."

"Do you want to catch a killer or not? If it's someone in this house, a show like this will do the trick. If it's someone outside the house, they'll hear the news. Jack is back."

John's hand raked through his hair, rubbing his scalp in irritation. He wanted to sleep alone. Before now he would have given anything to sleep with the beautiful creature standing in front of him, but he was confused. He needed time alone to think.

"What if I try to strangle you again?"

"I'm willing to take the risk. You know you're Jack now. I don't think there'll be a repeat of that night."

John hadn't been having nightmares about the past lately. Sighing, he turned in her direction. "I'll get my things."

Julia's smile brightened. "Great. I'll just take a shower and meet you in bed."

She was being deliberately provocative. How was he going to resist making love to her? He couldn't count on her resistance now that she knew his true identity, but for some reason he didn't feel right about touching her. There was a nagging voice whispering in the back of his mind, whispering a warning to keep his distance.

John took his time retrieving his belongings from the guest room. He walked around the room twice, looking for items he had missed even though he knew he wouldn't find anything. His overnight bag was perched on the edge of the bed, waiting for him.

He collapsed next to it on the bed and tried to catch his breath. Julia would be in the shower. He pictured her body covered in suds, her hands sliding over slippery flesh.

John mentally shook himself. He had to keep his hands off of her tonight. Perhaps he would try reciting *Hamlet*. No matter what she did, he couldn't allow himself to respond.

He returned to her room with a plan. He tossed his shirt to a nearby chair. It missed, hitting the ground instead. His hand went to the zipper on his jeans. Then he froze. What was he doing? He couldn't sleep nude, not with her in the same bed. Struggling, he slid, half dressed, between the sheets.

John closed his eyes, squeezing them tightly shut. He wanted to convince her he was asleep. At the moment sleep was his only defense against her charms. He wished he could make pretense into reality, but with her near enough to smell he doubted he would get any rest.

He heard the bathroom door open. Her soft footsteps fell on the heavy carpet as she crossed the room. He listened to her every movement carefully, daring not to breathe. He tried to imagine what she was doing, picturing her getting ready for bed. Each frame became a torture in erotica.

She brushed her hair and he relived the day he had helped her comb through the tangles. Long silky tresses had slid between his fingers. He had wanted to wrap it around his digits, pulling her to him for a passionate kiss.

Julia moved away from her vanity. He heard her robe slide to the floor and his heart picked up the pace. The sheets stretched, pulling tight over his abs. His breath quickened. The mattress sagged.

John worked hard to keep his body stiff. He concentrated on his breath, sliding it in and out in normal fashion.

Julia closed the space between them. She moved until the full front of her scantily clad body was pressed against his nude back, and his heart nearly stopped. His breath caught in his throat.

One of her arms rested on his side. Her hand played with the springy hair on his chest, gently tugging on it until he thought he would go insane. He prayed she would stop.

Relief flooded him when she withdrew her hand, but it was short-lived. Her mouth took over. She started with his shoulder, licking her way to his throat. Her lips parted over the throbbing pulse working in his neck. She sucked in a bit of flesh and lightly bit down on it.

A groan ripped from his lungs, leaving them empty. He sucked in a handful of air. What was she doing to him?

Julia giggled. She pushed him over onto his back and straddled his waist. Her strong thighs clamped down on him. Dislodging her was going to be a problem. His body was enjoying the contact with hers.

She hadn't turned off the lamp. He watched in fascination as she pulled the straps of her nightgown down her arms. The front hung open, revealing shapely twin globes. The centers were light pink and the dusky nipples puckered under his gaze as if on cue.

John groaned again. She was killing him. His hands itched to caress her, to possess her. His body hardened. She smiled down at him, feeling the change.

Julia rotated her hips slowly, testing his control. With a wry grin she bent forward to taste his male nipples. Lapping at them like a cat, she nearly sent him over the edge.

John's frame spasmed. He bucked upward hard, nearly knocking her off. His sudden movement caught her by surprise. Her hands grasped his strong arms, holding on to him as her tongue continued to tease him mercilessly.

He had wanted to wait until he knew why he'd left her, their marriage, behind. But he couldn't wait a second longer. He had to have her.

Chapter Fifteen

The old Julia had been unsure, insecure in her role as a femme fatale. During their years of marriage it had never even occurred to her to initiate sex. She was an old-fashioned girl, brought up to follow the man's lead. But she wanted John and left up to him, they'd never make love.

When she first stepped from the bathroom, she knew John was feigning sleep. She had been married to the man. She knew the rhythmic sound of his breathing while he slept. The light snoring. The easy rise and fall of his chest.

Finding him still in his jeans didn't surprise her as much as it should have. She straddled his waist slowly, fearing rejection.

Teasing him proved difficult. He held back what she most wanted from him. A response. It was odd, yet strangely exciting to have his hungry eyes on her as she stroked his chest, silently begging for his fingers and lips and tongue. She teased the corners of his mouth with a fingertip, daring him to ignore her.

Now John's large hands weighed her breasts. She threw back her head in sweet agony. He wanted her. She reveled in the knowledge. He wasn't going to leave her cold and unfulfilled as she had feared.

The wicked man was intent on prolonging her torture though. He scraped her engorged nipples with his palms, building friction by rubbing in a circular motion. She leaned forward, wanting more. She wanted his mouth on her, but didn't know how to ask.

She stifled a moan.

He said, "Don't do that. I want to hear you. I want to hear you cry out for me."

Julia wasn't sure she could do it. Knowing her son and others were nearby made her self-conscious. As paranoid as it was, she feared someone might be listening. She couldn't get over the embarrassment. Her complex went back too far to change in one evening.

John read her reluctance. A mocking smile curved his sensuous lips. His golden head lifted from the pillow, and his mouth fell open. She closed her eyes, waiting for the delicious moment that his silky tongue would touch her sensitive flesh.

John sat up, settling her in the pocket between his thighs. His mouth hovered over her breast. He blew on the nipple. His hot breath hit the peak and it raised higher, seeking contact. A shiver raced up her spine. He was driving her crazy.

Julia's fingers dug into his hair. She tried to force his mouth closer, but he wouldn't budge. He wouldn't give in to her deepest desire. She arched her back, pushing herself closer.

His tongue flicked out, teasing, feathering the tip with a light stroke.

Her body screamed for release. Every nerve ending grew to a fever pitch of excitement.

She knew him, almost everything about him, and yet it was like making love for the first time. His body was the same, but his moves had changed.

His tongue snaked out and boldly circled the pink areola. His teeth scraped the sensitive peak, eliciting a soft cry from her lips.

He laughed against her creamy flesh. "That's it, baby. I want to hear you. I want to know I'm pleasing you."

An inner voice demanded she tell him how much he pleased her, but her vocal chords refused to participate. Her lips sprang open. A tiny whimper escaped. It was enough confirmation for John.

He nibbled lightly on the extended nipple, a reward for her response.

Julia arched her back again and this time he took her deep into his mouth. He turned to a strong sucking motion that had her insides melting. Her stomach muscles contracted sharply. Pleasure and pain merged into one stunning sensation.

He finished with one and turned his attention to the other. She cried out and her back bowed. If he didn't take her soon, she would explode. Spontaneous combustion.

One of his hands vanished beneath her nightgown. His fingers pushed aside the flimsy cotton briefs, and he touched her. She began to tremble uncontrollably. She was ready for him. More than ready. She could no longer wait to rediscover the power of his possession.

But John had no intention of hurrying his pace. He worshipped her body with his hands and with his mouth. He touched and tasted, caressed and kneaded, nibbled and sucked until she thought she would shatter.

He wrung moan after moan from her. She rotated her hips, begging him to satiate her desire. Her fingers fumbled with the zipper on the front of his jeans. She was shaking so badly she couldn't get a firm grasp.

He laughed and raised up, kissing her firmly on the lips.

His tongue thrust inside, mimicking what was yet to come, the final act of possession.

She tore her mouth from him and cried, "Now!"

With an arrogant grin he flipped her onto her back and hovered above her. Julia tried to lift herself off the bed, seeking him, but he held her hips steady. She couldn't move. She squirmed, afraid he would prolong the torture.

He rained kisses over her face as he gently glided forward. He joined with her slowly, inch by inch. She was filled by the heart of him with agonizing slowness.

Her arms wrapped around his waist and her legs trapped his hips. He was at home inside of her. She knew it was where he belonged. They were joined, one flesh.

John's breathing turned to shallow gasps. He moved harder, faster, against her. His mouth slanted over her own. One last thrust and he collapsed on top of her. The desire still burned within her, but she no longer cared. She was in her husband's arms again. The world could explode and she wouldn't notice.

But John wasn't through with her yet. His hand insinuated itself between their bodies. He touched her, loving her with his hand until a vortex of color swirled around her.

And then the world exploded.

WATER FROM THE SHOWER hit him in the face like stinging hot needles. He tilted his head back. The water poured over his hair, rinsing out the soap. It flowed down his spine and legs, ending with a swirl around the drain. His toes curled. His entire body tensed as another flash of memory fought its way to the top.

A flash of silver and then it was gone. He couldn't hold on to it. He wasn't sure he wanted to, because along with the memories came pain. Sharp, repressed pain stabbed at him behind the eyes.

John's head fell forward. A wave of dizziness struck him. He could feel another memory pushing forward, racing toward him like a runaway train. There was no way to avoid a collision. All he could do was hold on until it was over.

He remembered another time, another shower.

HE COULD BARELY STAND in the shower stall. Half a bottle of bourbon had taken the edge off of his pain. He scrubbed at his hands in an effort to remove the mud. There was dirt embedded under his fingernails. No matter what he did he couldn't seem to get it all. He stood in the shower, still wearing his jeans.

His father was dead! He had found the shallow grave by accident. Jack didn't need a forensic team to tell him it was his father. He knew. He knew the truth in his heart, had known for months. His father was dead.

His tears mingled with the spraying water. He leaned against the wall and cried. He hadn't cried since he'd been a small child. His father had disapproved of men displaying what he saw as weak emotion. His father had been tough on him, on both his sons, but he'd also been fair.

Jack went down to his knees in the tub.

How could he tell his mother? She had insisted his father would return. She'd never given up hope. Now what would she do? What would she believe in?

The shower curtain flew back and Julia stood there, gazing at him with a pale face. Without a word she climbed into the tub and held him. Her clothes got soaked, but she didn't seem to notice. Her attention was focused purposely on him. It felt good to hold a warm body in his cold arms.

He said, "Dad's dead. Gunshot to the head. Billings thinks it was a professional hit."

"What would Billings know about that? He grew up here, same as we did. I think he watches too much TV." She stroked the wet hair away from his damp face. "Anyway, you don't know it was John Senior. Not for sure. It could be someone else."

"It was him, Julie. I know it was him. He's dead. The DEA talked him into helping them out on some stupid case for old times' sake, and now he's dead."

She stiffened. "What are you talking about? No one knows why John disappeared the way he did. He didn't say anything to anyone. He didn't even leave a note."

"He told me. I was the only one. He asked me to watch out for Mom and take care of the ranch. He told me it might be a few months. He made me promise I wouldn't say anything to anyone. I would have told you if I could have."

"So tell me now."

"The case had something to do with drugs. Smuggling, I think. He hadn't gotten all the details yet himself."

"I don't get it. Why get your dad involved?"

He said, "Dad worked for the DEA once in a while. It was a secret. He joined after leaving the military. They only used him on special occasions."

"And your mom doesn't know?"

"Of course not."

Julia said, "You better never keep a secret like that from me."

He grimaced, remembering the odd cases he had helped his father on. He had done it for the adventure. He had kept it from Julia because she would have worried about him, and she would have made him quit.

Julia tugged on him. "Come on. Let's get you into some dry clothes. You smell like you drank a gallon of whiskey."

"Half a bottle."

She shook her head. "You mother will have your hide if she sees you like this. You know she doesn't allow drinking in the house."

"I wasn't in the house," he said. "I was in the tunnel. Great place to think. No one to bother you."

"Do I bother you? I'm your wife. You should be able to talk to me about anything. I can help you."

He shook his hard head, suddenly suffocated by her love. "You can't help me! You can't bring my father back!"

She slammed the door on her way out. He'd hurt her. But wasn't that what he'd intended to do?

JOHN HELD his throbbing head between two fists. The memories were getting clearer, but clarity came with a price. His head felt as if it was going to explode. A dull knife dug into his temples until he wanted to scream for it to stop.

The curtain flew open. A sense of déjà vu nearly knocked John off his feet. Julia stood in front of him in his old robe. It hung open, baring half a breast. Hunger welled up inside of him. He couldn't possibly want her again so soon.

She asked, "Are you okay?"

His hand reached out of its own accord and his fingers brushed her soft cheek. "Do you want to join me?"

A pink hue colored her cheeks with embarrassment. "You don't look like you're up for it."

"Look again."

Her eyes reluctantly drifted down his nude body. Her face went from light pink to bright red. "You were reluctant to make love to me. Now you're acting like a man on his honeymoon. What's changed?''

He shrugged. ''Don't join me then. I'll join you.''

John stepped out of the shower and grabbed a towel. He wrapped it around his narrow hips. His eyes didn't dare stray from Julia's face. She looked like a scared rabbit ready to bolt.

He went around her, giving her some space. He wondered why she was so uncomfortable. He didn't remember anything of their sex life before. There were a lot of things he didn't remember.

She asked, ''When can we tell everyone it's you?''

''Depends on what you mean by 'everyone.' I thought we should keep it to ourselves for a day or two, come up with a plan.''

''The family. We need to tell them. J.J. will be confused. I swore you weren't Jack.''

John froze in mid-motion, his hand raised to stroke her cheek. He had a son. The news of his identity had stunned him to the point where he couldn't remember clearly. J.J. was his son, and he didn't know anything about the kid.

Julia asked, ''What's wrong?''

John sank to the edge of the bed. How were they going to explain the situation to the boy? Julia had insisted John wasn't his father. Now they knew different. How could they possibly make him understand?

''Do you have any ideas why I would leave you? Billings thought I was going into witness protection, but got shot instead. I could have called you. I could have written you. Why didn't I?''

Her smile was tight. ''I don't know. Maybe you were afraid I would be killed by the Scarecrow. You were very protective of me.''

"Was I?" He glanced away. "Why can't I remember? If I loved you so much, why don't I remember it?"

"'If'?" He could feel her mental withdrawal before she took her hand from his. "You don't believe you loved me?"

"I'm sorry. My emotions are tangled up right now. Don't take it personally."

He put some distance between them, using the time to get dressed. Sylvia had given him more of Jack's clothes. *His* clothes. He pulled on the unfamiliar items, feeling more of an impostor than ever. If the woman sitting behind him on the bed was his wife, why couldn't he remember her?

"Don't take it personally? My husband stares me straight in the eye and tells me he doesn't believe he ever loved me, and I'm not supposed to take it personally. Are you insane? Did you suffer brain damage in that infamous car accident?"

John opened his mouth to respond. He was interrupted by a hard rap on the bathroom door. J.J. poked his head inside. He shot John a nasty glare. "Uncle Bob wants to talk to you downstairs. He's mad."

Julia asked, "What's he mad about?"

"Don't know."

John stepped forward. He wanted to go to the boy, to his son. He wanted to tell him everything, but something held him back. Perhaps it was the anger in the kid's eyes. He wasn't ready to listen. John cautioned himself against pushing.

"I wonder what Bob wants," Julia said.

John glanced sideways at her, distracted. "Only one way to find out."

He followed her down the stairs. His eyes were glued to her shapely bottom, and desire stirred his loins. She was an incredible woman. If their marriage didn't work out, it was going to be hard to extract himself.

THEY FOUND BOB in the living room, wearing a trail into the carpet. He headed for John, fists clenched. "I've had enough of this charade. You are going to admit you are Jack right now!"

Julia said, "Bob..."

His hand went up. "I'm sorry, Julia, but this has gone on long enough. I know I promised not to approach him yet, but I have had it." His hot gaze swung to John. "Well? Are you going to admit you're my brother?"

"Yes. I'm Jack Keller. So I admit it. Now what?"

Roberta gasped.

The two men tried to stare each other down. They stood in the center of the room, ready to attack. The brothers reminded Julia of a movie she had seen once on wolves and their habits. The animals had warily circled each other, preparing to strike. She didn't know what to do.

She said, "John didn't realize he was Jack until that Chalmers guy told us. He still doesn't remember."

Bob laughed bitterly. "You are so young and trusting, Julia, but I know him. He's my brother, and I can see the old resentment in his eyes. He thought we were lovers, but he was the one trying to sleep with my wife."

Roberta slunk out of the room.

John said, "That's not true. I never touched your wife."

"How would you know? I thought you couldn't remember, Jack."

John pulled a cigarette from his pocket. He rolled it between finger and thumb before placing the end in his mouth. "I'd prefer it if you would call me John. I'm used to it now."

"I don't believe this. You hated the name John. You

were the one who insisted on being called Jack. Do you have a screw loose?"

Julia repeated, "He doesn't remember anything. The amnesia is real. I would know if he was faking it."

Bob snarled, "Sure. Just like you knew he was screwing my wife!"

Julia paled, and John tensed, ready to defend her. "Don't you ever talk to Julia like that again!"

Bob said, "At least I didn't sleep with her. I oughta kill you for going after my wife. For leaving. For lying to us."

"You mean you wish you had succeeded the first time in killing me. You should have shot me from closer range. You should have aimed your gun more carefully."

The fight drained out of Bob; his arms fell limp at his sides. Bob shook his head, staring up at his younger brother in horror. He backed away slowly, as if he couldn't put enough distance between them.

"You think I tried to kill you? It was a figure of speech." Bob's confused gaze swung to Julia for help. "I tried to save you. I rushed you to the hospital. I did everything I could. We're brothers. We fight, but I would do anything for you."

Julia stepped between them. "It's true, John. Bob did everything he could."

Ignoring her, John asked Bob, "How do you know I slept with your wife? Did you ever see me with her? Did I tell you that I slept with her? Was there any proof?"

"I saw signs. The two of you stopped talking every time I entered the room. I saw you holding her on the porch one night."

"Did you ever ask me if it was true?"

"I couldn't. I didn't want to know. After you died Roberta hinted that it was true. I know she can be a flirt, but she loves me."

"Does she?" John asked. "Did it ever occur to you that your darling wife might be lying?"

"Lying about my brother trying to seduce her? Why would she do that? She even admitted to being tempted. Do you think she's lying about that? You really are mental, Jack. John. Whatever the hell your name is."

Julia said, "Maybe he's right. I've never trusted Roberta. No offense, Bob, but Jack has better taste. If he was going to cheat on me, he would have chosen better."

Bob groaned, "Why would she lie to me?"

Julia threw up her hands. "I don't know. I'm completely stumped. But she did lie. Perhaps out of spite. Maybe she was jealous of me or of Jack. You know her better than we do."

"I don't know her at all. She's done some strange things since we've been married. Sometimes she goes on shopping trips for days and she doesn't buy a thing. Not that I'm complaining. I just don't understand the concept of window-shopping. When I go to a store, I go for a purpose. I buy something. I don't browse. It's ridiculous."

John said, "Maybe it's a woman thing."

Julia playfully slapped his arm.

Bob said, "It is good to have you back, Jack—uh, John. Gonna take some getting used to. We'll talk later."

Julia said, "I think you should have a long talk with your wife first, Bob."

"I think you're right. By the way, Stu says he saw someone snooping around out by the caves again."

John lifted two fingers to his lips. "Shh."

He went around the sofa and dropped to his knees. When he stood, he had a tape recorder in his hands. The red light was on. They were being recorded.

Chapter Sixteen

Julia fumed.

J.J. had promised he would stop taping private conversations. She was going to have to have a long talk with him before he discovered the truth on his own. Somehow she had to explain Jack's return without traumatizing their only child. It wasn't going to be easy. She grimaced. It was going to prove more difficult than their sex talk.

Her gaze traveled up to John's face. He needed to be part of her discussion with J.J. He was, after all, the boy's father.

As if a light bulb had suddenly blinked on inside his head, John snapped his fingers. He hurried from the room without a word. Watching him go, Julia was torn. Should she follow him or track down her son?

She walked down the hallway, still not sure of her destination, when she noticed a light under the study door. Curious, she pushed the door open to find John gazing up at the bookshelves. He reached high, moved a few books out of the way and pulled a shoebox free.

Julia gasped. "I didn't know that was there. What is it?"

He said, "Only one way to find out."

John set the box on the desk and flipped the top off. There were papers inside. He riffled through them as if he knew what he was looking for. The intense expression on his face had her holding her breath. Whatever it was he was looking for, it was important.

He held a card up for her inspection. The Scarecrow.

Sylvia spoke from the doorway. "Yes, John received one, as well. It came in the mail along with an anonymous threat. My husband was too proud to call the authorities. Stubborn man thought he could handle everything alone. He was a partially retired DEA agent, and they don't need help from anybody."

Julia said, "You knew."

Sylvia smiled. "It's hard for a man to keep secrets from his wife."

John asked, "Did he tell me about the threat?"

"He might have," Sylvia said. "The two of you shared secrets more often than not. I was out of the loop. John loved me, but he was old-fashioned. He thought a woman's place was in the kitchen, not in her husband's business."

Julia blinked at the woman. She was stunned. It had been arrogant for her to believe she knew all there was to know about her family.

Sylvia added, "Anyway, what does it matter? You're back. Why can't we drop this before someone else gets hurt? I'm sure the killer isn't around anymore."

It wasn't like Sylvia to back down from a fight. Julia watched as she patted John on the back before leaving the room, excusing herself to check something in the oven. Julia stared after the woman, wondering if she knew her at all.

An icy coldness filled her stomach. If Chalmers had been telling the truth, someone on the ranch could be a killer. A family member. A friend. Although John had pointed out that possibility, Julia hadn't wanted to face it.

A tiny doubt had kept her from believing it. How could anyone in her circle take another human life? Jack's life.

Things would never be the same once the truth was revealed.

John tilted her chin up, forcing her eyes to meet his. "What's wrong?"

"Do you think she's right? Do you think we should drop the whole thing, continue on with our lives in ignorance? Should we just be grateful for small miracles? We're together now. What else matters?"

Her fingers dug into his arms. Her eyes pleaded with him for understanding. She just wanted the nightmare to end. She wanted to lie in his arms night after night without fear of losing him. Their marriage had been too short. A hundred years would have been too short. They needed more time.

He said, "I have to know the truth. My memories are gone. All I have left is the truth."

"You have me." She closed the distance between them. Her lips pressed against his throat. The throbbing pulse of his heartbeat raced against her mouth. Heat stirred her blood.

"I know." His arms went around her as he said, "But I need the truth. Help me find it."

She withdrew from his arms. A great loss enveloped her. Would she lose him once they found the truth? She couldn't bear the thought.

Julia fixed him with a solid stare. "Why won't you let us call you Jack? Do you still doubt you are Jack? Do you doubt you're my husband?"

"No." His fingers laced with hers. "You're mine, Julie. Regardless of what we discover, you will always be mine. Nothing can change that."

"I wish I was so optimistic. I have this horrible feeling the truth will drive us apart."

"That's because you aren't sure why I left you. You're afraid I might leave again. I wish I could guarantee it won't happen, but…"

"There are no guarantees." She finished his sentence.

John returned the card to the box. He put it back where he'd found it and replaced the books.

She said, "Wait a second. How did you know that was there?"

"I haven't given it much thought. I just went to it."

J.J. raced into the room. "Mom, I can't find my tape recorder."

Hand on her hip, eyes narrowed, she nodded. "As a matter of fact, I did find it. I thought we decided you weren't going to tape any adult conversations anymore."

"Oh." He shifted from one foot to the other. "I didn't do it on purpose. I forgot where it was."

John knelt in front of the boy. "I bet you have a lot of interesting things on those tapes. What do you do with them after you listen to them?"

"I hide them in my closet."

John said, "I'd like to hear them. Will you get them for me?"

J.J. looked skeptical. He glanced at his mother and she nodded. She didn't know why John wanted them, but she knew he must have a good reason.

J.J. raced down the hall to retrieve the tapes and she asked, "What are you up to?"

"I think we may find an unexpected clue on one of those tapes. If your son—sorry, if our son—taped enough conversations he may have stumbled across something. If the killer lives in this house or works on this ranch, we might find a sort of confession on one."

She nodded warily. Fear of what they might overhear had her heart thundering within her breast. There were so many things she still wanted to say to John. She should say them quickly while she had the chance. She had hesitated once in the past and it had cost her two years with the man she loved.

Julia's mouth opened.

J.J. blasted into the room. "Here they are!"

Her eyes widened in disbelief. There were dozens of them. She scowled down at him. Exactly how long had her son been intruding on private conversations?

Before she could chastise him, John patted him on the head, removing the box from his arms. "Thanks, kiddo. I'll return them as soon as I've listened to them."

Return them? Julia's opinion of his parenting skills declined with a sudden swoop. What kind of father was he going to be? Certainly not the sort of father Jack had been.

She snapped out of her silent reverie when John started to leave the room without her. "Wait for me."

He said, "I want to listen to them alone. Besides, you need to talk to J.J. about the upcoming changes in his life."

Changes? But they had yet to discuss these changes. What if John decided he didn't want to play family man? What if he decided to leave after J.J. was attached to him? How would she pick up the pieces?

John vanished through the doorway and J.J. turned bright, curious eyes on his mother. "Did you want to talk to me?"

She hesitated, not sure where to begin. Damn John for leaving her to do this alone. She muttered, "Coward."

"Huh?"

"Not you, honey. I just wanted to ask you how you feel about John. The other day you were pretty adamant about not wanting him around. Would you be happier if he left?"

J.J. took a long time thinking it over. He finally shrugged. "No, he's okay. He can stay."

She knelt beside him. "Honey, you remember when I

told you John wasn't your dad, that your dad was dead? Sometimes your mom is wrong about things. I was wrong about John. He is your father.''

J.J. didn't seem very surprised. "Yeah, I looked at Dad's pictures again and you know what?''

"What?''

"His teeth are the same. Even if John's face was fixed by a doctor, his teeth wouldn't be the same. Right?''

Out of the mouths of babes. Why hadn't she noticed that? He was her husband for heaven's sake. She should have been the first to realize he was her husband, not the last.

She stroked her son's hair. "Daddy has amnesia. He doesn't remember us, but I'm sure he will.''

He smiled at her, but she could see the uncertainty behind it. They needed Jack back.

JOHN LISTENED to the tapes one by one. He almost fell asleep twice. Sylvia was his mother, but her discussions on needlepoint and her favorite recipes hit a hundred on the snooze meter. He also found Roberta's take on life quite boring. Did the woman ever shut up?

Actually she hadn't said a dozen words to him lately. She was abnormally quiet when he was in the room. Perhaps he was wrong about her. Maybe he did sleep with her while married to Julia. If he had slept with the woman, he needed to have his head examined. She was an obvious hustler.

He slipped in another tape, cringing when he heard Roberta's whining high-pitched voice.

"Have you seen my *Cosmo?* I haven't taken the quiz yet. I don't remember what it was on, but it was important. Something about shopping.''

"No," Sylvia responded. "I have not seen your *Cosmo.* I have something in the oven. Excuse me.''

There was a long period of silence. John was about to switch off the tape, assuming everyone had vacated the room.

"It's me. Stu is pressing me to tell Bob about our affair. His conscience is bothering him."

John didn't recognize the voice. It was soft with a husky timbre. John assumed it had to be Roberta. Why would Julia or Sylvia have to tell Bob they were having an affair? If it was Roberta, what had happened to her annoying squeak?

"I can't do that!"

There it was! The shriek was back with a vengeance. Who in the world was she talking to?

"I'll take another shopping trip. Don't worry. I've got it under control."

The door opened and John flicked off the recorder. Julia moved into the room, graceful in her tight jeans and soft blouse. He wanted her again, but it was the wrong time. He had to set his plans in motion.

She sat next to him on the bed. "Well? Did you find anything?"

"It's too soon to tell."

Her eyes sharpened. "You thought you were going to hear something damning about me, didn't you? Are you disappointed?"

"Not in the least."

"What did you hear? Why won't you tell me? Don't you trust me now?"

Surprisingly he did trust her. Something deep inside him warmed under her heated gaze. He grabbed her by the shoulders. An experiment. His mouth crushed hers. His lips ground against hers, almost angrily.

Julia struggled. She shoved at his chest with her fists. "Stop it. What's wrong with you?"

"I'm sorry. I just wanted to be sure."

"Of what?"

"Do you love me, Julie? Do you love me as much as you loved him?"

She cried, "You are him! You and Jack are the same person. Why are you trying to make me choose between you now?"

"Maybe you need to choose. Maybe I need to know it's me you love and not a memory. I'm a flesh-and-blood man. It's me or your memories of what I was. You can't have both. I'm not Jack. Not the Jack I used to be. I may never be Jack again. I need to know how you feel about me."

She shook her head violently, trying to escape, but he wouldn't release the tight hold he had on her arms. She couldn't face his probing gaze right now. Couldn't deal with the questions. "Let me go. You're hurting me. Jack didn't push me around."

He released her as suddenly as if she'd burned him. She nearly fell off the bed, but he didn't reach out to catch her.

He didn't want to touch her. If she didn't want him for himself, then he didn't want to be with her.

Rising, John slammed out of the bedroom. The sound of the echoing door reverberated in his mind, bringing the past to the present. He remembered everything. He knew why he had wanted to leave Julia in the first place. He knew why he hadn't returned to her until recently. The memories assaulted him like hammers until he caved under the weight of them.

Finally he found peace as darkness blanketed him.

"DARLING? How do you feel?"

Julia watched in relief as John's eyes flickered open. The magnificent blue hue nearly stopped her heart, but it had nothing to do with their color. It was the emotion she barely caught a glimpse of before he turned his head. Had she imagined it?

"Where am I?"

She replied, "You're in my bedroom. Our bedroom. I think you fainted. I was worried there was something actually wrong with you."

"Men don't faint. We lose consciousness." He lifted his head from her pillow. His eyes darted around the room as if he expected to find another occupant. Once he was satisfied they were alone, his gaze swung back to her face. "Have I told you lately how incredibly beautiful you are?"

She blushed. "I don't think so. Did you hit your head?"

"No, I just opened my eyes. How in the world did I keep my hands off of you for so long?"

She wasn't sure what had gotten into him, but she liked it. The raw desire in his eyes lit an answering fire in her heart. She leaned forward, offering her lips freely.

John's mouth glided over her lips, teasing them with a slight brush of a kiss. His fingers dove into her thick waves. He held her head steady as he kissed her cheeks, her nose, her eyes. Everywhere but the one place she wanted to feel those lips.

She pulled at his shoulders with an urgency she hadn't experienced in a long time and his mouth took hers in a fierce kiss. His velvet tongue stabbed between her lips. She groaned, moving closer to him. She couldn't get close enough.

John was the first to pull back. "Do me a favor."

She grinned and promised, "Anything."

"Send J.J. away for the night. Have him spend the night at a friend's house."

"Why?" she asked in breathless anticipation.

"I have a feeling everything is going to come to a head tonight. I want him somewhere safe. As a matter of fact, I think you should go, too."

Her green eyes narrowed. "No way."

"Honey, I want you to be protected."

She snuggled tighter into his arms, wrapping herself—arms and legs—around him. "I'm safer with you than I am without you."

"I'm not so sure."

She kissed the steady beat in his throat. "I am."

"Well, at least send J.J. away."

When she didn't respond, he dumped her gently back onto the bed and stood. He could feel her eyes on his back as he moved in the direction of the door.

He was leaving her. She suddenly got a blinding flash of premonition. He was in danger. If they stayed, something terrible would happen to him.

She hurried to him, the fear of losing him clawing at her throat. "Listen to me. We can all leave. We can all be safe. Let's just pack up and go. We can go anywhere you want."

"The danger will still be here when we return," John reminded her.

She shook her head hard. "We don't have to come back. I don't mind living somewhere else. Anywhere, as long as I'm with you."

"Well, I do mind. I have no intention of leaving the ranch. Not ever."

"Since when?" The dangerous glint in his eyes took her back to days with Jack. But he wasn't the same man anymore. She had to remember that. He was different from Jack, but her feelings for him had magnified a hundred times over. He had to know. She opened her mouth to tell him.

And they were plunged into total darkness. The bedroom light had been extinguished. She might have thought John had turned it off it wasn't for his grunt of surprise.

She heard him open the door and latched on to his arm.

He wasn't going to leave her alone in the dark. The hallway wasn't lit, either. In fact, no lights in the house seemed to be burning.

Sylvia called, "Does anyone have a flashlight? Jack, can you tinker with the fuse box? I think it's the fuses."

"Sure, Mom."

Julia stiffened beside him, hearing the words tumble from his mouth so naturally. Something had changed in the way he reacted to his environment, but she would question him later. At the moment she was more worried about her son. "I'd better find J.J. I don't want him getting hurt in the dark."

He grabbed at her, catching her wrist. "Before you go, can you get the flashlight under the bed?"

Julia hurried to fetch it. She hit her shin on the bedpost. Cursing under her breath, she crawled under the bed to retrieve the flashlight. She swiped at nothing. Finally her fingers clutched the cold metal. She flicked it on. Nothing happened.

"The batteries are dead," she lamented as she returned to the hallway. "I think there are some left in the kitchen. I'll get them."

John said, "Forget it. I'll manage without it."

"How are you going to do that? You might fall down the stairs and break your neck."

"I've been down those stairs a thousand times. I won't fall. Go and check on J.J."

She listened as his footsteps faded. Then he was gone. She felt her way along the hallway, using the wall to guide her. She hoped J.J. wasn't frightened. He was probably asleep.

John's strange comments echoed in her mind. He had been down the stairs "a thousand times"? He had known the flashlight was kept under their bed.

A soft cry ripped from her throat. He remembered. He

remembered their love, and the louse hadn't bothered to mention it to her. She was going to wring his neck.

Julia quickly checked to see if her son was okay and found him asleep. She went downstairs. Although her heart was beating like crazy and she wanted to rush to her husband's arms, she took each step carefully. Her hand slid down the smooth banister.

"John?"

Sylvia's voice reached up from the darkness. "I think he's gone down to the basement. I found some batteries for the flashlight. Where are you?"

"I'm on the landing."

She stayed where she was, hand held out. Sylvia found her easily enough. The woman handed her the batteries, and Julia shoved them into the flashlight. Relief flooded through her as the light blazed to life.

She hurried to the basement door, wanting to catch John before he broke his neck. She lightly pushed on the door. It swayed open in front of her. "John, I have the light."

She swung the beam of light down the stairs. John was nearing the end of the wooden steps. The light caught movement on the floor. Something slid across it. Several somethings. The floor was moving and John's foot was in motion to step off the last stair.

She screamed.

Chapter Seventeen

A beam of light cut through the darkness.

He had taken the stairs cautiously even though he remembered exactly how many steps there were and how much space was between each one. For all he knew, the wood could have rotted through in his absence.

The fuse box was a few feet in front of him on the far left. He'd made it to the last step with ease, relieved to have reached the bottom without falling. He would change the fuse and return to Julia's side. There were a million and one things that needed to be said.

About to step off the last stair, the beam of light illuminated the floor. It moved. Julia screamed. He tried to shift his weight backward to change direction, but he lost his balance and plunged forward.

Strong fingers wrenched his shoulder backward in midfall. His hands grasped at empty air as he twisted his body to keep from landing on top of Julia. They hit the stairs with a heavy thud. Pain ripped through his back and arms.

Julia's arm hit the banister and she lost her grip on the flashlight. It rolled to the slithering floor.

John stared in dumbfounded amazement at two small, beaded eyes. The mouth opened, revealing a white interior. The copperhead lunged at its intended target—his foot.

John jerked his foot out of the way in the nick of time. The hungry mouth snapped closed on thin air.

Julia screamed in his ear, jerking on his arm as she scrambled up the stairs. His hands went to her waist in an effort to keep her from tripping and tumbling them both back down the stairs. They reached safety together, working as a team.

John bolted the door behind them. They leaned against it, breathing heavily. His heart pounded angrily against his chest. He stole a look at Julia. She was pale, quaking like a leaf. He would have held her if his own hands weren't shaking too hard to close.

He gasped for air. "Funny. I don't remember the basement being overrun with copperheads before."

She glared at him in disbelief. "You rat! You do have your memory back! When were you going to tell me?"

He sighed, closing his eyes. There were so many things he wanted to tell Julia, but now was not the time. If he didn't miss his guess, someone had tried to kill him for the third time since his return.

He asked, "Who on the ranch has a fondness for snakes?"

"You think that was on purpose."

"The lights go out, the flashlight isn't working, and then we find a nest of snakes in the basement. What do you think?"

"Well, you don't have to snap at me. I was nearly scared to death down there."

He smiled dryly. "Sweetheart, I was almost snake food. Now who do we know that likes to play with snakes?"

The remaining color left her face, leaving him feeling like a complete jerk. She wasn't the one he should be barking at. She wrapped her arms around herself in a protective gesture and said, "I don't know anyone who likes snakes outside of J.J., and surely you don't suspect him."

Her eyes clashed with his in mutual challenge. Her mouth tightened and his eyes narrowed as he asked, "What do you mean, he likes snakes?"

She replied, "He reads about them. Sometimes he catches them. I've asked him not to. It frightens me to think of him messing with deadly reptiles." Her voice rose a notch. "But he's your son and he listens about as well as you do."

John asked, "What does he do with them once he catches them?"

"He usually puts them in a box he has outside. It's surrounded by rock and dirt."

"That changes things remarkably." He fished around in a nearby drawer until he found a candle. He lit it, holding it up so he could watch his wife's changing expressions more clearly.

Julia shook her head. "What are you saying?"

"Catching snakes and dumping a box down a flight of stairs are two entirely different situations. Someone who's afraid of reptiles might not mind the latter alternative quite as much."

"Oh, John, let's get out of here. Please. I'm frightened. I don't want anything to happen to you. We've already missed out on two years. I couldn't take it if we were reunited just to be torn apart again. I know you said you didn't want to run, but what's more important here? Your life or your pride? We can vanish. No one will ever find us. We can be happy again."

John stroked her soft face. "And what about Mom? What if the killer decides to hurt her?"

Her head dropped to his chest and his arms went around her. She leaned into him, defeated. She mumbled against his white sweatshirt. "I know you're right. I just don't want to lose you again."

He kissed the top of her head. "You won't. Don't worry. I won't leave you again."

A spark of hope lit her eyes. "Do you remember everything?"

A teasing smile touched his lips. He moved closer, caressing the naked skin of her upper arms. "Like what? Like the smell of your hair after you wash it? Like the sound of your moans while making love to me? Like the feel of your body next to mine? What exactly are you referring to?"

A furious blush colored her cheeks. "I can't think when you do that."

"You never could. I'm glad to see I haven't lost my touch."

"We don't have time for this, John. If we're going to stay and fight, we need to figure out who the Scarecrow actually is before he strikes again."

Sylvia raced into the room with her shotgun. She swung it around to face them. "What in the tarnation is going on? I heard a scream."

John easily wrestled the rifle from her grasp. "Mom, how many times have I told you to be careful with this thing? You aren't Annie Oakley."

Her hands trembled as they rose to cover her stunned mouth. "Jack? Has your memory returned? Do you know me?"

He laughed. "How could I forget the woman who taught me everything I know about girls?"

Sylvia embraced him as tears flowed down her cheeks. "Oh, Jack. I was afraid I wouldn't live to see this day. How are you and Julia now? Have you worked things out?"

He shot a look at his wife. She was trying hard to fade into the background. He had often wondered how a woman with her confidence could turn insecure in the blink of an eye. By accident or design, her head fell forward and the dark hair obscured his view of her face.

He said, "I'll get back to you later on that. At the moment Julia and I are in full agreement on one count. We need to find a killer before he finds us."

Sylvia asked, "What can I do to help?"

He didn't actually want his mother involved, but he knew she wouldn't agree to let him handle things alone. She was stubborn, like his wife. He would have to arrange a small task for his mom to do to keep her out of trouble.

"Well, Mom, you could keep an eye open for anything suspicious. Then let me know. Also, I'd like you to go upstairs right now and take care of our son."

She nodded eagerly. "Of course, dear."

"One more thing, Mom. I've been having trouble sleeping. Could you find me a couple sleeping pills for tonight? I think Roberta has some."

"No. No one in this house uses sleeping pills. I could call a doctor for you."

He shook his head. Hadn't Bob said something about his wife taking sleeping pills the night Jack had been shot? "No, thank you. I'm feeling better already."

"That's odd," John remarked.

"What is?" Julia asked.

"Roberta's alibi. I thought Bob told me she was under the influence of sleeping pills the morning Jack..." He rolled his eyes and continued. "I mean, the morning I was shot. Maybe I got it wrong. I guess I need to talk to him."

Sylvia said, "I'm quite certain no one in this house has ever used sleeping pills."

She walked away. Julia tried to follow, but John grasped her waist. He stood behind her and whispered into her ear, "We still need to get the lights back on. Call down to the bunkhouse. Ask some of the boys to corral the snakes for me and get the lights turned back on."

"But what do I say when they ask how we got so many snakes in the basement?"

"Play it down, honey. Let them think J.J.'s collection got loose on accident. We don't want to tip off the killer that we're on to him."

John tucked some loose hairs behind her ear. He wanted to kiss her, but he knew if he started he wouldn't be able to stop. There were too many things to take care of, too many things to talk about.

She said, "I want you to know that I—"

He placed a finger over her soft, luscious lips. "Not now. Gather Bob and Roberta in the living room for a little meeting."

Her eyebrows pulled together in concern. "What are you planning to do?"

"Do? Nothing. I just want everyone to know my memory is back."

"John, no! You can't. One of them could be the killer."

He smiled. "I thought you were certain it wasn't anyone in this house."

"Not certain enough to bet your life on it. Anyway, don't you know who it is? Chalmers believed you knew the killer's identity."

He said, "No. Chalmers told us I'd suspected it was someone in the family."

"Yeah. Bobby."

"An anonymous source named Bob as the killer, but I'm having trouble believing that Bob is secretly a professional hit man. He has trouble smashing bugs. They may have been trying to throw me off track." He took her slender hand in his strong one, stroking the fingers. "Sweetheart, I suspected it was someone close to me because they obviously knew I was looking for them. Every time I got close, the evidence would miraculously disappear. There aren't too many people that I trusted. You.

Mom. Bob and Stu. I didn't talk to anyone else. But that doesn't mean I was right. Maybe the phone was bugged. Or the whole house.''

She pointed out, ''That doesn't mean the people you trusted didn't trust the information to somebody else.''

He smiled indulgently as if he was talking to a small child. ''Did you repeat any of our conversations to anyone?''

She jerked her hand free. ''Of course not. What kind of a woman do you think I am?''

''The kind I can trust not to betray me. I can't see Mom or Bob spreading my business around, either, can you? As for Stu, he was like a brother to me. It's hard for me to imagine him repeating private conversations. I can't imagine any one of them being involved in trying to kill me.''

''But someone did.'' Julia lowered her voice. ''What exactly were you working on when you were shot?''

He replied, ''It's a long story. I'll explain it to you later. For now we need to assemble the cast. I want to play with the film a little, see if we can find the missing links. I think we can. If it is one of them, we'll hook them.''

She leaned into him, wrapping her arms around his waist. ''Then you and I can have some private time together? How do you feel about second honeymoons?''

He gently disengaged himself, avoiding her eyes. How was he going to make her understand why he had made the choices he had? He had ripped her heart out. How could he make up for that?

John flinched at the pain he saw in her eyes. The insecurity was back. She thought he didn't want her. He reached out for her. He would have kissed her until she couldn't breathe, soothing away her pain, but she slapped his hand away and left the kitchen.

He began to pace like a caged tiger. Working things out with Julia would have to wait. For now he needed to concentrate on his plan. If he slipped up, he would never discover the identity of his would-be killer.

ROBERTA WHINED, "What is this all about? Why isn't Sylvia here? Are we having a family meeting? I was sleeping. I need nine hours of sleep every night or I have dark circles under my eyes."

"Sylvia is upstairs with J.J.," Julia replied. Bob swung his tired gaze to Julia. "What is this all about? First the lights go out. Then we hear somebody scream. Now the lights are back on and we're all briskly ushered into the living room. There'd better be something terribly wrong."

"There is." Three sets of eyes snapped in the direction of the doorway to find John lounging against the frame, an insolent smile twisting his hard lips. "There is if you consider having a hired killer on the ranch as terribly wrong."

Roberta gasped. "What is he talking about?"

"Nothing but rubbish, lamb." Bob slowly pronounced his next words. "Don't mind Jack. His head was injured. He has no idea what he's talking about."

John interrupted. "But I do know what I'm talking about. My memory has returned in full force. Billings is on his way, and I'm going to hand the killer over to him. I have all the evidence I need."

"Well, if that's true," Bob growled, "then why are you harassing us?"

"I wanted you to know in front of witnesses that I never slept with your wife. I stand by my earlier denial. Roberta was whispering nasty things in my ear for over a year before my...sudden departure. She insisted you were sleeping with *my* wife."

Bob paled. "You can't be serious! You didn't think I was having an affair, did you, lamb?"

Roberta burst into tears on cue. Julia cringed as Bob

wound his arms around his wife. How could he be so blind?

Roberta sobbed. "You were spending so much time with her. You admired her. You even told me I should be more like her."

"I'm sorry, honey. I never should have said those things. You know you're the only one I want to be with."

John cut in. "Before this goes any further I think you should hear the rest. Roberta tried to seduce me on several occasions. She claimed we would be getting even with you, setting things straight. Those were the times when we stopped talking upon your arrival, Bob. When I refused her advances, she found someone else."

Bob's eyes widened, mirroring Julia's stunned expression. He shook his head. "You must be mistaken."

Julia felt curiously as if she'd walked into a movie halfway through the plot. She shook her own head in confusion, staring at one man and then the other. Why was Jack telling Bob these things now? She thought they were supposed to be talking about the return of his memory.

John said, "I'm afraid not. Roberta has had an affair with Stu. Among others. I think Gray Macready was even in there somewhere, wasn't he, Roberta?"

She cursed, "Damn you, Jack! Why didn't you stay dead? You rotten lowlife."

Bob blinked. "Is it true? You cheated on me?"

Roberta cooed, "It didn't mean anything. You know I love you. I thought you were being unfaithful to me. I needed someone to turn to. I needed to feel like a woman again."

John said, "I need to talk to you when you get through here, Bob."

He pulled Julia from the room, shutting the doors behind them. The angry voices rose. Julia didn't want to leave Bob alone with the barracuda, but she needed to talk to her husband. She had the feeling he was holding something vital back from her.

Had he fallen in love with someone else? Had he remembered his love for her had died?

They stepped inside the bedroom they had once shared with insatiable need. The door swung shut. John opened his mouth to speak. Julia couldn't bear to hear the words. She crossed the space that stood between them in a heated rush and mated her mouth with his, testing him.

John resisted at first. His cold-hearted denial of passion challenged her to push it further. Her hand went to the back of his neck, pulling him closer. She nibbled on his lips and teased him with her tongue.

A hungry growl was torn from his throat. His arm went around her lower back and lifted her into a tight embrace. His tongue stabbed between her lips. She accepted it, matching it thrust for thrust.

He pulled back. His husky voice cut through her passion like a chainsaw. "We need to talk. Now."

She lifted a hand, silently begging him to stop talking. "I can't. Not right now. Please, just hold me."

"We need to talk first."

She put some distance between them. "Don't you want me? I know you weren't exactly keen on sleeping with me before. I had to practically jump you, but you know who you are now. Things are different. Aren't they?"

"What are you talking about? Of course I wanted you before." John's expression softened somewhat as he moved toward her. He cupped her face gently between his hands. "I'm sorry. I was holding out because I was afraid I would lose you later. You weren't exactly impressed with me when I was plain old John Smith from nowhere."

"That's not true. I was bowled over by your charm."

"You could have fooled me. You resisted every pass I threw at you."

"Not every pass," she reminded him. "In truth, I found you absolutely irresistible. Only I was afraid. I was afraid you would leave me once your memory returned. I was afraid you were married. I couldn't stand the thought of losing you twice, and even though I didn't know it was you, I did. Does that make any sense?"

He nodded, pulling her closer. "It does to me. I guess I felt that way, too. I didn't feel like I could compete with a ghost. You seemed so untouchable when I first arrived. I wanted to awaken the fire I knew you were hiding behind that icy smile, but I knew I'd be risking my heart to give it to a woman who was still in love with her dead husband."

She stared into his soul, searching his blue eyes. She wanted him to read the sincerity in her words. "I fell in love with you all over again these past few weeks. I wanted to tell you earlier, but the lights went out. Do you understand what I'm saying? I fell in love with John Smith. Honey, I love you both. Now how's that for weird?"

"Only about as odd as a man falling in love with his wife without knowing she is his wife. I'd marry you all over again. Without question."

Her breath caught in her throat. "Do you love me, Jack? I'm sorry. I mean, John."

There was an awkward silence as they both tried to find another direction to look in.

Her barely audible whisper reached out to him. "Make love to me."

"Your wish is my command." His mouth crushed hers and his hands went to work on her bra, stealing under her cotton shirt. He unsnapped it. Then his hands went to the front of her jeans. He roughly pulled on her clothes, baring her creamy flesh. "The hell with the killer. We can bar the door."

"Oh, no." She said, "I can't believe I forgot someone

out there is trying to kill you. What sort of woman am I? He could be lurking around out there somewhere right now."

He breathed hoarsely in her ear. "The hell with him. I'll lock the door. I'll put the damn dresser in front of it. We'll be perfectly safe. I've been dying to make love to you. You drive me crazy, woman. I want you now."

She shoved him backward, catching him off guard. He lost his balance and fell, landing at the foot of the bed in an undignified heap.

She gasped. "I'm sorry. Are you okay? You must think I'm crazy."

She sat beside him and, placing a hand on his thigh, said, "Maybe I wouldn't feel so insecure if I knew why you'd left me in the first place. Tell me everything. I can take it."

"I didn't exactly leave you. I was shot."

She said, "Billings mentioned the Witness Protection Program. You were planning on leaving without saying a word. Once you were gone, you didn't rush back to my side."

John shook his head and sighed. "I can't talk to you about it right now. We don't have time. You want to think the worst of me. Did we ever trust each other?"

Her eyes widened in hurt surprise. "What do you mean by that? Of course we trusted each other."

"Did we?" He laughed with bitter regret. "I suspected you of cheating on me. You probably thought I was cheating on you." He threw up his hands. "Where's the trust in that?"

Her eyes clouded with tears as she watched him leave the room. She took a deep breath to steady herself. Perhaps she should leave him alone for a while. They could talk later, clear up misunderstandings.

JOHN STEPPED from the shower, dripping water on the floor. He casually wrapped a towel around his lean hips. Stalling for time, he brushed his teeth and shaved. He wasn't in any hurry to leave the bathroom. Julia would either be crying her eyes out or she would be getting ready to hand him his head. He didn't know which was worse.

His talk with Bob hadn't exactly gone the way he'd planned. There was still a great deal of mistrust between them. John wasn't sure he had gotten through to his stubborn brother. If only…

A loud crack echoed throughout the house, bouncing off the walls. A gunshot. The familiar sound blanketed him with dread. The gun had gone off in the house. Several horrible scenarios came to mind. His mother might have reloaded her shotgun and accidentally shot someone. The killer might have come for another victim.

Since his talk with Bob he had been expecting to hear a gunshot, but it still worried him. Plans didn't always follow the path you set them on.

John dropped his razor. It clattered to the sink. He took the time to pull on a discarded pair of dark blue boxers before running from the bathroom at full speed. He flew down the stairs, not daring to stop until he reached the living room. The scene stopped him in his tracks, freezing him to ice.

Bob was lying on the floor. Standing over him, holding a gun in her hands, was Julia.

She raised frightened green eyes to meet his startled ones. She shook her head slowly, but didn't say a word in her own defense.

Chapter Eighteen

Julia turned the gun in her husband's direction.

Her hands trembled on the cold metal, the betrayal in his eyes a knife in her heart. She prayed he would realize she would never hurt him. He had to know this wasn't real.

His cold blue eyes dropped to his brother's body. "Is he dead?"

Roberta cried, "Thank God, you're here, Jack! She's crazy. It was Julia all along! She tried to kill you so she could be with Bob, and now she's going to kill me! Bob told her he still loves me, so she shot him. Do something! Help me-ee!"

Julia wanted to protest, but she couldn't get her lips to move. A barely audible whimper passed between them. If John heard, he gave no indication of it. She prayed they lived long enough for her to explain.

John took a step forward.

Julia shouted, "No! Stay where you are!"

The gun shook in her hands, growing heavier by the minute.

Puzzled blue eyes swept over her. She silently pleaded for him to remain where he was. She couldn't risk sending him a more obvious signal. If they were going to live, he had to trust her. Her eyes begged for his trust, the one thing she wasn't sure he was capable of giving her.

Roberta turned away from him, but Julia saw her smug smile.

Julia prayed he would hear the silent message. She forced her voice to remain steady. "I want you to leave, John. I know you aren't my husband. Your little plan didn't work. I know you aren't Jack. Leave before I shoot you, too."

His eyes widened, then narrowed on her as he seemed to reach an understanding of the situation. "Okay."

Roberta yelled, "Wait a second! What are you two trying to pull? I know you're Jack. I saw the card trick. Jack used to do that all the time. I think you should stay, Jack. Don't you think so, Julia? You don't want him to miss out on the fun."

Sylvia's voice echoed down the hallway. "What in tarnation is going on now? I heard a gunshot."

John turned his head sideways to intercept his mother. "It's okay, Mom. It's nothing. Go back to bed."

"Are you sure?"

Half of his body was concealed by the wall, but his face was visible as he repeated, "Go back to bed. Everything's fine." Perhaps he would signal Sylvia to call the police with his hidden hand.

Sylvia said, "Okay. I'll see you in the morning."

They listened to her footsteps fade. Julia took a deep breath. For a moment she had pictured both Sylvia and John dying because of her. Whatever happened to her, she had to make sure they lived. She loved them. She loved John more than she had the day she'd married him.

She blinked away the tears, trying hard to steady the gun with her quivering hands. The gun grew heavier by the minute. She wasn't sure how much longer she could hold it.

John glanced from Roberta to Julia to Roberta again. "So what's the verdict, ladies? Do I stay or do I go?"

Roberta dropped her whining act. Her voice turned husky. "I think you should stay, Jack. Come on inside with us before your nutty mother returns with her shotgun and gets you killed. Don't do anything clever."

John's eyes widened as innocently as a newborn babe's, but Julia wasn't fooled. "Excuse me?"

Roberta sneered. "You know what I mean. I saw the way you looked at me. You knew all along I was behind it. Didn't you?"

"Not all along," he said. "I suspected you after I overheard a phone call. Were you calling your partner? For a professional hit man—or should I say, woman—your lack of caution borders on the absurd."

Roberta leered at his nearly nude state. "Well, at least I know you aren't hiding a weapon on your person. Get in here."

Julia almost dropped the gun. "Hit man? She's the Scarecrow?"

"That's right, sweetheart. This is the infamous Scarecrow. She kills people on her little shopping trips. Then she hides out here beneath a very clever disguise. Who would suspect a ditzy blonde of pulling off some of the country's most notorious hits?"

Roberta asked, "What gave me away?"

"It wasn't any one thing in particular. There was your odd change of voice, your trips to the barn. A woman like Roberta Keller wouldn't go into such a dirty place. Then there was the check to Straw Man, Inc., for fifty thousand dollars with Bob's signature on it. You wanted us to think he paid the Scarecrow to kill me. When the truth is, he gives you blank checks all the time so you can enhance your wardrobe.''

''Clever,'' Roberta said. ''Yes, I could always count on good old Bob for a check. Too bad I had to kill him. You know I always liked you, Jack. Killing you won't bring me any pleasure.''

Before anyone could take a breath, John pitched forward with Sylvia's shotgun in his hands. He trained it on Roberta. Julia cried out a warning.

The man concealed behind the door, Roberta's partner, placed the muzzle of his gun in the hollow behind John's right ear. John froze, and the man laughed.

Roberta joined in on the laughter. She took the rifle from John's hands and turned it on him. ''You were speaking of caution, Jack? Perhaps you should have taken some of your own advice. Very sloppy. Now it's my turn to be disappointed in you. A DEA agent shouldn't make such stupid mistakes. Didn't you wonder why your wife was pointing a gun in your direction?''

He shrugged. ''I thought it was because I hadn't given her flowers in a long time.''

Julia dropped the gun, the empty gun, to the floor. ''They wanted me to convince you I was the killer. They were going to let you live.''

He winked at her. ''I know, honey. Don't worry about it. I knew you wouldn't shoot me.''

Roberta gagged. ''How very touching.''

John tried to turn his head to get a look at the partner, but the gun pushed his face back in the other direction. John asked, ''Don't I even get an introduction? Should I guess? I know it isn't Bob. Mac?''

Roberta laughed with unrestrained glee. ''Macready? What made you think it was him?''

"The tunnel leads to his place. I figured you were taking the drugs there. His place is closer to the county line."

"Drugs?" A horrible thought occurred to Julia. "Did you kill Jack's father?"

"As a matter of fact, yes."

John shook his head. "Why? Who hired you to kill my father?"

Her shrill laughter taunted him. "Hired me? No one hired me. Killing John Keller was necessary. I wanted Bob to inherit everything. I also wanted to get him alone. He was so much easier to handle without all of you constantly interfering. Your father was the worst when it came to sticking his nose where it didn't belong."

She took a breath and continued. "Anyway, I tried to get to you, but you had to be faithful to your wedding vows. If you had given in and become my lover, things would be so different now. But you couldn't see any other woman outside of Julia. I had to kill you. I guess the FBI was tipped off somehow. They planned a getaway for you, but I got you first. I heard rumors last year that you were still alive. I didn't care…as long as you stayed away."

Roberta smiled. "Now it's my turn to ask questions. How did you survive, and why did you come back?"

John said, "After you shot me, Dr. Pascal was contacted by the FBI. He falsified my death certificate. He arranged for my 'body' to disappear. I recovered in a hospital in Dallas. They wanted to put me in the Witness Protection Program, but I declined. I wanted to catch my father's killer. The DEA allowed me to work for them full-time on this case. It took us down to South America."

John turned to Julia and explained. "That's where I got the scars. Chalmers and I found the drug dealers who were sending drugs up here to the Triple K. I just didn't know who they were sending the drugs to. But that was why I decided to return. I had to protect you and J.J. I wanted to find the Scarecrow and the drug dealers and stop them.''

He took a deep breath before continuing. ''I had to place myself in dangerous situations. Drug dealers are even more paranoid than you've accused me of being. I had to gain the trust of one in particular. They have games of initiation to prove a man's worth. One of those games meant placing a lit cigarette between my arm and that of a trusted employee. The first man who moves away loses face.''

Julia shuddered, wrapping arms around herself. ''That's barbaric.''

''Yes, but it had to be done. I would have tried anything if it meant coming home.''

''It must have hurt.''

''Nothing compared to the pain of losing you.'' He added, ''I got into a knife fight in a tavern after drinking, and that's where the scar on my back comes in. I was drunk, missing you. It had nothing to do with the job. It was my own stupidity, but I accomplished something that night. I overheard the guy who cut me talking about the Scarecrow's operation. I found out where it was located, and I went there. I met a few of the Scarecrow's employees, got them to talk. It led me straight back home.''

Roberta said, ''Well, now I have to move my operation somewhere else, thanks to you. But first I'm going to have to kill you all. I can't leave witnesses.''

John's eyes turned to ice. Afraid he was going to try to strangle Roberta and get himself killed, Julia threw her arms around his bare waist. ''No. Please don't do anything stupid right now. I want to grow old with you, not because of you.''

The tension coiled inside of him relaxed somewhat in her desperate embrace. She felt him swallow down the rage. He said, ''Go on. Fill me in on the rest. You're going to kill us anyway. I want to know how you managed to keep the authorities at bay for so long. You must have had someone inside the law helping you out. A DEA agent perhaps?''

Julia glanced at the man standing behind John. ''Billings is her partner.''

Billings said, ''I thought you'd figured that one out already.''

Billings allowed John to turn around and face him. John shook his head in disbelief. ''But you knew I was alive. That's why I didn't suspect you of trying to kill me. You knew I was living somewhere under an assumed name.''

Billing corrected him. ''I wasn't certain. Even if I knew you were alive, I thought I'd never see you again. I don't believe in killin'…unless it's necessary. When the authorities asked for my help in sending you into witness protection, I couldn't believe my luck. I'd be rid of you one way or another. The DEA called me and told me you were on your way back to town. They wanted me to help you. I sent word for Roberta to come home and finish the job.''

Roberta laughed. ''I had to return from shopping just to fill you with lead. No telling how much money that cost me. I'd had a big buyer lined up that weekend.''

Billings added, ''The cops from El Paso gave me a holler when you left the program and headed this way. I should have killed you myself. You're a jinx for Roberta. She just can't seem to kill you, but I won't have a problem.''

''Sorry to be such a hassle.''

''I wasn't sure it was you when I ran your car off the road,'' Roberta said. ''Luck was with me that day. I saw you outside of El Paso and I followed you. When I got the chance, I ran you off the road.''

John said, "You didn't mind killing an innocent person if it wasn't me?"

"Jack, grow up. No one past the age of ten is innocent." Roberta laughed. "I didn't know it was you until I saw you do the card trick. That was a dead giveaway. Pardon the pun."

Julia asked her, "Why live here? You must have a lot of money. Why not live in a big city?"

"This place is a great cover. Who would look for a world-class killer in the middle of nowhere? It's perfect, and Bob was the best patsy. Thanks to you, I'll have to find myself another one now."

"Was Chalmers in on this, too?" Julia asked. "He told us Bob was the killer."

John said, "He didn't say Bob. He told us it was Bobby. He meant Bob*ie* as in Roberta. I was tipped off anonymously by phone. I didn't believe it. I knew Bob wasn't the killer. I didn't make the connection to Roberta…until recently."

Roberta said, "Some of my closer clients call me Bobbie. One of them must have turned on me."

Julia asked, "But what about the file in Cecily's office. Why did it have B. Keller on it? It said psychotic. It couldn't have been about Bob."

"You're right," John replied. "The file was on Roberta. I had told her things about Roberta, as well as the other suspects, and she'd tried to come up with a profile on each of them."

John asked, "What happened to Pascal?"

Billings said, "When you turned up after your accident, the good doctor called the FBI. You took off on your own, and they relocated him. Too bad. I would have liked to have broken his dialing finger."

Roberta interrupted. "What do we do about Sylvia? She's probably calling the police."

Billings glared at her as if she was stupid. "My deputy will call it in to me. I'll tell him I'm taking care of it myself. We'll blow the house up. I'll tell everyone John here went crazy when he found his wife in his brother's arms. Killed the lot of them, including himself."

Julia's arms tightened around John's waist. She didn't care for her own life, but she needed to know her husband and son would live. J.J. needed at least one parent. John would take good care of him.

John said, "You still haven't told us how you did it. And why drugs? Wasn't the business of murder paying enough?"

Julia gazed up at him. He was stalling for time. Had Sylvia gone for help? Hope nestled in her heart. She leaned her head against John's chest while he stroked her hair and she listened to the steady beat of his heart. He wasn't worried and she trusted him.

Roberta took a long breath and said, "We have men who smuggle the dope into the country. They bury it in the tunnel. Once we know we're safe, we uncover it. I take it to the city inside my little ships on my shopping trips. I sell it to dealers. They sell it to the little guys. It's America, the land of opportunity."

John said, "So Mac has nothing at all to do with this? I think I'm disappointed. After the way he swindled Julia out of her father's land, I wanted to bust him."

Roberta snorted. "That guy is dumber than you are. He caught me on his land once, and I told him I got lost. He actually believed me."

Julia asked, "How do you go from being a hit man to being a drug dealer?"

"It's not hard. Billings turned me onto it. He used my

services to get rid of his wife ten years ago. Remember, he's the one who introduced me to the Keller men. He offered me a steady job. I took it.''

Julia turned to John. ''Were you working with Cecily then? Didn't you know Roberta was the killer when you went away?''

''No, honey.'' John explained, ''I had no idea it was Roberta. Cecily and I had files on everybody. She works for the DEA, too. Maybe she's finally figured out that Roberta wasn't using sleeping pills, proving her alibi on the day I was 'killed' false.''

''Enough,'' Billings growled. He grabbed Julia's arm, wrestling her from John. ''Now if you will please stand in the corner. We'll shoot you first and be done with it.''

JULIA TRIED TO FIGHT, but Billings was too strong for her. She couldn't understand why John was so passive. He wasn't even trying to help her. She took a deep breath and controlled her fear. She trusted John. He wouldn't let her die.

''Are you going to shoot her with your own gun?'' John asked.

Billings glanced down at the weapon in his hand. He turned to Roberta. ''Shoot her with the rifle. It has to be done with their gun. Otherwise it'll look suspicious, and I won't even be able to cover it up.''

Julia's mouth dropped open. Why was he helping them? Had he lost his mind?

Her head quirked to one side and she squinted at him suspiciously.

HE HELD BACK a smile. It served her right. She had nearly stopped his heart when she'd raised that gun in his direction earlier. For a split second he had thought she might have lost her mind.

John would have rather been killed by Julia than live life without her. She was everything to him. If there was more time, he would have told her. A woman needed to hear the words. Especially a woman such as Julia who hid her insecurities behind a brave smile. He wished she could believe in him.

Billings ordered, "Shoot the woman!"

Julia's eyes filled with tears. She held her hand out as if to touch him even though he was on the other side of the room. It killed him to see her so distressed. He wanted to comfort her, but he couldn't.

Roberta aimed the rifle at Julia's chest. A slow smile spread across her lips as she eased back the trigger. Julia closed her eyes, squeezing them shut.

Click! Roberta's eyes widened a fraction. She jerked on the trigger again. Nothing happened.

Bob sprang to his feet and knocked the rifle barrel up toward the ceiling. In her confusion Roberta lost her grip on the weapon. Tossing the rifle aside, Bob threw her to the ground. He straddled her, holding her down.

Bob wasn't dead. He wasn't even injured. Julia stared at him in amazement.

An astonished look had captured Billings's face when he'd heard the empty click of the rifle. He'd spun around, but was too late. John had been waiting for the telling sound. He expertly kicked the loaded gun from the sheriff's hand.

Billings swung a meaty fist in John's direction.

John ducked. He planted two hard punches into the sheriff's soft gut and was rewarded with a grunt of pain.

Billings hit John in the jaw.

John's head snapped back. Blood trickled down his chin.

He staggered on his feet, but refused to fall. Billings threw another punch. This time John easily avoided it. He rammed a fist into the sheriff's belly and then hit the man with an uppercut to the chin.

Billings fell like a stone.

Julia ran to his side. She wrapped her arms around his waist, holding him as if she'd never let him go. She stared up at him with concern. His breathing was erratic and his heart was racing like a Thoroughbred's. He hitched up the sliding boxers, wishing he had taken time to dress before coming downstairs. He felt utterly ridiculous surrounded by fully clothed people.

"Are you okay, Jack?" The name slipped from Julia's lips. She seemed to tense, waiting for him to correct her. He stroked a thumb down her cheekbone.

Bob, his eyes never straying from his dangerous wife's angry face, said, "I can't believe it worked. I thought we were dead for sure."

"How long have you two been working together?" Julia asked.

John ignored her question. "Can you handle things here until the police arrive?"

Bob nodded. "Sure can. Stu is on his way. I saw him through the window when I jumped Roberta. He probably went to get his gun and call the police."

Julia shook her head in wonder. "But I thought Stu was involved. Why did he have a check from Straw Man, and why was he drawing pictures of the Scarecrow?"

Roberta grunted from beneath Bob's body. "That check was a phony, you idiot. I put it there for you to see. I wasn't sure you would buy that Bob was trying to kill you, so I made it look like Stu might be involved, too. Stu and I were lovers for a short time. He found a Scarecrow card in my bedroom and became fascinated with it. The idiot has been drawing it over and over in charcoal. I couldn't make him stop without arousing his suspicion.''

Bob sneered. "I sure can pick 'em, can't I?''

Julia said, "Don't be so hard on yourself. She had us all fooled.''

"Not to mention the FBI and the DEA," added John.

John pulled a protesting Julia from the room. Halfway up the stairs he stopped to kiss her. His mouth hungrily covered hers, firmly silencing her questions. His hands roved her body in passionate exploration. His tongue thrust into her mouth, eager to reclaim previous territory.

Julia groaned, pulling him closer. Her fingers slid up over his naked back and she kneaded the muscles with deliberate pressure.

He wrenched his mouth free and breathed, "Upstairs. We have to go upstairs." He growled, "Now."

They sped up the stairs, halting once more outside of the bedroom as John rocked her back into the wall, lifting her feet off the ground as his mouth hungrily crushed hers. He was between her thighs. His hips moved against her in an erotic rhythm.

Her hands vanished into his thick, brown mane. Her fingers tangled around it, tugging on it gently.

He withdrew, allowing her to slide down his body until her feet reached the floor. She sighed. Her head swam in dizzy circles. She clutched at his shoulders, unsteady on her legs.

They entered the bedroom, John in the lead. She expected John to immediately strip her clothes off in his haste to make love to her. But once again he surprised her. He leaned against the door, chest heaving with every tortured breath. His eyes slid over her, apparently content to look before he touched.

Julia suddenly felt self-conscious. It was an odd feeling.

Jack had looked at her a thousand times. He had seen her naked. He had made love to her as two different men. But she had never seen him look at her the way he was gazing at her now.

A single tear slid down her cheek. He loved her. He not only wanted her. He truly loved her.

She opened her arms to him, welcoming him home at last. He walked to her, a beautiful smile on his face, and his arms went around her as he pulled her into a loose embrace.

John rained kisses over her jaw, neck and face. He kissed her closed eyelids. He kissed the corners of her mouth. His lips went to her ear and he whispered, "There are so many things I need to tell you."

"You can tell me anything."

That made his smile grow. Tiny crinkles appeared around his blue eyes. It was going to take her a while to get used to the changes in him. It was more than a few endearing wrinkles. There was also a change in attitude. John didn't smile as much as Jack had, but she was going to help him with that. She wanted to make him happy again.

"I need to tell you why I didn't try to contact you after I was shot."

"You don't have to explain. You wanted to protect me and our son. I get it."

"I want to explain." He pulled her down beside him on the bed. She sat next to him, crossing her legs demurely. She didn't want to talk. She wanted to love him, but he continued to speak. "I didn't stay away because I thought you were unfaithful. By the time I was shot I had already decided Roberta was lying to me about that. I disappeared because I couldn't let you give up your life here for me."

She protested, "You were my life."

"We would have been running forever. That's no life for a child. J.J. belongs here on the ranch. I wanted him to grow up like I did."

She said, "Don't you think the decision should have been mine? J.J. is a strong, resilient child. He could deal with moving around a lot better than he could deal with losing a father. And what about the killer running around loose?"

"I figured you would be safe until I could catch the guy. Besides, I had agents watching you the whole time." John kissed her passionately. He sighed. "I thought I was doing the right thing at the time. I wanted to find out what happened to my father, and I knew how stubborn you could be. I knew you would go with me if I asked. That's why I didn't."

Julia understood how strongly Jack had wanted to find his father's killer. He had been torn apart by his father's death. No son could have been more loyal.

"There's one more thing I don't understand. It seemed like a big conspiracy. People were either denying they knew you or vanishing into thin air. What happened to Cecily Carpenter? What happened to Officer Nader? What about Pascal? Who relocated them?"

"I did."

Julia shook her head in wonder. "What?"

"I didn't want anyone hurt because of me, so I told the DEA they'd better relocate everyone fast because I was returning to help my family. Once I made up my mind to return to you regardless of the danger, I let the agency know. I didn't give them much warning because I knew they would try to stop me. There was a frantic rush to do just that."

She asked, "What did they do?"

"They had the police arrest me. You remember the big

officer behind the desk in El Paso? He and Nader threw me into a holding cell and called Chalmers. Chalmers picked me up, but when we got outside I knocked him out. He was a good man. It was my idea to put his file on the deactivated list so he could give me help with the Scarecrow if I needed it. I wish I'd left him out of it now. He'd still be alive. But he was stubborn, like you. He probably would've come after me anyway.

"Pascal had helped the DEA several times in the past. He was always well compensated for it. I think he enjoyed the adventure of playing spy a bit much. He called the DEA when I turned up at the hospital after my accident." He sighed. "I know how the DEA works. They probably thought they could have him tell me my face was redone, have the local police cart me off somewhere safe while they pretended to search for my closest relatives. I'm sure Pascal was paid well for his part in it. He's probably somewhere exotic, taking it easy until the Scarecrow is behind bars. He'll be able to return home now."

"I think they were using you," Julia said. "The DEA could have picked you up any time they wanted to. Sounds to me like they wanted you stumbling around in the dark, searching for the Scarecrow without backup."

John gave her conclusions some thought before nodding. "You're probably right."

"I can't believe any of this." Julia paced the length of the room with her arms wrapped tightly around herself. "All of this time the killer was right under our very own roof. There were times when Roberta was alone with our son. She could have hurt him."

John shook his head. "No. Remember, Roberta is a professional. She doesn't kill for sport. She's cold-blooded, but she kills for money."

"You were wrong when you complained there was no

trust between us. I knew you weren't going to let Billings kill me. I knew you had a plan. Although, I admit my heart nearly stopped when Roberta pointed the shotgun at me. I trust you with my life, John.''

"Jack," he corrected her. "I'm home again, darling. I want you to call me by name. You say it so sweetly.''

"I trusted you with my life, Jack. How much more trust do we need?''

"You have to be sure you want me back. Once you open your arms to me, I won't ever leave again. Not even if you want me to. Please be sure.''

Julia stood and went to the door as if she intended to go through it. She turned to face him. She would never forget the look on his face. Fear and anguish clouded his soft blue eyes. He thought she'd actually meant to reject him.

Julia didn't need to consider the options. Jack was the only man she would ever love. No separation, not even death, could banish him from her heart. He meant everything to her. He always would.

She raised her arms and opened them, giving him the answer without words. Jack sucked in a harsh breath. His eyes were bright with tears, mirroring her own. He crossed the room in five quick steps. Then she was in his arms, kissing him as he had kissed her.

Jack engulfed her in his strong embrace. He whispered words of love, barely audible, into her ear while his hands tunneled through her hair. He grabbed handfuls of silky waves and buried his face in it, breathing deep. His entire body was shaking with relief.

He said, "Oh, baby. I was so afraid I'd lost you forever. I never should have left you. I swear I'll never make a decision that affects both our lives again without your input.''

She laughed happily. "And I'll never take you for granted again. I love you so much, Jack."

He pulled back slightly and smiled. "I love you, too, Julie."

She pushed him away and her brow furrowed. "Wait a second. I don't get something."

He narrowed the gap again and nibbled on her neck. "You don't get what?"

"Why did she shoot Bob?"

"Bob and I talked things over. We put it all together and set her up. Bob told her he wanted a divorce. We thought she would tip her hand after hearing that, run out and gather up her drugs. We didn't actually think she would try to kill him. It was a good thing she used Bob's gun. He had loaded it with blanks after we figured out she was involved somehow."

Julia said, "What about your mom's shotgun?"

Jack laughed until tears formed in his eyes. "Honey, Mom's shotgun has never actually been loaded. She pretends it is, and we go along with it."

Julia's eyes clouded over, tinged with sadness. "Too bad Roberta didn't try to use the shotgun when she shot you the first time. She would have been caught and we would have had the past two years."

He stroked her cheek. "Don't think about the past. Think about the future. You and I are going to have a wonderful life together filled with laughter and love and lots of babies."

Her eyes widened and a smile curved her lips. "Oh, wow. I thought J.J. would be my last. Now I can have as many babies as I want."

Jack cautioned her, "Don't get carried away now. I was thinking one or two more."

Julia shook her head. Her fingers went to work on his neck, massaging the tight cords. "I want at least twelve."

Jack sputtered, "Twelve!"

"Okay. Make it thirteen. A baker's dozen."

He shook his head and she reveled in his beautiful smile. He said, "I married a crazy lady."

"Are you complaining?"

He didn't answer the question. Instead, he took her to bed and removed any doubt.

Epilogue

"Where are the kids?"

Julia sat in a corner of the living room, curled up in her favorite reading spot. She glanced up from her book to see her handsome husband standing in the doorway. Her breath still caught every time she looked at him. It was amazing to have him back in her life again, back home where he belonged.

She set the book aside and said, "Stu's taken J.J. out on the range. He's trying to teach him to rope a moving cow. The twins are upstairs asleep. Can you believe it? I finally got them to settle down for a nap at the same time."

He grinned. "And you thought you would fill in the time by relaxing and reading a book. Well, I'll just go back outside and find something to do."

"Don't you dare." She stood and crossed the room to wrap her arms around his middle. With three children, they didn't get much quiet time alone anymore. "I can think of other ways for us to relax and enjoy nap time together."

"You want to take a nap? I am bushed."

She playfully punched him in the gut. "You know that isn't what I meant."

Julia began with the buttons on his shirt, sliding one after another through the holes.

Jack watched her, seemingly amused. He asked, "Mrs. Keller, are you making a pass at me?"

"And if I am?"

His eyes went to the ceiling as if he could see through the solid mass. "Are you sure the twins are out?"

She nodded and tugged his shirt off. "Oh, yes."

"And how long do you suppose they are going to stay that way?"

"Hmm." She sighed as he nibbled on her ear. Her reply came out breathy. "If we're lucky, an hour. Maybe even two."

His grin widened. "I'm feeling very lucky today."

"Oh, yeah?"

He picked her up and headed for the staircase. She squealed in protest. "Jack, you're going to hurt your back."

"Nah. You're light as a feather."

She rolled her green eyes. "I still haven't lost all the baby fat yet."

"You're beautiful. Perfect."

Jack laid her down on the bed they shared and rested next to her. His eyes locked with hers as he said, "When I was John, I imagined you like this. Do you think about him anymore? Do you miss him?"

Julia shook her head. "You are a nut. You are John. I see parts of him in you every day, and even though losing you for two years was tragic, I'm grateful that it brought us closer together. You share things with me now that you never did before. You talk to me, open your heart to me. This is how I always dreamed it could be."

Jack said, "I'm sorry I was such a jerk when Dad died. I should have talked it over with you. I had no idea my silence hurt you so much. I'm glad we can talk now. And there's also the issue of trust. I guess deep down you and I had a problem trusting each other, but now I trust you completely. With my life.''

Her eyes misted over. "Oh, Jack."

He smiled. "Get ready to say that again, but louder."

His mouth went to the sensitive part of her neck.

The sound of a baby crying ripped through their intimate moment. Jack buried his face in her throat, laughing. She slapped him on the arm, then pushed at him.

She said, "Move, Jack. I have to go see what he or she wants."

He got up instead. "I'll do it. You stay where you are. I'll sing to the kid and in five minutes, he, or she, will be begging to sleep just to make me stop."

Jack left the room and Julia smiled, closing her eyes. During those two years when Jack had been gone she couldn't imagine ever being happy again. Now she was happier than she'd ever imagined being.

A happy ending at last.

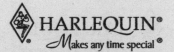

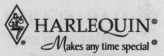

Two women fighting for their lives...
and for the men they love...

INTIMATE DANGER

Containing two full-length novels of enticing
romantic suspense from top authors

Susan Mallery
Rebecca York

Look for it in September 2002—wherever books are sold.